THE EXCALI

ERNEST DEMPSEY

ENCLAVE PUBLISHING

ERNESTDEMPSEY.NET

ISBN: 978-1-944647-13-1

Prologue
Jerusalem
AD 1100

The king's final orders began with a fit of coughing, as did nearly everything he'd said in the last three days. A thin line of blood oozed from the corner of his mouth into the dark blond beard, his pale face the ghastly color of eminent death.

Godfrey stared at the far wall, eyes bloodshot and sagging. He'd been propped up on a stack of pillows to make him more comfortable, but the cushions did little to ease the pain from the illness ravaging his insides. Ever the warrior, Godfrey didn't give in. He hardened the muscles in his face so as to not show weakness to the others in the room.

His younger brother, Baldwin, stood nearby with hands folded. He wore a solemn expression—lips drawn into a frown, eyes sullen and full of pity.

No one was sure what had happened.

Godfrey was a relatively young man, only forty years of age. Up until the day he first noticed the symptoms, he'd been in near-perfect health.

Baldwin searched the eyes of every man and woman in the room, hoping to find a traitor in their midst on whom he could place the blame. He suspected poison, but there was no way to be certain. There was also the fact that he'd never seen symptoms like this before from any poisoning. That didn't mean it could be ruled out. They were strangers in a strange land. The rules were different here.

"Brother," Godfrey said after the violent stretch of coughs ended. "Come to me."

Baldwin gave a nod and stepped close to the bed. "Yes, my king."

The line pried a dismissive snort from Godfrey's nose. He forced a feeble smile across his face and shook his head. "I've told you before, Brother, I do not deserve the title of king. There is only one king of Jerusalem, and that is Jesus Christ. I am merely an advocate and defender."

Another series of coughs racked his body as soon as Godfrey finished the sentence. Baldwin reached out to steady his brother and give him comfort. When the fit subsided, Baldwin waited for a moment before he spoke again.

"Brother, what would you have me do?"

Godfrey looked into his brother's eyes and pinched his lips together. He was in a tremendous amount of pain, and it was all the great leader could do to not scream. "Leave us," he said and waved to the others. "I would like a moment with my brother."

Baldwin watched as the assistants, nurses, and military advisers filed through the door and disappeared into the hall, leaving the two brothers alone in silence.

Godfrey swallowed. “There is something...something I need you to do.” He struggled to speak.

“Name it, Brother, and by God it will be done.”

Godfrey admired his brother’s loyalty, his fierce determination. He would make a great leader for Jerusalem. “For many years now, I have waged war on the Muslims, fighting for God and His kingdom.”

“And fought well, you have.”

Godfrey raised a weakened hand, signaling that he wasn’t finished. “I believed in the war. I still do. And that is why you must do exactly as I say.”

“Name the task.”

“First, I must make a confession to you, my brother. I...I have kept a secret from you...from everyone, all these years.”

Baldwin frowned, his eyebrows knitted together. “A secret? What kind of secret?”

Godfrey grinned as best he could. “A secret that bears enormous power.”

Baldwin wanted to ask what kind of power, but another string of coughs cut him off.

Godfrey’s body sagged, and for a moment Baldwin thought his brother’s life had come to an end. A quiet whistle seeped out of Godfrey’s nose and told Baldwin his brother was still alive, albeit barely.

Godfrey drew in a deep breath and did his best to straighten up. “This power does not make one invincible, as you can see for yourself. At the end of this day, I will be dead. Nothing can stop that now.”

“Don’t talk like that, Brother. The nurses—”

"The nurses do not know what is wrong with me. My race is run. I accept that and look forward to meeting my God. There is something, however, you have to do for me. And there is something you must know."

He paused for a moment, reflecting on something from the past. What it was, Baldwin didn't know.

"Jerusalem will fall to the Saracens again, Brother. No matter how strong our line, no matter our defenses, they will return, and they will overrun us."

Baldwin started to refute the notion, but Godfrey went on. "I do not wish that to be the case, but I know that is what the future holds. Things always change, Baldwin. They cannot stay the same forever. That is not the way of the universe, and certainly not the world of men."

Baldwin's head bowed low. "Will this happen in my lifetime?"

"Difficult to say. I think not, but it is possible."

"What can I do to stop this?"

Godfrey's eyes narrowed. "You must lead the people as best you can, Brother. Be true to God and to them. Let that be your guiding principle."

Baldwin waited a minute before he spoke again. "You mentioned a power."

"Yes. It is the great secret. Eight others possessed it before me. It is a relic of incredible importance, and must never fall into the hands of the Saracens. Were that to happen, I fear the worst."

"I...I don't understand. If this relic is so powerful, why not use it to fend off the Muslims? We could destroy them forever."

"It does not work that way, Brother. Its power is not infinite. It fades. I do not know how to describe it other than to say that this relic must be returned to its home until it calls to another."

"Calls to another?"

Godfrey gave a slow nod. "I never told you this. In fact, I never told anyone. You must promise to keep this information secret until the day you die. Is that understood?"

Baldwin hesitated and then nodded his agreement. "I swear."

The answer was good enough for Godfrey. "I remember it as if it were yesterday. I was out for a ride on my horse—you know, the path that runs through the forest on our family land."

Baldwin's head rocked up and down. "I do."

"The great leaders of Christianity were calling for soldiers to lead a Crusade against the Saracen hordes in Jerusalem. I was uncertain whether or not I should go. Of course, I knew the answer. It may surprise you to know that I had a good amount of fear in my heart."

That did surprise Baldwin. He'd never known his brother to fear anything. On more than one occasion, Baldwin witnessed his brother overcoming incredible odds on the battlefield. One such occasion was during the main assault on Jerusalem. While many leaders would have stayed near the back of the lines, Godfrey led the men into battle, cutting down enemies from atop his steed. Even after losing his horse, Godfrey fought on, hacking his way through enemy lines as if some kind of divine power coursed through him, surging him forward without ever tiring. Baldwin recounted times when his brother had even fought off wild beasts with his bare hands, killing ravenous animals three times his size.

"Fear is a natural thing, Baldwin. It is the point in the road in which men make a decision to be courageous, or cowards." He let the words sink in before he continued. "During my ride through the forest, I decided to take a moment to pray. So I got off the horse and knelt by a large oak, one that has been on our land since long before we were born. I prayed that God would give me strength to do what is right, and to fight for Him in all things. When I arose and opened my eyes, I was surprised to see a man in gray robes standing less than twenty feet away."

"A man in gray robes?"

"Yes. I drew my sword and demanded he tell me who he was and what he wanted. I told him he was on my land and that by rights I could cut him down for trespassing.

"The man drew back his hood and revealed an old face, worn with the wrinkles of time. His beard and hair were white like snow. But his eyes were full of peace. I knew he meant no ill will."

Baldwin had been sucked into the story and leaned in close. "What did you do?"

“I lowered my sword and asked him what he wanted. The man told me he had a gift for me, and me alone. I asked what kind of gift, but he wouldn’t answer. He merely stepped forward and produced a map from an inner pocket of his robe.”

“A map?”

Godfrey nodded. “Yes. I asked what the map led to, what area it depicted, but he would not answer. When I took a moment to look over the map again, the man was gone, as if the forest had consumed him. I mounted my horse and looked everywhere, but the old man was nowhere to be found. He’d vanished.”

“What did you do?”

Godfrey’s lungs wheezed like he might cough again, but the fits didn’t return. “I deciphered the map and used it to find something incredible, something that helped me during the Crusades. Without it, we would have surely lost.”

The buildup was tugging at Baldwin’s curiosity. “What is it?”

“A sword. But not just any sword. It is a sword that commands incredible power. For a time, the one who wields it cannot be destroyed.”

“For a time?”

“That power fades, remember? It needs to be returned to its home until the world needs another leader to rise against evil. That is the task I ask of you, my brother. You must return the sword to its home. Keep it hidden. Keep it safe. You must tell no other human about this. If evil were to find it, the world as we know it would end.”

“But how could evil use it if the power fades?”

Godfrey forced a smile across his lips. “When it is returned to its home, the power renews itself. Then the sword becomes the ultimate weapon once more. Whoever wields it will be unstoppable.”

“Where do I take it?”

Godfrey raised his hand to a golden necklace clinging to his chest. It was a circle, surrounded by five half circles. The jewelry gave the appearance of a golden sun. Godfrey ripped it from his neck and handed it to his brother.

Baldwin stared at the object in his palm as Godfrey’s cold, clammy fingers pulled away.

“The location…is inside. Remember, Brother…you must never tell a soul. Only God can reveal the location to His sword. He chooses who will wield it next, not you or I.”

Godfrey’s breaths came quicker. His face tightened, and Baldwin knew his brother was on death’s doorstep.

“The sword, Brother. Where is it?”

“It is safe, in a place only you would know where to look. When we were children, remember the trick I played on you with your favorite toy?”

A tear formed in the corner of Baldwin’s eye. He remembered the event well. Somehow, Godfrey had taken his favorite toy sword and put it in his own scabbard. Wearing it in plain sight, Baldwin never suspected. After allowing his younger brother to search the house for the faux weapon, Godfrey gave away the hiding place by tapping his finger on the hilt.

Baldwin stood up straight and glanced down at the weapon. Then he looked back to his brother. In the rush to get to his brother's side, he'd not even noticed the difference.

Godfrey gave a weak nod. "It was the safest place for me to put it, Brother. Take it back to where it belongs. That is my last request for you."

Suddenly, Godfrey's body tensed. His lungs gurgled inside his chest. He shook violently for several seconds, fighting death's grip as long as he could. Then, as suddenly as it began, the fit ended, and Godfrey's eyes settled on a random spot on the ceiling.

Baldwin stared at him for a second and then reached out his hand. He took Godfrey's in his own and held it tight. The skin was cold, like the stone of a wine cellar back in their homeland.

"Brother?" he said.

There was no response.

Baldwin leaned in and listened to Godfrey's chest. It was deathly silent.

He straightened up, fighting back the tears. "Nurse!" he yelled.

People flooded the room once more. Wailing soon commenced. The military leaders paid their respects and then immediately began the discussion concerning Godfrey's successor.

Baldwin heard his name more than once, but he didn't care about that at the moment. He had a mission to complete, the last request of his brother.

He stepped out of the room and wandered down the hall until he found an empty room on the right.

It was nothing more than a simple cell, a place where one of the maids slept. He stole a quick glance down both directions of the corridor and then slipped inside, closing the door behind.

He stared down at the sword in the scabbard. How it had gone unnoticed to him was still a mystery. In hindsight, he had never given much thought to putting on his belt and scabbard. It had become second nature, an unconscious action in a multitude of routine things he did every day.

Why would he have noticed?

Now, as he stared down at the hilt, he could tell the difference. The silvery metal handle was shinier than his own weapon. The thing looked as if it had never seen the wear and tear of battle.

With a twinge of fear in his heart, he wrapped his fingers around the handle and eased the blade out of its housing. Remarkably, the edges were still perfect, and the steel still gleamed as if it had just come out of the smith's polish.

Baldwin held the sword at waist level and noticed something etched into the blade just above the hand guard. His eyes narrowed with curiosity, and he raised the weapon so he could read the lettering.

There were three lines, one in Hebrew, one in Greek and one in Latin. The first two were languages Baldwin didn't speak. He had a feeling they all said the same thing. His eyes widened as he read the last line in Latin.

Caliburnus.

Chapter 1
Bellevaux, France

Tommy's wide eyes stared unblinking into the gaping hole in the rock. His team from the International Archaeological Agency had been working alongside teams from all over the world to uncover centuries-old ruins, buried just a few hundred yards from an eleventh-century castle, or what was left of it. The location was perched atop a steep mountain. It was framed by picturesque views of the Lac de Vallon and the surrounding hillsides covered in green coniferous trees.

Their painstaking efforts had resulted in not only the discovery of structures that predated the castle but dozens of artifacts including pottery, glassware, and remnants of weapons. They'd also found a section of rock in the basement of the ruins that had been carved out by human hands. Inside was a stone sarcophagus.

Never had Tommy expected to find anything like this in an historically remote location. Sure, he'd hoped there would be some artifacts or relics on site, but to find an actual sarcophagus was beyond anyone's wildest dreams.

The team of workers cleared a path and set up a series of lights inside so Tommy and his assistants could see more easily. He moved down the temporary wooden steps onto the lower landing, followed closely by three others. Two were men from Oxford. A third was a female anthropologist from Switzerland.

The buzz grew quickly and soon a daily crowd of onlookers arrived outside the roped area surrounding the site.

Tommy wasn't accustomed to people watching as he and his team did their work. He preferred to take care of things in secret. This project, however, wasn't his baby. Most of them weren't, although the people who brought in his team typically let them operate however they wanted.

Cameras flashed around the four as they entered the floodlights' pale glow coming from the corners of the cave. Only a few people from the media had come to cover the story. The number didn't matter. What mattered was the discovery itself.

Tommy had already taken a look at the stone box, but that didn't keep the sight from stopping his breath as he stepped closer and beheld the shield engraved on the surface. A Templar cross was cut within the shield's borders, surrounded by four other, less elaborate equilateral crosses. It was a symbol synonymous with the legendary Crusader, Godfrey of Bouillon. Tommy thought it, though he didn't say it out loud. He didn't need to. The fact that the symbol was here in France made no sense. The great leader was purportedly buried within the confines of the Church of the Holy Sepulchre in Jerusalem.

Then Tommy reminded himself of where he was. This land would have fallen squarely into the area that was considered part of Godfrey's property.

Was this the true burial spot for one of the greatest leaders of the Crusades? Or was it one of his followers? Tommy had put off the answers until he had more time with the evidence. He was only seeing the tip of the iceberg at this point.

The other three hadn't seen the surface of the sarcophagus yet and were unaware of the engraving. Tommy had kept that a secret to only be revealed by their own eyes.

"Incredible," said one of the men from Oxford. His gray hair and beard were badges of honor in a world where one's depth of knowledge was dependent on years of experience. This was Dr. Tim Hathaway, an anthropologist from London. He'd been an expert in his field for more than 30 years.

The other man—one of similar age and manner—was Dr. Nicholas Remming. He nodded in agreement. "Well done, Tommy. Well done indeed. A Templar burial site. Astonishing." Remming had been a professor of medieval studies for 22 years and had taken part in more than a dozen digs across Europe.

"Not just a Templar, Doctor. These perfectly align with images often associated with Godfrey of Bouillon."

The older man raised an eyebrow and fired a suspicious look Tommy's way. "We'll see."

The researcher, Dr. Cherie Sauvad, took a few pictures with her smartphone and then began putting on gloves she'd brought in. Her graying brown hair was pulled back into a tight bun. The hairdo stretched the shallow wrinkles on her forehead, almost making them disappear.

"I hope you gents are ready for this," she said.

The other three nodded, and she motioned for two of the workers outside to join them in the sepulcher. The men—both of Asian descent—hurried inside with crowbars and shovels.

Sauvad motioned to the sarcophagus lid. "Be very careful," she said. "Make sure the lid doesn't fall into the box. The last thing we need is to crush the remains."

The two Oxford men took a nervous breath as the workers wedged their tools into the seam between the top and the bottom of the box. When they were satisfied with the depth, they leveraged the iron, and the lid came off its housing. The workers nodded at each other and slid the top a few inches toward the far wall. Dust tumbled out and over the lip of the sarcophagus. The two older men covered their faces with handkerchiefs to ease their breathing.

Once there was enough room for the workers to get their fingers under the lid, they set down their tools and took up positions opposite each other on either end. With a curt nod, they hefted the heavy object and slid it to where it was slightly less than half off the bottom. There, they held it in place, letting most of the weight rest on the sarcophagus's rim.

"Perfect," Sauvad said. "Just hold it there for a moment."

The two workers pressed down on the lid's edge to keep it in place as she moved closer.

When the dust settled, the cave's occupants all stared inside to see what secrets the stone box held.

They all expected bones, probably wrapped in medieval clothing or armor.

Instead, what they saw was a dusty shield. No skeleton. No armor. Just a shield.

Everyone in the cave frowned.

“Where’s the body?” Sauvad asked. “I don’t understand.”

Dr. Remming glanced over at Tommy. “You’ve kept this area secure since its discovery, yes?”

“Of course,” Tommy stammered. “We’ve had video surveillance and guards posted around the clock. If someone tried to get in here, we’d have known about it.”

Sauvad continued gazing into the sarcophagus. She reached out and ran a gloved finger along the shield’s edge, wiping a thin layer of dust from the surface. Her action revealed a pale yellow metal.

“Gold leaf on the edge,” she said. “If someone broke in here to steal something, they would have taken this with them.” She looked closer and wiped her hand across the breadth of the shield. “What’s this?”

She repeated the action three more times until everyone in the chamber could see clearly the image on the metal surface.

It was a black eagle, a symbol used by one of the greatest kings to ever live: Charlemagne.

“Wait a minute,” Tommy said. “That can’t be right.”

“It must be a forgery,” said Hathaway. “Charlemagne is buried in Aachen. Everyone knows that.”

"Yeah, but there's no body here. Maybe this wasn't meant to be a burial chamber."

"Why, then, is there a sarcophagus?" Remming asked. "And why is it on Bouillon land?"

Tommy put his hands on his hips and stared at the shield. "Dr. Sauvad, may I use your gloves for a moment?"

"Certainly."

"What are you doing?" Hathaway asked, his voice full of uncertainty.

"Just having a look."

Tommy lifted the shield from its resting place and stared into the shadow underneath. A yellowish object caught his attention. Propping the shield up with one hand, he used the other to reach under. A moment later, he laid the shield back down and held up the object he'd removed.

It was a circular medallion with five half circles surrounding it. Every eye in the room stared at the small treasure.

"What is it? Who was the owner?" Sauvad asked.

"Where is the owner?" Remming asked.

"Look," Tommy said. "On the back. There's something inscribed on the metal." He peered closer. "It looks like Latin."

Sauvad read the lines out loud before the others had a chance. "It says, *All who draw the sword will die by the sword.*"

"Why in heaven's name does it say that?" Hathaway asked.

The two workers suddenly drew pistols out of their jackets and pointed them at the other occupants.

"Hand over the medallion," one of them said in heavily accented English. "Do it now, and don't try anything stupid."

The two Englishmen took a moment to process what was happening.

"What is the meaning of this?" Remming demanded.

Tommy answered for them. "They're stealing this artifact. Which, I don't have to tell you two, is a bad idea. You won't get out of here with it."

"We'll see," the worker who'd spoken before said. "Medallion. Now."

His voice grew louder but still not loud enough to be heard outside the cave.

"You two positioned yourselves perfectly," Tommy said. "Nobody can see you thanks to where the walls cut off. But they'll see you come out. Then what's your plan?"

"Not your concern. Now give me the medallion, or I kill her." The worker pressed the muzzle to the side of Sauvad's head.

She trembled but didn't dare move.

"Okay, just take it easy," Tommy said. He held out the object and moved his hand slowly toward the gunman. "Point the gun at me, not her. She's not the one holding what you want. I am."

"Shut up," the gunman snapped.

When Tommy's hand was at full extension, the gunman shoved Sauvad out of the way and snatched it from the American.

"Now all of you step back into the corner." He waved his gun. His partner sidestepped toward the entrance, circling around the sarcophagus.

Tommy watched the second man's movement and instantly recognized an opportunity. As the silent partner neared the other gunman, Tommy slid his hand on top of the sarcophagus lid as if to brace himself. When the other three researchers were safely behind him, he pressed down hard on the lid's corner and stepped back.

The heavy object immediately slipped off its housing and crashed to the floor, crushing the second gunman's foot in the process. He howled in agony. His trigger finger instinctively pulled and fired off a shot that ricocheted around the room.

Ironically, it struck the shooter in the side of the head, and within seconds he slumped to the floor. Tommy clambered over the lid and twisted the weapon out of the dead man's hand. He spun around to aim at the other guy, but all he saw was the man's feet as he sprinted up the stairs.

Tommy shook his head like a dog. "I usually have a guy for this."

He jumped over the dead man's left leg and took off.

People gasped, and one person shrieked.

Tommy imagined the gunman wielding his weapon to clear a path. He burst from the cave and charged after the thief. Another woman in the crowd of onlookers screamed at the sight of Tommy running with a gun.

"It's okay," he said, putting up a dismissive hand as he ran by. "I'm one of the good guys."

His disclaimer did little to ease any minds. People still ducked and scattered.

Tommy didn't have time to worry about that.

He had a thief to catch.

Running up another section of steps sent his heart rate to its max capacity as he reached the third and final tier.

Tommy gasped for breath, forcing himself to keep going. His legs felt like bags of sand, growing heavier and heavier with every step. The thief appeared to be unaffected by the stair sprint. He'd lengthened the gap to nearly twenty yards, and it wasn't getting any better for Tommy.

The only way down from the dig site was a narrow one-lane road that wound around the mountain, circling it until arriving at the bottom, and a slightly wider road leading out of the rural village.

The thief was making his way toward one of the few cars parked nearby. If he got in, stopping him would be nearly impossible.

Tommy took a few more steps as the thief skidded to a stop at the driver's side of a red sedan. He reached for the door handle but was halted by a loud pop. The bullet smashed into the front quarter panel. Another gunshot sent a round through the windshield.

The thief took cover behind the next vehicle in line and waited. Tommy was crouched on one knee, aiming carefully with his weapon. Now that the other guy was behind another car, he didn't have a clear shot. And Tommy was out in the open, completely exposed.

Without warning, the thief rose quickly and fired four successive shots. Tommy did the only thing he could. He dove and rolled as the dirt erupted around him. As he tumbled sideways, he managed to extend his weapon and squeeze the trigger five times.

The shots were wildly inaccurate, most sailing off into the ether, or wherever errant bullets go. Two, however, made themselves useful.

One found its way into the front left tire of the red sedan, rendering the getaway car useless. The second round snuck under the vehicle the thief was using for cover and struck the man in the shin.

He instantly dropped to the ground, howling in agony. The fingers on his free hand wrapped around the bloody wound. He didn't release his weapon, though.

Tommy seized the moment. He dragged himself up and ran as hard as he could toward the car on the far end of the row. Gunfire erupted again from the thief's weapon, but Tommy dove for cover before any of the bullets even came close.

Safe for the moment, Tommy tucked in behind the front tire of an SUV and waited a second.

"Okay. Stay on the offensive," he whispered.

He took a deep breath and peeked around the vehicle's front end. Instead of seeing the man writhing on the ground from the bullet wound,

Tommy was shocked to see the guy hobbling desperately toward the curve in the road.

"Seriously?"

If the situation hadn't been so dangerous, he would have thought it a hilarious sight.

Tommy crept out from behind his hiding place with his pistol held waist high. He still panted for air, but the run had been a short one and in the time he'd been hiding, his legs had mostly recovered.

"I have got to start working out more," he said and took off after the thief once again.

In spite of the wound to his leg, the thief had picked up speed and was already nearing the bend in the road. He looked back over his shoulder and saw Tommy bearing down on him. He raised his weapon and fired a salvo at the big American.

Tommy's reaction was almost catlike. He'd seen the guy's intent when he turned around. The only place Tommy could take cover was a large boulder on the side of the drive. Bullets splashed into the gravel and pinged off the boulder until no more shots rang out. Tommy wasn't as good at counting enemy rounds as his friend Sean, but he was pretty sure the thief's gun was empty.

He popped around the corner, fired a reply of his own, and caught the thief in the middle of checking his pockets for a fresh magazine. Startled, the man took off again, running down the road.

Tommy dashed after him, like the worlds slowest 100-meter sprinter coming out of the blocks. His lack of speed didn't matter now. His prey was injured, and that tilted the odds in Tommy's favor.

The thief panicked as Tommy closed the gap to less than ten yards. Then he did something unexpected. He spun to the right and veered toward the cliff's edge as if he planned to jump.

Tommy's eyes widened as he saw the man draw closer to the ledge. There was no time to lose. If the guy jumped, the medallion could be lost forever to the depths of the lake below.

With only two yards between Tommy and the thief, and only one yard between the thief and the precipice, Tommy pushed all his weight onto his left foot and leaped forward with arms outstretched. The thief looked back in time to see the big American flying at him. He tried to jump away, but it was too late. Tommy's right arm struck the man's heel. The heavy force tripped him and sent him tumbling toward the precipice.

Tommy kept his head up as he hit the gravel. The thief rolled toward the ledge only a few feet away. Without a second to lose, Tommy reached out and grabbed a handful of the thief's jacket just as the man's momentum carried him over the steep drop-off.

For a second, the thief's dead weight pulled Tommy downward. Tommy kicked his toes hard into the gravel as he was dragged toward the edge. Luckily, his foot caught on a rock embedded in the ground. With his upper chest hanging over the precipice, he was faced with a six-hundred-foot drop down an 80-degree slope. Even though it wasn't straight down, the odds of surviving such a fall were slim to none.

The thief's good foot was planted on a narrow ledge about six feet down. Apparently, he was having second thoughts about jumping.

"Grab my arms," Tommy said. "I'll pull you up."

The man's narrow eyes were full of angry determination. He said nothing in response.

Tommy's fingers and forearms strained to keep the man's weight up even though the guy had a fragile foothold.

"I can't hold you like this forever. Let me pull you up. Then we'll talk."

"There is nothing to talk about, American dog. Soon, the world will bow to us and the Dear Leader."

"Dear leader? Listen, you can tell me all about it. Just take my hand, and let me pull you up."

Tommy twisted one hand, trying to get a better grip on the inside of the man's jacket. He grunted and felt his foot sliding off the rock that was the only thing keeping him from going over the edge as well.

The thief's eyes blazed as he stared into Tommy's. "For the leader," he said in a menacing tone. He reached up with both hands to grab Tommy and pull him down, but his foot slipped off the ledge below.

Tommy's fingers instinctively let go. For a bizarre second, the thief hung in limbo as gravity wrapped its hands around him. His eyes went wide as he suddenly felt himself being dragged downward.

For a second, Tommy watched as the man tumbled through the air until he saw the man's head violently crack against the rocky slope. Then the thief's somersault instantly sped up as he plummeted to the water below.

Tommy shimmied back to safe ground before the man hit the lake. There was a faint splash in the distance, signaling the thief's fate. Tommy breathed hard for a minute. Then he propped himself up with one hand on the ground.

His eyes caught a glimpse of something on the gravel a few feet away. It was yellowish and glimmered in the sunlight peeking out from behind white fluffy clouds above. He crawled the short distance over to the medallion and picked it up, holding it to the light. Underneath the engraved words was one number: a nine.

When he spoke, it was in a whisper. "What secret are you hiding?"

Chapter 2
Aachen, Germany

Dr. Jann Heimrich stared at the screen in disbelief.

He'd been working on the DNA sequencing project for more than two years. It had begun with getting the appropriate paperwork and permissions, and wading through miles of other red tape.

That was to be expected when dealing with the remains of one of the greatest kings who ever lived. Getting access to tissue and bone samples of Charlemagne was one of the most ambitious things Heimrich had ever taken on. After months of interviews and appeals, he'd finally gotten permission to examine a small portion of the king's body.

The Aachen Cathedral had been roped off one evening, which wasn't a huge problem since few parishioners visited after dark. Under careful supervision, Heimrich had taken the samples from the remains, stored them in the appropriate containers, and then transported them to his lab on the other side of town.

The process, the years of waiting, had all led to this, this incredible revelation.

"That can't be right," he said.

He adjusted the view on the screen by zooming in closer.

The adjustment didn't change what he already knew to be correct. "That's impossible."

"What's impossible, Doctor?"

The voice startled Heimrich, and he instinctively spun around to make sure it was his assistant.

"Oh, Michael. You frightened me."

"Maybe if you weren't working alone in the dark in an old laboratory after nightfall...."

Heimrich snickered. "Good point. What are you doing here so late? I thought you would have gone home for dinner."

"I just had a few things to clean up before I left for the night. What are you doing?"

"Come, come. You must have a look at this." He beckoned his Korean assistant to the computer.

Michael obliged and padded from the doorway over to the workstation. Heimrich scooted his rolling chair to the side so his assistant could get a better view.

"See?" He pointed at the screen as Michael leaned over and examined the display. "The DNA, it's..."

"It's not human."

Heimrich shrugged his head to one side. "Well, not exactly what I was going to say. It definitely *is* human."

"Not like any human DNA I've ever seen."

"Correct. You're correct on that."

Michael leaned in closer to the computer. His face was less than a foot away from it now. "Are you talking about some kind of evolutionary mutation, Doctor?"

"You know me better than that."

It was true. Heimrich didn't subscribe to the theory of evolution. He'd studied the evidence on both sides of the argument and chosen the side with an architect.

"What, then?" Michael asked.

"I'm not sure. Whatever this is will be a big discovery for us." He pointed at some of the dots on the screen. "This could prove that certain people from history were more than just ordinary humans."

"Are you saying that Charlemagne was more than a man?"

Heimrich stared at the screen. "What I'm saying is that he was no normal man. With these additions to the sequence, it's possible he could have been smarter, maybe even stronger, than an average man."

"That would certainly account for his military prowess. How did this happen?"

Heimrich absently rubbed the scruff on his chin as he considered the question. He'd been thinking on it long before Michael entered the room.

"Have you ever heard stories about relics that gave human beings incredible powers?"

"Of course," Michael said, standing up straight again. He tweaked his neck to the left and right to get the kinks out. "It's one of the reasons people are searching for the Holy Grail."

"Right. An excellent example. There are people who believe that if they find those relics, the objects can give them some kind of power. What if the power a person receives is actually a genetic transformation, something that makes them—as you said—more than human?"

Michael raised a dubious eyebrow. “Doctor, you don’t actually think there is something out there that could cause this sort of mutation in a human being, do you?”

“All I’m saying is that something changed Charlemagne’s DNA. And like you said, that *could* account for his incredible success as a warrior.”

“Yes, but he died.”

Heimrich raised a finger. “Aha. I had the same thought.” He maneuvered the mouse and clicked it a few times to zoom in on the image. “You see here how some components are somewhat smaller than the regular pieces of code?”

“Yeah...”

“It appears they deteriorated, probably over time.”

“So what does that mean, exactly?”

Heimrich fell back in his chair and put his thumb to his chin once more. “I’m afraid I have no idea.”

They lapsed into silence as Michael considered the doctor’s theory. “All of the samples had this same result?”

“Every single one,” Heimrich said, nodding. “They’re all consistent. The mutation happened throughout the entire code. What I wouldn’t give to have taken a blood sample from Charlemagne himself. Then we could have confirmed what was going on.”

Michael sidetracked the conversation to public relations. “Are you going to announce this discovery?”

"Hmm? Oh, yes. Yes, of course. We'll set up a press conference, get all the appropriate people involved. The scientific journals will be extremely interested in this find. Obviously, it will stir up a good amount of wild theories, but that is to be expected. At least the officials who gave us access to the remains will be glad to see something incredible came out of it."

Michael listened, keeping his face emotionless, like stone. When Heimrich finished, Michael crossed his arms and gave a nod. "I'm sure you'll be world famous as a result of this find, Doctor. This is going to be huge."

Heimrich blushed. "Well, thank you, Michael. I don't seek to be famous, although some of the money that may come with fame would be nice. Have to pay the bills. But yes, I should think the news of this discovery will go far and wide."

Michael unfolded his arms and in doing so revealed a black pistol with a lengthened round barrel.

Heimrich frowned at the sight of the weapon.

Michael spoke before the doctor could say anything. "We can't have the world knowing about this little secret, now can we, Doctor?"

The muzzle flashed four times, brightening the laboratory for a half second with each squeeze of the trigger. Michael lowered the weapon and stared at his handiwork. Three rounds to the chest and one to the head made sure Heimrich was dead.

Michael glanced back into the corner near the door. He'd disabled the camera earlier. The little red light on the side no longer glowed. There would be no evidence, no witnesses as to what just happened.

Hurriedly, he put away his gun and set about collecting the samples of mutated DNA. He found a medical cooler he'd placed in the room under one of the tables and put the samples inside. It was still very cold in the box, which would protect the DNA long enough for him to get to the drop-off point.

Next, he deleted all the computer files that contained anything about the Charlemagne DNA. The last thing he needed was for the police to accidentally find what the doctor had been investigating.

Satisfied the information was secure and all the samples taken, he grabbed the cooler and strolled out the door into the hallway. All the cameras in that wing of the building had been disabled so he'd have a clear path to his getaway car.

Soon, he would return to North Korea a hero.

Chapter 3
Venice, Italy

A small section of the building's corner exploded in a burst of debris and dust as the bullet smashed into the decades-old brick. Sean ducked his head and jumped into the alley as his pursuer fired another round—this one sailing wide of the corner and into the façade of the building next door.

He drove his legs harder, pounding the concrete with the balls of his feet as he approached the next intersection of the sidewalks.

Sean had visited Venice several times in the past. That didn't change the fact that the mazes of causeways, sidewalks, and canals were extremely confusing—even for Venetians. Based on his previous tack, another canal would be up ahead on the right. That or he'd find himself—quite literally—in a dead end.

He clutched the brown paper package tight in his right hand and tucked it under his armpit like a football as he darted toward the next turn.

The gunman behind him fired again. The bullet ricocheted loudly off the concrete close to Sean's right foot. Another bounced off the windowsill near his left elbow.

He reached the turn and ran ahead, finding a bridge that spanned one of the old city's many canals. A few tourists stood on it with their elbows on the railing, probably talking about how romantic the city was or how they'd like to stay another day if they could.

Other than for its historical value, Sean didn't feel the same way about the old city on the water. It smelled in the morning and—as mentioned before—was extraordinarily confusing to navigate. He didn't particularly care for the people either, noting that the Italians farther to the south seemed to be much friendlier.

Maybe he'd just been to Venice for the wrong reasons. Like the one under his arm.

He cut to the left and found himself staring at steps that descended into the water. No sidewalks lined this canal.

"Crap."

He heard the footsteps of the gunman approaching the bridge. The guy was running at a furious pace.

Sean stuffed the package into his jacket pocket and pressed his back against the building nearest him, and waited. He didn't have to wait long. As soon as Sean felt the pursuer was close enough, he spun around the corner, extended his arm, and clotheslined the guy squarely across the throat.

The gunman flipped 90 degrees, his face smacking the ground as he landed. His weapon tumbled through the air, struck one of the steps leading into the water, and plopped into the murky liquid.

Disoriented and desperate, the gunman grasped at his throat. Sean knew he'd crushed the man's larynx. Without immediate medical attention, he would be dead in less than ninety seconds.

Apparently, the gunman didn't care.

He kicked his leg and caught Sean off guard, squarely in the ankle. Sean fell to one knee. Alertly, he sensed the next attack and raised his elbow in time to deflect the man's downward punch. The momentum brought the attacker too close. Sean instantly twisted his body, getting as much force behind the counter as possible, and drove his fist into the man's gut.

The two tourists on the bridge stood in awe for a moment and then took off running in the other direction, the woman yelling something in Serbian.

Sean rose quickly and swung with his right fist. His target was hunched over yet still managed to deflect the first punch. He couldn't stop the second one. Sean's left fist snapped like lightning, striking the man's jaw. His head rocked back, and he staggered toward the bridge rail. Sean pressed the attack, landing a second and third blow until the man could barely stand.

Sean stared at him for a second with fists still up and ready. The guy's nose bled, his right eye already swelling. He wavered—gasping for breath—and then collapsed, prostrate, onto the sidewalk.

A nudge with his shoe against the man's side told Sean the guy was dead. Sean took in a deep breath and sighed. He picked up the object he'd dropped during the fight and stared at the wrapping.

He considered opening it but knew he should wait.

Sudden movement in the corner of his eye confirmed his caution. He ducked back for cover as another pursuer fired a pistol. The bullet thumped into the building on the left across the bridge.

"These guys just don't give up."

He drew his weapon and whipped around the corner. His finger squeezed the trigger three times, unleashing a deadly metallic volley at the second gunman. Sean didn't wait for the man to return fire. The second he saw the guy duck for cover, Sean sprinted across the bridge and into the next alley.

More gunfire erupted behind him, but the shooter was too far away to be accurate. No doubt the man was trying to chase while shooting, which would only make it worse.

Sirens whined from somewhere beyond the buildings. The tourists must have alerted the police. Of course, it could have been the gunshots that alerted the citizenry to trouble.

Either way, Sean had no desire to deal with the authorities. He had to get away.

He ducked down a pathway running alongside one of the canals and then turned right into another parallel alley. He didn't need to check what time it was. Sean knew he was at least five minutes late. Fortunately, there was no way his ride was going to leave him.

He burst through one of the archways of Saint Mark's Square and into the crowded plaza. Dozens of pigeons sprang to life, startled by his sudden appearance. The flocks of birds flapped their wings furiously as they climbed into the air and swirled over the piazza.

Sean kept running, now leery of an attack from above *and* behind.

Tourists pointed at the mass of birds as they took flight. But some continued taking pictures or drinking their morning coffee. Only one or two people noticed the American running at full stretch as he turned toward the harbor.

Another gunshot echoed from the square as Sean cleared the last pillars and crossed over the main thoroughfare on the edge of the city. A woman screamed from behind him, but he didn't turn around to see what happened. His focus was straight ahead, on a brown speedboat waiting at one of the docks.

A man off to his left yelled something in Italian. Sean knew what the word meant, but he didn't care. He wasn't going to stop. His eyes stayed locked on the boat less than forty yards away. He sensed the police rushing toward him. Fortunately, the gunman fired again, and their attention immediately turned his way.

Sean didn't see the bullet strike an innocent tourist in the leg just a few feet away from him. With the police now on his side, Sean pumped his muscles faster.

The tapping of his feet on concrete and stone changed to thumping as his shoes repeatedly pounded on the wooden dock. In the boat, he could see Adriana was looking his way.

"Start the boat!" he yelled.

She didn't need to be told twice. Adriana twisted the key in the ignition and the motor roared to life.

She'd only tied off the back end. She stepped over and loosed the rope, dropping it on the deck. Then she stepped back to the wheel and wrapped her fingers around the knob to the side.

The sirens grew louder. Sean noted the police boats splashing through the waves as they drew close to the docks. The spotters were pointing at the crowd of people near the piazza.

He took two last steps and then dove from the dock into the boat, rolling to a crashing halt against the gunwale.

Adriana didn't wait for an order. She shifted the knob forward and eased the boat out of its slip. The motor groaned and lifted the bow several feet. Adriana guided the craft out into the open water, keeping her eyes forward just in case the police had noticed her escape. Looking casual was the first step in remaining anonymous.

Her dark brown hair was pulled back tight into a ponytail, but a few loose strands had pulled free and flapped around in the wind.

When they were clear of the busy channels, she turned the wheel and steered toward the backside of the nearest island across the way. She glanced down at Sean and flashed him a bright smile.

"Had some trouble back there?" she asked in her Spanish accent.

Sean was still catching his breath. He sat up enough to look out behind them at the chaos surrounding San Marco Square. "A little. It wasn't easy; I'll say that."

"Is it ever?"

He shook his head. “Almost never.”

She gazed out over the water as the bow rose and fell in the two-foot swells. “I’m assuming it’s in your jacket. That or you dropped it in your mad dash for the boat.”

Sean chuckled and reached into his jacket. He produced the object, still wrapped in its brown paper. He held it up triumphantly and shook it with a flick of the wrist.

“Aww, that was nice of you to gift wrap it for him.”

“I thought he’d think it was a nice touch,” Sean said, continuing her sarcasm. “A brown bag was the best I could do. Thought it might help to disguise it.”

“Did it?”

“Not even close.”

Adriana snorted. “Well, Tommy should be happy. I imagine he’ll get a good amount of press for this one. Not to mention some powerful friends.”

“Yeah. And enemies.”

Chapter 4
Pyongyang, North Korea

Han-Jae Pak strode through the dark corridor, wearing the smile of a triumphant warrior. He carried a small metallic case in his right hand, locked to his wrist by a thin chain and cuff.

None of the soldiers saluted as he walked by. He wasn't an officer, not that they knew of. Pak's job was entirely undercover, only known to the highest of officials in the North Korean government. Not even the Chairman knew who he was or what he did.

His boss made sure of that.

Pak stopped at the pair of elevators and pressed the button. It didn't surprise him that the door to the right opened immediately. Due to the lateness of the hour, he doubted anyone would be out and about. Curfews made certain that the city's citizens were off the streets well before midnight.

After a slow ride up to the penthouse, Pak stepped off and turned to his left. One of the guards—a low-level soldier in the North Korean army—greeted him with a nod and moved aside to allow Pak to pass.

Pak recognized the man but didn't say anything to him. There was no time for chitchat. He had something of extreme importance to share.

At the last door on the right, Pak stopped and knocked three times. A moment later, an older man in a gray shirt and pants opened the door. His black hair was slicked back. The cheeks below his eyes were slightly swollen and his neck a tad pudgy.

Pak wasn't surprised. The only people in the country who tended to eat well were the ones who ran it. General Ku Min-Woo was one of those. When the general had first approached Pak about a secret mission, the younger man had been wary. After a little convincing, however, Pak started to see things the general's way.

What they were doing wasn't some piddly little thing, either. It was clear-cut treason. If the Chairman found out about it, they'd both be dead men, along with at least a dozen or so others who'd been in on the conspiracy. For most of those involved, it was worth it, including Han-Jae Pak.

He'd worked as a spy for nearly a decade. The general knew he was one of their best operatives, but that wasn't the only reason he'd chosen Pak. He knew that Pak had a desperate family who was—at this very moment—probably starving to death. A promise of extra rations would make people do things they'd normally scoff at. Especially in North Korea. The rules here were different.

Since Dear Leader had done nothing to assist Pak's family, he figured it didn't matter if what he was doing was treason or not. In reality, the Chairman had betrayed his people. Now it was time to set things straight.

Han-Jae wasn't anti-government. He was proud of his heritage and believed North Korea should assert its power on a global stage, but in the pursuit of vainglory, the government had forgotten its most important responsibility: its people.

"You've done well," the general said. He moved aside and motioned for Pak to enter.

Once he was inside, the general closed the door and led the way to a dining room table in a corner just beyond the kitchen. The condo was minimally decorated, as were those of most officials who worked in government. General Min-Woo, however, had a much larger living space than the average citizen. The condo featured three bedrooms, two baths, and a living room that was the size of most apartments in Pyongyang.

Pak set the metal case on the table and pulled a small key out of his right pocket. He loosed the cuff from his wrist first and then inserted the key into the hole on top of the case.

"There's nothing dangerous in there, correct?"

"Of course not, sir. All of the samples are currently in our labs under safe watch."

Min-Woo gave an approving nod.

Pak flipped the snaps holding the two halves of the case together and lifted the top. Inside was a stack of printed images and papers.

"The reports you asked for," Pak said. "Along with images of the DNA samples, straight from the German's lab."

Min-Woo picked up the documents and pored over them. He set them down after a rudimentary glance and pinched the corner of one of the images. He held it up to the light and stared at the genetic sequence.

"The mutated blocks are smaller than the others."

“Just as you predicted, sir. Your theory about the source of the mutation fits perfectly with this evidence.”

Min-Woo’s head rocked back and forth absentmindedly. He was mesmerized by the picture. “I knew it. And even so, I couldn’t believe it was real until now, having seen it with my own eyes.”

“This will make us a world superpower, General. No one will be able to stand in our way.”

“In time, Han-Jae. In time. There is much work to be done before that can happen. And we must operate with the utmost secrecy. If the Chairman were to find out about our clandestine operations, he would have us both shot.”

No other person in the city would dare speak of performing secret operations outside the scope of the Chairman’s knowledge. But Min-Woo was not an average citizen. He personally swept his condo for bugs every other day, making sure no one was listening in on his schemes. Of course, he’d found devices. It was easy enough to remove them, place them somewhere quiet when he needed to, and then put them back where he found them. That way, whoever put them there would find them upon checking in every now and then.

He knew exactly how things worked. After all, he’d been running similar operations to catch traitors for nearly thirty years. It wasn’t his primary job, but it was certainly part of it. Because of that, Pak trusted the general implicitly and knew better than to ask whether the room was clean or not.

“Any word from the others?”

Min-Woo's face lengthened into a troubled scowl. "Unfortunately, they were not able to complete their part of the mission."

"How is that possible?" Pak's eyebrows knit together, wrinkling his forehead.

The general set the image back in the case and put his hands behind his back. "They'd been working the site with the archaeologists from America. It seems when the sarcophagus was opened, somehow the Americans seized control. One of our men was shot and killed immediately. The other made it out of the cave with the medallion, but he fell to his death off a cliff."

"Were the French authorities able to identify them?"

"It's unclear at this juncture. All I know is that they're dead and the Americans have the medallion. Their leader, a man named Tommy Schultz, was the one responsible. We believe he's received permission from the French government to do further research on the object before turning it over to them."

Pak crossed his arms over his chest. "Sounds like I need to pay them a visit."

"I have others I can send. You just got back. You need to rest."

Pak knew what the older man was saying was a test. He'd seen it before, hundreds of times. Weakness was never rewarded in their culture.

"I'll be ready to leave within the hour, General."

Min-Woo feigned considering his operative's offer. "Very well," he said after a moment. "Take your best three assets with you. This research is extremely important, but none of it matters without that medallion. Understand?"

"Clearly, sir."

"Good." Min-Woo pointed at a folder on the edge of the counter in the kitchen. "You'll find everything you need to know about Schultz in that file. He's had a history of encounters with dangerous people. So don't let his appearance fool you. Schultz is a problem. Once you have the medallion, kill him."

"With pleasure, General."

Chapter 5
Atlanta, Georgia

Tommy stared out the window of the seventeenth-floor office window. The city bustled below, like it did nearly all hours of the day. Atlanta had turned into a sprawling epicenter of capitalism over the last few decades. The city had grown so much that all the peripheral towns became monstrosities in their own right. Buckhead had been nothing more than a cool hangout when Tommy was in college. Now it had its own downtown area.

He looked over to the left where the rubble of the old IAA building was being transformed into what would be their new headquarters. The foundation had already been laid. With that done, things would progress rapidly.

The doorknob clicked and Tommy spun around, wrested from his thoughts. He was surprised to see Sean at the door.

"Where in the world have you been?" Tommy asked as he stood up.

Sean's eyes danced over the room before settling on his friend. He gave Tommy a short hug and then sat down in one of the guest chairs. "I already told you; we were in Italy, working on a project."

Tommy raised a suspicious eyebrow. "One of Adriana's Nazi art things?"

"No," Sean's head moved side to side. "This was something different."

Tommy's eyes went to the black leather-bound box under his friend's arm. "Is that it?"

Sean ignored the question for a moment. “I have to say, I like the new digs.” His eyes wandered again, taking in Tommy’s temporary office and the view of the city. He pointed at the construction site a few blocks away. “Keeping an eye on things from above?”

Tommy snickered and glanced back over his shoulder out the window. “That’s not why I rented this space.”

“Didn’t hurt either.”

Tommy’s lips cracked a thin smile. “True.” He decided to change the subject. “So, I found something interesting while I was in France.”

“Yeah, I saw your text.” Sean had received the text message from Tommy before returning to the United States. “You were a little vague as to what you found. And by a little, I mean you gave me nothing to go on.”

Tommy’s grin widened as he raised both eyebrows. “Seems like we both have something interesting to share. That reminds me, by the way, I could have used you in France.”

“Oh yeah?”

“Yeah. Turns out two of our assistants on the dig weren’t vetted very well. They tried to steal the artifact we found in a sarcophagus.”

“Sarcophagus? What sarcophagus?”

“That’s the part of the story you’re interested in? Not the fact that I was almost killed, along with several other people? What about a priceless and mysterious artifact almost being lost to antiquity?”

Sean snorted and bowed his head. “Yes, I apologize. Go on. Tell me what happened.”

Tommy hesitated and motioned at the object on the desk, his curiosity getting the better of him. “No, I’d rather see what you brought me first. The box is nice.”

He stared at the leather-bound box, analyzing its shape and size.

Sean smirked. His friend had always struggled with patience. They’d known each other since childhood, their bonds tested through Tommy’s parents’ mysterious death when they were younger.

“Fine, go ahead,” Sean said. “Open it. Just stop making it weird. I’m not asking you to marry me.”

Tommy’s eyebrow twitched upward. “You sure?”

Before Sean could reach out and take back the box, Tommy snatched it off the table. Sean crossed his arms and watched with a smug grin on his face.

Tommy carefully pulled the lid off the box and set it to the side. He stared into the container for a second and then looked up at his friend. “So, seriously, you’re not asking me to marry you, right? Because this looks like a yellow diamond.”

“It is.”

“This can’t be a real diamond,” Tommy said, shaking his head. “I mean, I’m no gem expert, but something like this would be incredibly expensive. Which, again, I’m just curious why you’re giving it to me.”

Sean’s smirk broadened. “You don’t recognize that rock, do you?”

Tommy held the box closer to his face. He tilted his head one direction and then another, trying to get a better angle to analyze the precious stone. He gave up after less than a minute.

"No," he said with a shake of the head. "I mean, if this is real—and I'm still not sure about that—it's probably one of the biggest diamonds I've ever seen. Where on earth did you find it?"

"Funny you should ask," Sean said as his friend continued staring at the yellow-hued gem. "I tracked it down to some guys in Venice. They run a crime syndicate there. Jewelry isn't really their thing, but I guess for this one they made an exception. Normally, they deal in paintings, which is how Adriana and I found them."

"So you used your girlfriend's connections."

"Don't hate the player," Sean said with a shrug. "Do what you have to."

"I'm still confused. Why should I know what this is, and why did you go looking for it?"

Sean crossed his arms. "Honestly, I'm disappointed in you, Schultzie. I really thought you'd recognize the Florentine Diamond right away. It's one of the more famous missing jewels in the world."

Tommy looked up from the box and gazed at his friend, appraising him to see if Sean was lying or not. "Florentine Diamond? You can't be serious."

Sean's stare never wavered; his pressed lips gave no sign of dishonesty.

Tommy's eyes returned to the diamond, then to Sean, then back to the diamond once more. "It can't be. No one has known where this thing is for—"

"Almost a hundred years," Sean finished the thought. "Yeah, I know. I thought you'd be a little more excited about it than this."

"Sorry. I just…is this for real?"

Sean burst out laughing. "Yes, buddy. It's real. Promise. You're not on some television practical joke show."

"This…this is incredible. We'll have to set up a press conference, contact the Austrian government to make sure it's returned safely…this is a huge get, Sean. Well done." Tommy's face beamed with delight. Anytime his agency could deliver something of incredible historical value to the world, he got as giddy as a little boy on Christmas morning.

Tommy Schultz had built the International Archaeological Agency with the money his parents left him upon their untimely deaths. With shrewd investments and good public relations, he'd grown that amount into the hundreds of millions in a relatively short time, though most of that growth had been in the last year or so.

"I'm just so excited. Thank you, Sean. Thank you."

"Don't mention it. Seriously, don't mention my name when you announce this. Okay?"

"As always."

Sean Wyatt preferred to remain anonymous. He'd made enemies all over the globe during his time with Axis, a small government agency now based in Atlanta. While most of his enemies were either terminated or in jail, some were still hiding in the shadows, waiting for him to reveal himself.

"Now," Sean said, interrupting his friend's excitement, "didn't you have something you wanted to show me?"

Tommy shook his head, snapping back to reality. "Right. I almost forgot. I mean, it pales in comparison. The kids are working on getting more details right now, but we don't have some of the resources yet that we had in the old building. New hardware will be here later in the month."

He stood up, sidled over to the center of his desk, and pulled out the middle drawer. Next, he removed a plastic bag with a golden medallion stuffed inside. "Here," he said, extending the baggie to Sean. "Have a look."

Sean's eyebrows lowered as he took the bag and held it to the light. "Looks pretty old. Five, maybe six hundred years? Where'd you find it? That dig in France?"

Tommy nodded. "Yep. Found it up on the mountain above the lake. And it's older than six hundred years. We think it belonged to Godfrey of Bouillon. The sarcophagus had an eagle on it that looks remarkably similar to Godfrey's crest. Plus, it was on old Bouillon land. No body in the crypt, though. Very strange."

Sean listened as he continued inspecting the medallion. When Tommy was done, Sean pointed out the writing on the back. "I assume you already translated this Latin."

"Yep," Tommy said. "It's a reference to a verse from the *Bible*."

"Matthew 26:52. But why is it on this medallion? And what does the nine mean?"

"Good questions. We don't have all the answers yet, but we're working on it. Godfrey of Bouillon was a Crusader. Actually, he was *the* Crusader. He led a massive siege and subsequent assault on Jerusalem and captured it. Then he was named king. Godfrey was a religious man and didn't want to be called king. He said the only king of Jerusalem could be Jesus. That medallion," Tommy pointed at the object, "was included in several portraits of Godfrey. What you're holding in your hand is something that belonged to one of the greatest military figures in history."

Sean gazed at the object with his mouth agape. "I have to say, Schultzie, I thought I brought you something nice. This, though. This is incredible." He paused a second to think. "That story still doesn't explain the engraving on the back."

"Right. We had to do a little connect-the-dots work on that. As it turns out, Godfrey is part of a group of men referred to as the Nine Worthies or sometimes called the Nine Good Heroes."

Tommy slid into his desk chair and pecked away on the computer. Then he clicked the mouse twice and turned the laptop screen around so Sean could see it.

"That is a picture of a thirteenth-century sculpture in the rathaus in Cologne, Germany. It features the Nine Heroes."

Sean stared at the image for a long minute before speaking. "Who are all the others? And why haven't I heard of this?"

"Oh, you know of most of them. The other eight men are Joshua, King David, Judas Maccabeus—"

"The Jewish rebel?"

"The very same. The carving features three Jews, three pagans, and three Christians."

"Dogs and cats living together."

Tommy snorted. "Anyway, Hector, Julius Caesar, and Alexander the Great make up the pagans. The three Christians are Charlemagne, King Arthur, and our friend Godfrey. Best we can figure, that is the nine the medallion refers to."

Sean frowned. He rubbed his chin. "Yeah, but two of those guys are fictional. I mean, maybe Hector was real, but King Arthur? Come on. That whole Merlin story is a fairy tale."

Tommy rolled his shoulders. "I'm just telling you who they are. It certainly accounts for the number on the back of that medallion."

"Right. I get that. It's just hard for me to get past the fact that King Arthur—and probably Hector—weren't real."

"For now, that's irrelevant. Each of these nine men exhibited chivalrous qualities of one kind or another. That's why they're called good heroes and not just heroes. Some were kind to women, others were very generous, some were merciful."

Sean set the medallion down carefully on Tommy's desk. He pondered the information and then crossed his arms. "Well, that's a nice story. And congrats on getting two incredibly important artifacts in a single week. That's gotta be some kind of record for you."

"Yeah," Tommy said. He sounded crestfallen.

"What's the matter?"

"I don't know. It just seems like there's more than meets the eye to this thing. The riddle on the back of that medallion..."

"Okay, hold on. There's no way we know that's a riddle. It's probably just a way of honoring those other eight guys, you know? I wouldn't look too much into it, buddy. Be happy you made another historic discovery. I can't wait to see you on the History Channel."

Tommy let out a half-sincere laugh. "Yeah, but something doesn't feel right. I told you about the guys who tried to steal this."

"Yeah."

"They were Korean."

"So?" Sean shrugged. "Who cares where they were from? A thief's a thief, right? They probably just wanted to sell it."

"They were North Korean," Tommy said.

That changed things. "North Korean? Are you sure?"

Tommy nodded slowly.

"How sure?" Sean double checked.

Tommy opened a side drawer of his desk and pulled out a folder. There were pictures inside along with files on both thieves. "They were North Korean spies. Interpol had been watching them for some time. CIA, too. Not sure how the two men slipped by all those eyeballs, but they did."

"And we hired them."

"Don't beat yourself up over it. I paid them."

Sean's head twisted back and forth. "I don't understand. Since when did Pyongyang care about archaeology?"

"And since when did they use some of their highly trained spies to attempt to steal artifacts? I'm afraid right now we have more questions than answers. I've been talking back and forth with my connections in Europe. They can't seem to piece together a motivation."

"Did you call Emily?"

"No. I thought maybe you'd be better suited for that phone call, seeing how you two were partners and all."

Emily Starks was the director of Axis. She'd worked her way up through the years as a field agent. Sean and Emily had worked several assignments together. When Emily became the director, Sean walked away. He always maintained the two occurrences were coincidental. She knew him well enough to know he wasn't lying. He'd had enough of the spy game. She saw it in his eyes the day he resigned.

"Sure, I'll give her a call and see what she knows. If the CIA has them on a list, Emily probably does, too."

The phone on Tommy's desk started ringing.

He reached over and picked it up. "Hello." After a second he said, "Hold on, Tara, I'll put you on speaker."

Tommy hit the speakerphone button and set the receiver back in its housing. "I've got Sean here with me, Tara."

Tara Watson and her research partner, Alex Simms, were among the best in the business when it came to digging up hard-to-find facts and evidence. They almost never left the lab, except to get coffee—something that had saved their lives in one instance.

"Oh, hi, Sean. Glad to see you made it back from Venice safely."

Tommy glanced over at his friend. "She knew?"

One of Sean's shoulders raised for a second. He pouted his lips. "I had some questions along the way."

Tara interrupted. "So, Tommy, we've been working on this thing with the Nine Worthies, like you asked."

"How's it coming?" Tommy said.

"Slow. We started by digging into each character in the Cologne carving. There's a good bit of information on most of them, except Hector and Arthur, which is what we expected. That's not why I'm calling, though."

"Oh?"

"Get online, and do a search for Charlemagne."

Tommy waited for a few seconds to see where she was going with the conversation.

"Are you doing it?" she asked.

"Oh, sorry. Yeah. I thought you were going to say something else." He spun his monitor back around and set to work typing.

"I am." She paused and listened as Tommy pecked away at the keyboard. "See anything unusual in the headlines?"

The screen flickered and produced the search results. Two of the top links were articles about a murder in Aachen, Germany.

"A couple of news outlets are reporting a murder in Germany. There's an article about Charlemagne..."

"Stop," she said, sounding a tad more commanding than intended. "Click on one of the articles about the murder."

"Okay..." He clicked the blue link and a second later was taken to the news site. After scanning the article, Tommy said, "That's terrible. Why would someone kill that poor guy?"

"Yes, it's tragic. I know. But take a look lower down in the article. The killer switched off all the cameras in the building. He even went so far as to delete any footage that could possibly have him in it."

"Let me guess," Tommy said, "now he's disappeared, and the police don't know who they're looking for."

"Yes and no. He was able to take out the cameras in the research building. However, he didn't know there was one across the street that happened to catch a full view of him. The image is lower down in the article. It's a little fuzzy, but the cops know he's

Asian. They're looking for him now. He's the prime suspect."

Tommy's interest piqued. "Asian?"

"Probably Korean descent."

Tara might as well have run a truck through the office. The room fell into a somber silence.

"You don't think?" Sean said.

"That there's a connection between the guys who tried to steal that medallion and the death of a scientist in Aachen? I know. If it's a coincidence, it's a creepy one."

"This article says the scientist was doing research on Charlemagne's DNA," Tommy said. "It doesn't say anything about the results of his work."

"Alex did some digging around. The reason the article doesn't mention results is because almost everything related to the study was stolen from the lab. The killer took all the specimens and data."

"So we don't know what he might have found."

"Actually," Sean interrupted, "Tara said almost everything was taken. Tell me this guy slipped up."

"Always so astute, Sean. Correct. Investigators swept the entire place. They found something underneath the dead man's workstation. He'd taped a slide underneath his desk—they assume for safekeeping."

"He must have known someone might try to kill him," Tommy said.

"It certainly appears that way. Or maybe he was paranoid. In any case, the authorities confiscated the specimen and are holding it as evidence."

Sean thought for a moment before speaking again. "I don't suppose they bothered checking to see what was so special about that particular slide."

"I'm not sure at this point. They may have, but if they did, it's being kept extremely quiet."

"Okay, Tara. Thank you, and tell Alex I said thanks, too."

"No problem, and will do. I'll let you know if I find anything else."

Tommy hung up the phone and looked across the desk at his friend. It was a look Sean had seen many times during the course of their friendship.

Sean spoke before Tommy could. "I know what you're thinking, and it's not a good idea."

"What? I was just going to see what you had planned the next few days."

"Look, Schultzie. Just because a scientist was killed researching Charlemagne's DNA and Charlemagne happens to be on this sculpture doesn't mean there is any sort of connection to your medallion."

"It doesn't mean there's not. Plus, if the killer was North Korean, that makes the connection way stronger. It can't be a coincidence."

"Maybe. But then you have to ask yourself, why? Why kill that guy and take his research? And what does he or his research have to do with that medallion? One was dealing with Godfrey of Bouillon and the other Charlemagne. It feels a little like you're reaching on this one."

"Come on, buddy," Tommy said. "What else do you have going on right now? Huh? We go to

Germany, have a look around, and if there's no connection, then we spend a few days taking in the sights and then leave. What's the big deal?"

Sean sighed. "I'll talk to Adriana."

Chapter 6
Atlanta

“Sure, sounds like fun,” Adriana said in a cool voice.

Sean raised a dubious eyebrow at the comment. “Um...first off, I thought we were going to try to take a little time off from danger and adventure. You know, do some normal people stuff. And second, it wasn’t an invitation.”

Adriana put a hand on each hip and slowly shook her head. “You’ve been singing that song since we met. We both know you and I aren’t cut out for normal life. Remember your kayak shop in Florida?”

“Yeah.” Sean sighed. “How can I forget?”

“You thought moving to the beach and running that place would be relaxing. The whole time you were there, all you could do was pace around waiting for something to happen.”

“I know.” His head drooped. “But this time, I’m serious. I don’t like the idea of you getting shot again.”

“Oh, so this is about me?”

He stepped toward her and wrapped an arm around her waist. “Yeah. A big part of it is.” He pulled her close and felt her breath against his skin.

She looked up into his cool blue eyes. “When you put it that way, you almost sound like a nice guy.”

His grip on her lower back tightened at the joke. He snorted a quick laugh. “I can be nice.”

“I think you need to go with Tommy. It’s been a few months since you did anything with him.”

"Oh, so you're trying to get rid of me?" he asked, pretending to be offended.

She put her hands on his chest and pushed him playfully. He didn't budge. "No. I'll come along for the ride."

"It's up to you. I'd prefer you stay somewhere safe."

"As sweet as that is, we both know that's not going to happen. And besides, how unsafe can it be? Aachen is a nice place."

"A safe place where a scientist was murdered in his lab."

It was Adriana's turn to sigh. "I know. Honestly, maybe I need to be there to have your back. I know Tommy will be there, but you can never have too many allies."

He knew she was going to get her way no matter what he said. If he was honest, he'd rather she be with him than off doing her own thing. She'd been looking into a new mystery lately, a painting that went missing during the early years of World War II. Adriana had made quite a name for herself in the art underground. She'd successfully discovered and returned more priceless works of art than any other single investigator in history. As a result, she'd also picked up a few enemies of her own.

"So when do we leave?" she asked before he could fire off another protest.

Sean sighed. "Tommy's getting the details sorted out on our end. He'd like to get access to the crime scene. That's not going to happen. I spoke with Emily about the North Koreans. They're trying to get more information on the case, but right now it's coming at a trickle. Hard to get any real intel on that country since they're so closed off from the world."

"Look at it this way: we'll have time to pack." He offered a weak smile.

"I already packed."

The front door opened, and a moment later Tommy entered the room. "Well, it looks like everything's all set on my end. Heard anything new out of Emily yet?"

"Not yet," Sean said, giving a quick shake of the head. "She'll keep me in the loop."

"Well, I've got some news. Under tight security, some scientists at the university near Aachen have analyzed the remaining sample. The results should be ready by the time we get there."

"Well done, Schultzie. What does that mean?"

"It means we can find out what that scientist was learning about Charlemagne. By doing that, we can try to draw a connection between his murder and the North Koreans at the dig site in France."

Adriana cocked her head sideways and passed Tommy a dubious, narrow-eyed glare. "Did *you* order the sample analysis, or were they already doing that and you're just taking credit?"

Sean giggled. His friend was busted.

"Okay, yes," Tommy confessed. "They were doing it independently. But I did have to request access to the analysis. I would love to be able to get into that scientist's lab."

"Won't happen," Sean said. "With a full-on murder investigation, I doubt the German authorities will be happy to have us poking our noses around. It would be best if we get in with your friend, get what we need, and get out of there."

"What is it we need, anyway?" Adriana said.

Tommy fumbled for an explanation. "Well..."

"He doesn't know," Sean answered for his friend. He turned to Tommy and shook his head. "Honestly, this feels like a wild goose chase. If you think you're going to find any connection between your medallion and some DNA samples from a guy who's been dead for a thousand years, you're drifting toward the crazy side of the river."

"Look, I know it's a stretch, but let's see where it goes. I mean, Germany is nice this time of year. Maybe we can relax, get out and see the sights."

"You found a girl!" Adriana said out of the blue.

Tommy was taken back by the sudden comment. "What? That's silly. Me? A girl? Come on."

Sean crossed his arms and stared at his friend with disbelieving eyes. "Seriously, you're an awful liar."

"What's her name?" Adriana asked.

Tommy sighed. "What? No. You know what? Just...no, I'm not doing this. We're going to Germany to investigate a potential connection with a probably priceless artifact. This has nothing to do with a woman."

"Oh, so there *is* a woman?"

Tommy's face flushed red. "Look, can we just get back on task? We're going to Germany to investigate why an innocent man was killed and a possible connection to the medallion I found in France. End of story."

The other two remained silent for a moment, so he continued. "With any luck, the university will have already come up with some answers."

"So she's a professor at the university," Sean said with confidence.

"You know, I don't have to listen to this. We're dealing with a very serious matter."

"You're right, buddy. I'm sorry."

"We both are," Adriana added, desperately fighting back the smile that was trying to escape.

"Yeah," Sean agreed. "We both are. You're right. Let's just go over there and figure out what's going on with this medallion thing."

"Thank you," Tommy said, exasperated. He was visibly relieved they'd finally dropped the subject.

Sean's eyes narrowed and his lips curled in a mischievous smirk. "And while we're there, if we happen to bump into a lady friend of yours, that's just a bonus."

"All right, you know what? Yes. Yes, there's a woman at the university who happens to be a friend of mine. No, I wouldn't mind seeing her again. Okay? But nothing ever happened between us."

Adriana turned sympathetic. "Oh, why? Why didn't it work out?"

Tommy put his hands out wide. "Isn't it obvious? We live a few thousand miles apart. I can't just drop what I'm doing, hop in the car, and drive out to meet her for dinner."

Sean understood. Distance had strained things with him and Adriana. Not to mention the fact that Adriana's hobbies were extremely dangerous. Fortunately, she'd been spending most of her time with him in the States lately. They went a few weeks without seeing each other, but those times usually happened after long stretches together.

Still, Sean was curious how Tommy had been able to keep this a secret. He decided not to press the issue for now even though it itched his mind like a flea on a dog.

He'd get to the bottom of it sooner or later.

Tommy struggled to get them back on topic. "Can we please focus?"

His guests nodded.

"Please continue," Sean said, fighting back the urge to giggle.

"Okay. What we know is that the verse on the back of the medallion is from Matthew 26. It's a quote from Jesus when Peter cut off a man's ear in Gethsemane."

"When they were about to arrest Jesus," Adriana said.

"Right. The guy who lost the ear was Malchus. Of course, Jesus reattached it for him. It was one of the last miracles He performed. Anyway, that's beside the point. The thing is; why was Peter carrying a sword?"

Tommy let the question hang in the air for a moment while his friends considered it.

Sean and Adriana exchanged a questioning glance.

"Funny," Sean said. "I never really thought about that before. I mean, I've known that story since I was a kid, but it never dawned on me that Peter was armed. Of course, I knew he was. Just never bothered to ask why."

"Exactly!" Tommy exclaimed. "He was armed, carrying a weapon right there on his belt. Why? Up until then, the entire mission of Jesus had been about peace and healing and hope for eternity. Why would one of His closest followers be carrying a weapon?"

"Some of the disciples were zealots," Adriana offered. "They were ready for a rebellion against Rome. At least in their minds they were."

"That's a good thought," Tommy said, "and we know that a few of them were zealots, for sure. Peter had all the makings of one."

Sean interrupted. "I feel like you're about to refute that theory."

"Am I that transparent?" Tommy asked. "Okay, fine. Yes, the zealot thing is a good theory. The verses, however, don't suggest that any of the other men were armed. If they had been, wouldn't they have tried to fight off the authorities for their messiah? You have to figure the brothers known as the sons of thunder would have done something about it had they been armed."

"James and John, right?" Sean said.

"Correct. They were known to have a temper, as was their father. It would seem much of their angst was against the empire."

"So it would follow that they would have been armed, or at least tried to fight."

"Exactly," Tommy said. "If they were carrying weapons, seems likely someone else would have been hurt."

"Okay," Adriana interrupted. "What are you getting at? Peter was the only one carrying a sword. Fine. So? What does any of this have to do with Charlemagne and your medallion?"

"So we come back full circle to the mission of the messiah. See, most of the disciples believed that Jesus was here to set up an earthly kingdom. They were hoping He was going to overthrow the Romans and set up the new Jewish empire. He had to correct them on that belief constantly. Even when He did, they wouldn't accept it."

"You're saying Peter was ready to be the first soldier for the new Jewish nation?" Sean asked.

"At first, I thought maybe that was the answer. Now, I'm not so sure. He would have talked with the others. The entire group would have been carrying weapons if that was the consensus." Tommy shook his head. "No, Peter was the only one. That makes things interesting."

"Looking forward to seeing where you're going with this."

Tommy raised a finger. "I thought you might be. Remember how I told you about the sculpture in Cologne?"

Sean gave a nod. "Yeah. The nine heroes."

"Yes. The Nine Worthies. There is something peculiar about that sculpture. Before you ask, I'll just go ahead and tell you. Every single man depicted is carrying a sword. While the clothing and facial hair are all somewhat skewed to the era in which each of the heroes lived, their swords are all the same."

Adriana raised an eyebrow. "You mean they all look the same?"

"I mean they all *are* the same," Tommy said. "That makes no sense. The sword that Joshua carried had to be different than the one Charlemagne took into battle."

"Maybe it's just an artist error," Sean said. "That sort of thing happens all the time. Much quicker to keep it uniform. Plus, Charlemagne's sword is on display in the Louvre."

"A valid explanation," Tommy admitted. "I thought the same thing at first. Sidebar, I'm impressed you know where his sword is. Then I started analyzing the rest of the sculpture. The clothing, while somewhat similar, does have unique traits that date it to the appropriate time frame. Same with the shields, the crowns, even the hair on their heads. Why then, if the artist was so meticulous about everything else, would he make the swords identical?"

Sean's mind connected the dots rapidly. "Wait a minute. You're telling me that all of those guys carried the same sword?"

"It's possible. Or does that sound crazy?"

"Kind of. You're talking about a sword that would have been passed down through millennia. Not only would it have had difficulty surviving the hundreds and thousands of years, but how would it have been passed down from generation to generation without eventually getting lost? Not to mention it would have worn down over time."

Tommy smirked as if he knew Sean was going to out all those things. "I'm not saying it's correct. All I'm saying is that it's interesting to consider. Look at the facts. Every man in the sculpture experienced incredible military success. They were nigh unbeatable in battle. What if their abilities were something more than human?"

Sean and Adriana were both taken back by the question.

"What do you mean, more than human?" Adriana asked. "You don't mean they were extraterrestrials or something?"

"No," Tommy said, shaking his head. "I'm not saying those men in the sculpture were from outer space. The sword on the other hand..."

"So you're suggesting that the sword—the one Peter had—was the same sword used by all those guys from the Nine Worthies? Not only that, you're saying it had some kind of power?"

Tommy could see the doubt on his friends' faces. He'd doubted the theory himself when he first made the connection. Now, he wasn't so sure he was wrong.

"There can be no denying the facts. These men were all men of incredible military prowess. They were nearly unbeatable in battle, in spite of overwhelming odds. It was almost as if they had an unfair advantage."

"Yes," Adriana said, "but let's say that sword does have some kind of otherworldly power. How does that transfer to one person's entire army?"

"It wouldn't have to do much," Tommy said. "Look at the story of the three hundred Spartans at the battle of Thermopylae. Those three hundred soldiers held off tens of thousands from the Persian army."

"They had a tactical advantage with the bottleneck in that spot, though," Sean argued.

"Sure. But fighting all day, every day? Had to be exhausting."

"Are you saying Leonidas had the sword, too?"

"No," Tommy said. "But I'm saying it wouldn't take much—if there were something that could help a small group of troops—to turn the tides of battle."

The others considered his point, and the room fell into a long silence.

Tommy's phone rang in his pocket, interrupting the quiet moment.

"Hello. Tommy here."

Sean and Adriana watched and listened as their friend went through the motions of his phone conversation. When he ended the call, Tommy's eyes burned with a grave intensity.

"That was Helen and Joe."

Sean grinned. "Mac and Helen? How are they?"

"They're good," Tommy said in a serious tone. "I put them in charge of the dig site in France. They said they found something."

"What?" Sean asked.

Tommy stared blankly beyond his two friends. "It was in a stone cylinder."

"What was?" Adriana said.

"A vellum codex. The writing had faded, but was still visible due to the way it had been completely sealed in wax. They said they're still working on the entire translation, but it references all nine of the heroes from the sculpture by name. It was stamped with a Templar cross. And it mentioned the sword."

Adriana broke the stillness after a minute of contemplation. "Okay, just so I understand what you're saying, this codex mentioned Templars. Does that mean we're looking for the Holy Grail now? Or a sword?"

Tommy shook his head. "Not the grail. I think we're looking for Excalibur."

Chapter 7
Aachen

The dramatic church spires soared above the rest of the old city. Wet cobblestone streets curved in and out between the buildings. Cafes made of brick stood across from taverns built from stone. In spite of the rain that fell earlier, the cafes still had their outdoor sitting areas open, though no one took the offer. The empty chairs were a permanent fixture, something that probably couldn't be done in an American town. The seats would have been stolen long ago.

Europe had its share of thieves, but they were too busy picking pockets or targeting items that would fetch a higher price than simple street chairs.

Inside the tavern, a group of revelers laughed and shouted, sharing stories from the day or maybe from long ago.

Sean kept his eyes alert as he and the other two made their way down the street toward a cafe where they'd meet their German contact. Thing was, she wasn't actually German.

June Holiday was Tommy's friend, the woman he'd kept secret from Sean and Adriana for the better part of the year. She'd grown up in the United States but had attended university in Germany. Identifying more with the culture there, she'd remained in Germany ever since.

Tommy had met her when he first arrived in the border town before he began work at the dig site in France. He'd been in Aachen for a day, touring the university, when the person giving the tour introduced them.

June worked at the university as a researcher. Her specialty was in genetics, which intrigued Tommy. His initial thoughts were how he could get June to help with some of his own projects at IAA. There were many times they had to outsource genetic testing of samples. She could be his connection in Europe.

Of course, it wasn't just work that endeared Tommy to June. Her locks of golden blonde hair trickling down past her shoulders, her bright smile, the radiant blue eyes, and her enthusiastic personality made her impossible to resist.

Tommy just hoped he didn't screw it up.

When he was in France, he'd slipped across the border several times on weekends to take her out for dinner or coffee. They talked mostly about work, which turned out to be fine since they had a mutual interest in each other's careers. After the third date, however, things got more personal. During one conversation, the time passed so quickly they didn't realize they'd been talking for nearly six hours—until two o'clock in the morning.

Their connection was unlike any Tommy had ever felt with a woman. Part of that was due to the fact he didn't have much time to date since he was busy most of the time or out of town.

Being on the eastern border of France had opened the door to opportunity, and Tommy had walked right on through.

The three visitors rounded a corner and turned right down another street. A collection of black and white umbrellas sat over more chairs and tables in front of a cafe on the left a few dozen yards away.

“There it is,” Tommy said with a hint of excitement in his voice.

His traveling companions knew his exuberance wasn’t due to the meal they were about to have. It was the blonde woman sitting with her legs crossed, wearing a navy-blue sundress, tortoiseshell sunglasses, and a smile that seemed permanently stuck on her face.

She waved to the group and stood up from her chair in the corner. Tommy’s smile broadened as they approached. He ignored the hostess at the podium just outside the black railing surrounding the outdoor sitting area, and walked straight over to June.

Sean and Adriana paused and watched as the two hugged each other. There was a quick exchange of pleasantries before Tommy turned to his two friends lingering a few yards away.

He motioned them over and turned back to June. “June, these are my friends, Sean and Adriana.”

She smiled pleasantly to both of them and shook their hands. “It’s a pleasure to meet you both. I’ve heard so much about you. Especially you, Sean. Tommy says you two have been friends since childhood.”

“Oh, I’m sure that’s not all he’s told you,” Sean said.

Her teeth gleamed in spite of the overcast sky. “He said you have a penchant for getting into trouble.”

Sean raised an eyebrow. “Did he tell you that he’s the one dragging me into trouble more often than not?”

June cast a sidelong glance at Tommy, who blushed and put on his best *Who me?* face.

“He omitted that part.” She turned to Adriana. “You, he wasn’t so forthcoming about. But he did have some complimentary things to say.”

Adriana nodded at Tommy. “Aww. You’re so sweet.” She reached out and squeezed his cheek with finger and thumb.

“Okay. Enough with the introductions. Can we please sit down?” Tommy said.

“Is he always this testy with you?” Sean asked June.

“Always,” she said, taking a cue from Sean.

Tommy gasped, but before he could defend himself the server came by and asked for their drink order. Everyone ordered coffee. Tommy got his with a little extra milk.

“So you’re here to take a look at the Charlemagne DNA,” June said while the others looked at the menus.

She didn’t beat around the bush. There less than two minutes and straight to business. Sean appreciated that.

“Yeah. Your friend here,” he motioned to Tommy, “thinks there might be a connection to an ancient weapon of untold power." Sean ended the sentence with his best monster truck announcer voice.

Tommy scrunched his face at the comment. "What? I have no idea what you're talking about."

June's eyebrows shot up, and she twisted her head slowly until she faced Tommy. "You didn't mention anything about an ancient weapon. Something you forgot to say to me?"

He tried to shake off the question, but her gaze was going nowhere.

"Wait," Adriana interrupted. "You didn't tell her your theory?"

"Theory?" June said. "What theory? Yes, please. Tell me your theory, Thomas."

Tommy was cornered. And all three of his companions were enjoying watching him writhe.

"Yes, it's just a theory. Okay? Probably incorrect," he said finally.

"You sounded pretty sure about it when you told us back in the States," Sean said.

Tommy's face turned deep red. "Okay. Fine. You guys just love giving me a hard time, don't you? Yes, June. I'm sorry. I do think there might be a connection between the DNA sample you checked out and a very old sword."

"Not just any sword," Sean added.

Tommy flashed him an irritated look. "Would you let me finish?"

Sean put up his hands in surrender.

"Like I was saying, I did some research, and there are some really interesting bits of information that coincide with one very specific sword from history."

"Excalibur?" June asked.

Tommy's eyes widened. "How did you know?"

She snorted a laugh. "Seriously? I'm no historian, but how many famous swords are there? Can't be that many. I just guessed the one that sticks out most. What did I win?"

Tommy shook off his disbelief and scooted closer to her, more smitten than he'd been a moment before. "I'm impressed."

"Thank you?"

Sean chuckled at the way she'd phrased it as a question. "I like this one, Tommy. Try not to screw it up. Otherwise, we might have to ditch you for her."

Tommy tried to ignore his friend's joke. "Anyway, I didn't mention it because I didn't want to sound crazy, but yes, I think there might be a connection between Charlemagne's DNA and Excalibur."

"Interesting. At some point, you'll have to tell me where you came up with this theory. For now, you may as well have a look at the results from the testing we did on that sample."

"Sounds good. We'll just get something to eat and then head over to the university."

June's lips curled. "Actually, I took the liberty of bringing the results to you. Thought it might be best if we didn't interrupt a murder investigation."

"I could hug you," Tommy said.

"You can," she said. "After you look at these."

She reached down and pulled a green folder out of her laptop bag next to her chair. She laid the folder on the table in front of Tommy and nudged it toward him.

"Go ahead," she said. "Be my guest."

He paused for a second, apprehensive about opening the folder, partly because he was afraid the results inside might prove him wrong. When he finally got up the courage to flip it open, he was dismayed at what he found.

It was mostly a bunch of numbers, columns, and data points he didn't understand.

Before he could ask what he was looking at, June spoke up. "The sample we analyzed was definitely different than anything else we've investigated. This data shows that whatever Charlemagne had going on genetically was certainly something special."

"Special?" Adriana asked.

"Yep. We're not entirely sure what to make of it. However, it does seem to be some kind of mutation. I've never seen anything like it."

"This mutation," Sean said, "it kept him human, though. Right? I mean, he didn't become a monster or anything like that?"

"Not at all," June said. "It is definitely human DNA. If I had to guess, it just made him stronger, possibly a little quicker with his mind as well. Again, that's only a guess at this point. As it pertains to the legend of King Arthur and his fabled sword, Excalibur, are you suggesting that the sword may have caused Arthur to be stronger and smarter than other humans?"

"He's only one of them," Tommy said. "There were others who also had incredible abilities when it came to combat." He hesitated a moment and then went on. "You know the sculpture of the Nine Good Heroes in the Cologne rathaus?"

June had to think for a second. "Seems to ring a bell. I only went in there to do the touristy thing. This country has so many rathauses, it starts to feel like if you've seen one you've seen them all."

"This sculpture has nine men—three Christians, three Jews, and three pagans."

She smirked. "Sounds like the beginning of an epic joke."

Tommy was thrown off by the comment and then pushed through his laughter to continue. "True. Anyway, you know the names." He rattled off all nine of the men in the sculpture and the similarities of the swords they carried.

Then he took a plastic bag out of his jacket and placed it on the table. June's eyes were drawn to the golden object inside. "What is that?" she asked.

"A medallion I found in France when I was here last. I think it belonged to Godfrey of Bouillon."

Sean cut in. "Except that Godfrey is buried in a tomb at the Church of the Holy Sepulchre."

"Right," Tommy agreed. "So the tomb I found couldn't have been his."

"It was probably a relative then, right?" June said, looking up from the medallion as she pulled it closer.

"Possibly," Tommy said. "We're not sure. I've still got people on site in France looking around for more clues."

June squinted her eyes as she tried to process the information. "Okay, so let me get this straight. You wanted to know about Charlemagne's DNA, which I could have just told you over the phone or via email. Yet you flew all the way here to find out in person? On top of that, it's not just Charlemagne you're investigating. It's a whole series of ancient kings?"

"To be fair, Judah Maccabee wasn't a king," Sean offered. "And Joshua was more of a guide than anything. A ruler of sorts, but not a king."

Tommy ignored his friend's cynical comment. "We're also here to have a closer look at the sculpture in Cologne. I'm hoping there could be a lead there, a clue that could help us figure out the next place to look."

"To look for what? Excalibur?"

"I know it sounds crazy, but yes. I have reason—we have reason—to believe it might actually exist. Think about it. Every man in that sculpture had a similar sword. From what we know about the Arthur legend, it gave the one who carried it incredible power. If those leaders were able to get their hands on it, they would have wielded the same power."

"If I may," Adriana said, "I'm as skeptical as anyone when it comes to this sort of thing. Tommy makes a good argument, though. And I have to say, I'm definitely curious."

June sighed after taking it all in. "I have to say, this is pretty overwhelming. You three do this sort of thing all the time, running all over the world, chasing leads to old legends?"

"Well," Tommy said, "it's not the only reason I came to Europe."

"No?"

A sly grin crept across his face. "No. It was a perfect excuse to see you again."

It was June's turn to blush.

She reached over and touched Tommy on the arm. "That is so sweet."

Sean rolled his eyes. Adriana noticed and nudged him with her knee.

"Stop it," she mouthed.

"So do you want to come to Cologne with us?" Tommy asked.

June considered the offer. Before she answered, Tommy already knew what she was going to say. "I do. I really do. It sounds fun, but I have to work. If you're still here this weekend, maybe we could spend some time together?"

Tommy hid his disappointment well. "It's okay. And yes, I would definitely like to stick around over the weekend. I look forward to it. One of the perks of having a company jet is we can decide how long our stay will be."

Sean fought off the urge to remind his friend that he and Adriana would still need a ride home. Instead, he decided to let Tommy have his moment.

His friend hadn't had a significant love interest since college. And even then, Tommy was so absorbed in his studies that he didn't make time for dating. Those habits carried over into adulthood. By the time he'd started feeling lonely, the time he could have used to hone his social skills had passed him by, leaving him a bit awkward when it came to engaging with members of the opposite sex.

He still wasn't very smooth, but with June it didn't seem like he had to be. Deep down, Sean hoped his friend had finally found the right girl.

A different server approached wearing a black button-up shirt and matching pants. He appeared to be in his late twenties, maybe early thirties, with dark blond hair. "Has anyone helped you yet?" he asked.

"Yes," June replied in almost-perfect German. "The girl with the short brown hair took our drink order."

Sean's eyes had drifted to the people passing by on the street before the server began speaking. When he turned his attention to the younger man, it was already too late.

Sean saw the towel draped over the server's right hand. More importantly, he saw what it covered: a subcompact 9mm pistol.

Before Sean could warn the others, the server pulled the towel back so everyone at the table could see the tip of the weapon. The few passersby going about their morning routine or visiting touristy spots didn't notice.

"Now if you don't mind," the man switched to English, "slide the medallion over to me, as well as the folder. I'd prefer not to kill anyone."

"And yet you're pointing a gun at us," Sean said through clenched teeth.

Tommy eased toward June to keep between her and the weapon.

The server shrugged and tilted his head to the side. "I do what is necessary, Mr. Wyatt. If you want to protect your friends, you'll do what I say."

"I'm sorry," Tommy said. "Do you two know each other? Sean, who is your friend here?"

"Mr. Wyatt does not know me, Mr. Schultz. Nor do you. Again, give me the medallion, and no one gets hurt."

"You're not going to use that gun here," Sean said, his voice cool as the other side of the pillow. "You're bluffing or bullying, but you're not shooting. Not with this many people around. And if you know me, you know that if you pull that trigger, you'd better put one through my skull. If you shoot one of my friends, you'll be dead before you hit the ground. I can promise you that. But my money says that you have no intention of squeezing that trigger. Too many witnesses who've seen your face. So I think maybe you should put that peashooter away and walk on."

The gunman swallowed hard. His eyes turned to slits. Sean knew at that moment he was spot on. Whoever this guy was, he didn't want attention. Thieves rarely did.

"Here are your drinks," a familiar voice interrupted the standoff. The female server returned with a tray full of beverages and began setting them on the table. She noticed the man dressed like one of the restaurant workers. At the sound of her voice, he'd concealed the weapon once more.

"Would you like a menu?" the girl asked the gunman.

"No," he replied in German. "I was just leaving."

"That's right," Sean said. "Our friend here was just leaving. Although he might be interested in filling out a job application. He's already dressing the part. Isn't that right?"

The gunman's nostrils flared, and his jaw tightened.

He spun around and marched away without looking back.

"Guess he wasn't interested," Tommy said.

"Guess not," Sean said as he watched the gunman disappear into the pedestrian traffic. "But, I doubt we've seen the last of him."

Chapter 8
Aachen

"Who was that guy?" June asked with a tremor in her voice.

"I don't know," Tommy answered. "But we'll find out."

"He had a gun, Tommy."

"I realize that."

June gasped. "You say that as if you deal with this sort of thing all the time."

Sean raised an eyebrow at his friend but didn't need to say anything.

"It happens from time to time," Tommy said. "That's the risk involved with recovering artifacts of this nature."

"Risk? He had a gun, Tommy. He pointed it right at us."

"I know," Tommy said, putting his arm around her.

She slid to the side to get out from under his attempt at soothing. "I'm sorry, I need to go. I don't know what you all are involved with, but I'd prefer to not have guns aimed at me."

She stood up and collected her things.

"I wouldn't do that," Sean said.

"Sean, it's been nice to meet you. Adriana, you as well."

"He's still watching us," Sean added.

June's eyes widened. She glanced around the pedestrian street to see if she could find the man's face. He was nowhere to be seen.

"Look," she said. "Whatever that guy wants, he wants from you two...three. I don't want to have anything to do with it."

Tommy stood up and tried to put his hand on her shoulder again. She shrugged it off.

"When you decide to get into a career that doesn't involve deadly weapons, feel free to give me a call."

She started to walk toward the cafe's entrance.

"Second floor. Red building across the street," Sean said.

His words froze June in place. "What? What did you say?" She looked back over her shoulder at him.

"It's not the guy we just met. He's waiting for us around the corner. Doesn't need to be in sight because he's got a pair of eyes watching us from that red building over there."

She started to divert her gaze to the building he was referring to, but he stopped her.

"Don't make it obvious you're looking," Sean said. "Be casual. Second-story window, second one over from the white door below it."

June twisted her head slowly. Tommy and Adriana waited a moment before they stole a quick look. All three saw the same thing. A dark silhouette standing in the window moved suddenly, causing the cream-colored curtains to ripple in the window.

"He ducked out of sight, didn't he?" Sean said, staring into his cup.

June nodded absently.

"These guys rarely work alone," Sean said. "Come back over here, and have a seat. They're not going to hurt us. If they were, they'd have done it by now."

"Or they would have waited," Tommy said.

"Right. Which means these guys wanted us to know they're here."

"Why would they want that?" June asked, still held in place by fear.

"Who knows? Typically, they'll do that to make a statement. In this case, it's probably a warning."

"A warning?"

Adriana jumped in. "To get off the trail we're following."

Sean nodded in agreement. "That's a good thing. Means we're heading in the right direction."

"A good thing?" June blurted. "It's a good thing to have a gun pointed at you?" Her voice rose with her level of anger.

"That's not what he meant," Tommy said.

Before she could protest further, Sean urged her to return to her seat. "Please. Sit down, June. You're much safer with us than on your own."

"No. I don't think so. I think I was safer before I met you three. I'm going back to the lab. Please don't call me or follow me or whatever it is you do."

She walked toward the entrance to the outdoor eating area. Tommy stood up to stop her, but Sean kept him in place. "Hold on, buddy."

"Hold on?" Tommy said. "She's in danger if she leaves here alone."

"I know. Just give her a head start."

"A head start? I'm not using her as bait, Sean. She's a woman, a woman I happen to have feelings for. So I'm sorry if I don't agree with the whole give-her-a-head-start plan."

He stormed by Sean and hurried after June. She'd already merged into the increasing current of people walking down the cobblestone street.

"Would you use me as bait?" Adriana said, curling her bottom lip.

"Not unless I was sure you'd be okay."

She didn't seem surprised. "So you think June will be okay?"

"She would have been if Tommy had stayed here. Now they're both in trouble."

"We going after them?"

He nodded. "Yep. Just as soon as that guy across the street steps out the door."

Sean reached across the table and picked up the folder. He stuffed it and the medallion into his rucksack.

"Why do you think that guy was bluffing?" Adriana asked.

"Someone who intended to hurt us wouldn't have shown their face. They wouldn't have come after us in broad daylight. And they wouldn't have been so polite."

"Polite?"

"Yep. He clearly said he didn't want to hurt us."

"And you believed him?"

Sean's lips pressed together in a grin. "I've played cards long enough and been in this game long enough to know when a person is lying and when they're telling the truth. That guy wasn't lying."

"Which means what, exactly?"

“I don’t know,” he said, staring across the street through the passing bodies. “But it looks like the spotter is on the move.”

Adriana followed his eyes across the street to the white door in the red building. A man dressed in black pants, and a matching pea coat stepped out onto the street. His gaze was aimed in the direction Tommy and June went. The guy slipped on a pair of sunglasses and started after them, careful to stay close to the buildings to keep out of sight.

“Are we going after them now?” Adriana asked.

“Yep,” Sean said with a nod.

He fished some euros out of his pocket and put enough on the table to cover their bill.

“Shall we?” he asked.

“Sure,” she answered with a cute smirk.

They made their way out of the cafe and onto the street, keeping a careful eye on the spotter across the way. He was dipping in and out of sight between the other people walking along. Occasionally, he paused to pretend to look at fruit or some other items in the outdoor marketplace, probably because he thought his quarry had noticed him. All the while he never realized he was being followed. At least that’s what Sean hoped.

From Sean and Adriana’s vantage point, it appeared Tommy was trying to convince June not to leave as the two made their way toward the next street, where Sean was 99 percent certain the gunman was waiting. More than once, June spun around and waved her hand at Tommy. Sean read her lips as she told his friend to go away and leave her alone.

June turned right and started down an alley. The man across the street made a corresponding directional change and hurried to stay in pursuit.

"No, what are you doing?" Sean said.

"Going into an alley like that definitely isn't a good idea," Adriana voiced Sean's concern.

"Yeah. What do you think we should do?" he asked as he twisted sideways to avoid a rather plump man in a gray suit and tie.

"You're asking me?" She sounded surprised.

"Always open to good ideas."

"You go in behind this guy. I'll go up to the next street, run around, and cut them off."

"You sure you're fast enough?"

She lowered her head and gave him a playfully irritated look.

"Yeah. I'm fast enough."

Before he could question her, she took off, ducking and weaving through the pedestrians. It didn't take her long to reach the next corner, where she disappeared behind the row of buildings. Meanwhile, Sean peeled off into the alley behind the spotter as he pursued Tommy and June.

Now, in between the buildings on either side, June's voice resonated louder than it had on the main street.

"I told you, Tommy, I'm going back to work. Leave me alone. I don't want to get involved with whatever you all are up to."

"June, please. Just listen to me. I'm sorry," Tommy said. "Please. We really need to get back on the main street."

Tommy turned around and saw the man in the pea coat behind them. Sean ducked behind a garbage bin before his friend could see him.

Seeing the spotter following them, Tommy knew they were in trouble. "June, sweetie. I think it would be a good idea if we go back to the cafe and chill out for a bit. Just let me explain things."

"What is there to explain? You and your friends are obviously involved with something dangerous. I'd prefer to keep that kind of danger out of my life. My car is just around the corner, so I'll be fine."

She'd no sooner gotten the words out of her mouth than the gunman from the cafe stepped out from behind the corner ahead. His towel was gone, and now he held the weapon in plain sight in front of his waist, aiming it right at the approaching couple.

June stumbled to a stop. Tommy saw the threat and stepped in front of her.

"It would have been easier if you had given me the medallion at the cafe, Mr. Schultz. Now you've put yourself and your girlfriend in a bad situation."

"I'm not his girlfriend," June said.

"She's not my girlfriend," Tommy said almost simultaneously, though he sounded a tad hurt.

"I don't care," the gunman said. "Give me the medallion and the folder."

Tommy shook his head. "Like my buddy said, you won't fire that weapon here. Too many people will hear it. Police will be all over you within minutes. Then what will you do?"

The gunman flashed a toothy grin. "Well, we can't have that."

He reached around his back and produced a black cylinder. His fingers made quick work of the sound suppressor, and within twenty seconds it was attached to his weapon's muzzle.

Tommy swallowed.

The spotter stepped up from behind and grabbed June's arms. She shrieked for a second, but the spotter covered her mouth with a gloved hand. She struggled for a moment, until she felt something press hard into her lower back. Tommy spun around to rush to her aid, but there was nothing he could do. He saw the gun in the spotter's hand.

"Don't make this harder than it has to be," the first gunman said. He put out his hand with palm up. "Medallion. Now."

"I don't have it," Tommy said. "It's at the cafe with my friends."

"You must think we're stupid. You would never let something as valuable as that medallion leave your sight."

"What do you want with it anyway?" Tommy asked. "I guess a two-bit criminal like you plans to sell it on the black market. No one even knows what it is. I doubt you could get more than a few hundred bucks for it."

"We aren't interested in money, Mr. Schultz. You have no idea what you're dealing with."

Out of nowhere, a can of tomato sauce zipped through the air and struck the gunman on the side of the head. As he toppled sideways, the gun in his hand went off, sending the bullet into one of the wooden support beams of the building to his left.

The spotter shoved June aside and took aim at the corner from where the can had been thrown.

"Who's there?"

He heard rapid footsteps behind him and spun around in time to see Sean charging at full speed. Before the spotter could react, Sean plowed his shoulder into the man's midsection and drove him backward toward Tommy.

Sean let out a growl as he forklifted the guy an inch off the ground.

Tommy stepped out of the way as Sean drove the guy into the ground. The spotter's head smacked against the hard surface, knocking him out instantly.

The original gunman recovered from the can striking his head. After a few seconds of staggering, he regained his balance and took aim at the new threat.

He only heard two footsteps from his right before a foot snapped up and kicked the gun out of his hand. The gunman ignored the sharp pain in his hand and turned to face the adversary who dared interfere.

"Ms. Villa," he said, assuming a fighting stance.

"And you are?"

He swung a fast kick at her midsection. She knocked it down with a swipe of her fist. The kick was just a decoy to lower her defenses. He faked a jab, which she tried to block, and then sent a roundhouse into her right cheek.

Her head whipped to the side, and she stumbled backward. The man didn't relent. He jumped through the air and kicked hard with his right foot, landing the blow on the same cheek he'd just struck.

Adriana tripped and fell backward, crashing into three garbage cans next to the corner.

Sean and Tommy saw what happened and rushed to help. The gunman glanced over his shoulder and saw them approaching. He reached down, grabbed Adriana by the jacket, and yanked her up onto her feet. She winced in pain but was still conscious.

The man produced a knife and pressed the sharp edge against her neck. "Stay back," he warned.

Sean and Tommy skidded to a stop just ten feet away.

The man shuffled his feet backward. "I'm warning all of you. Leave this place. You do not know the power you're meddling with. Those who raise the sword will die by it."

His hands moved suddenly, and he threw something onto the ground. He shoved Adriana forward and dashed down the adjacent alley just as the little metal disk erupted in a searing white flash.

Sean grabbed her and dove clear of the blast radius. Tommy tackled June and covered her to keep any shrapnel from hitting her.

"Tommy, you guys okay?" Sean asked, unable to see anything as his eyes started the slow progression of adjusting back to normal light.

"Yeah, we're okay. You guys?"

"Yeah. It was just a flash bang."

Tommy sat up and waited for the world around him to slowly change back from bright white. "It looked like one of those disks you got from your buddy at DARPA."

"I was thinking the same thing," Sean said. The white light had already started fading. He helped Adriana to her feet and then half felt his way over to the unconscious man on the ground. "You hear what he said about raising the sword?"

He felt around in the guy's pockets, but found no identification, money, or credit cards. The only thing he discovered was a single key. It was certainly old, since keys like that were rarely used anymore except for historical buildings. At the end of the stem, an interesting design had been carved out of the metal: a sword and a crescent moon.

"Yeah. That verse from Matthew again." Tommy said. His eyes had begun adjusting, and he could see Sean was holding something. "What's that?"

"A key."

"Key? To what?"

"I'm not sure. But our friend here probably won't tell us anything until he wakes up."

Sean noticed something on the spotter's wrist and lifted the limp hand to get a better view. "Now that's interesting."

"What?" Adriana moved closer and looked over his shoulder. Then she saw what he was examining. "The other guy had one of those, too. It was on the same wrist."

"You're sure?"

She nodded. "One hundred percent. I noticed it when he put the knife to my throat."

Tommy helped June onto her feet, and the two made their way over to the others.

"They could have killed us, but they didn't. Why?" Tommy said. "No one would have noticed back here. Not for a while, anyway."

"Adriana said they have matching tattoos, just like this one," Sean answered. "That can mean only one thing."

"They're not North Korean?"

Sean snorted a forced laugh. "That, too."

"They're part of a secret society," Adriana said.

"Which means now we're facing two foes."

The faint sound of sirens whined in the distance.

"Three if you count the police," Tommy said. "I doubt they'd appreciate us here with this unconscious guy."

"Probably not," Sean agreed. "And I'd rather not answer any of their questions right now."

"You're just going to leave him here?" June asked, finally able to speak after several minutes of stunned silence.

Tommy and Sean glanced at each other and then up at her. They answered simultaneously. "Absolutely."

"Where do we go next?" Adriana asked.

Neither of the men had an immediate answer.

"Right now, we just need to get out of here," Sean said finally. "Quick, out that way." He pointed to the side thoroughfare leading out to the next street.

The four hurried to the sidewalk and then slowed down to appear less conspicuous.

Sean's eyes darted in all directions, keeping a lookout for more trouble.

"We should go to Cologne," Tommy said as the group turned right and meandered down the sidewalk. "We can investigate the sculpture of the Nine Worthies and see if there's a clue."

"Sounds like as good a plan as any," Sean said.

Chapter 9
Aachen

"What do you mean there's another piece in play?" Min-Woo's voice was full of fury. "How did someone else find out about it?"

"I'm not sure, sir. We're working on it." Han-Jae's face remained like stone as he stared into the alley.

The police showed up only minutes after the Americans left. He'd watched as the man on the ground was scooped up and taken away in an ambulance. If it was a crime scene, it was the sloppiest one Han-Jae had ever seen, and he'd observed plenty during his time as an operative in Europe.

"Well, you need to find out soon. The Chairman has grown suspicious of our activities. If we are going to strike, it must be soon. I cannot risk doing this without the sword."

"I understand, sir. I intend to find out exactly who these meddlers are. When I do, they will be dead. As will the Americans."

"Good. Don't call me until it is done."

The call went dead, and Han-Jae slid it back into his pocket. Two of his assets were standing behind him, leaning casually against the wall of a building opposite of the alley. Another one was across the street, taking a look around to make sure everyone was gone.

Han-Jae waited for the man to wave them over. When he did, Han-Jae motioned with a nod of his head for the other two to follow him across.

The three men joined the fourth and walked into the alley, leaving one just on the outer edge to keep watch.

Han-Jae took point, leading the other two to the far end of the narrow street. Their nostrils filled with the stench of garbage. Multiple bins were nearly overflowing with trash, stuffed by the restaurants and cafes on either side of the alley.

Something metal clanked on the ground around the corner, causing the two men with Han-Jae to draw their weapons and take aim in the general vicinity. They poked their heads around the building to make sure it was clear and found the source of the noise. A bird was pecking away at a nearly empty can on the pavement.

The operative on the left turned and gave the all-clear nod to his superior, then took up a position at the corner just like the guy at the other end.

Han-Jae stood in the middle of the alley for a moment, looking around for a clue as to who the mysterious gunmen were who attacked the Americans. He understood why the general was upset. New players in the game could mean additional problems. Then again, it could also work to their advantage. If these new men took out Wyatt and the others, the path to the sword would be clear.

The sun cracked through the gray soup above and for a moment sprayed rays of light on the world below. Something flashed on the ground, catching Han-Jae's eye. He frowned and took a few steps over to where he'd noticed the anomaly. Bending over, he discovered a burn mark surrounded by tiny pieces of metal. He picked one of the fragments up and held it up to the sunlight.

"What is it?" the man closest to him asked.

Han-Jae had watched the interaction between the Americans and the two strange gunmen. He'd seen the flash bang go off from across the street, far enough away that it only blunted his vision for a moment.

"Just pieces left from the device that man used to get away."

"What's next?"

Han-Jae looked out the other end of the alley at the people passing by on the street. "Let's see where our American friends are going now."

Chapter 10
Cologne, Germany

“Please, just talk to me,” Tommy begged. “You have to understand, I didn’t know any of that was going to happen.”

June had been silent during the entire car ride to Cologne. Fortunately, it wasn’t that far away. With very little traffic, the drive took less than an hour. June stared out the window at the approaching city.

The massive twin spires of the Cologne Cathedral dominated the skyline of the town next to the Rhine. At over five hundred feet tall, the cathedral’s twin spires were the tallest twin varieties in the world, and second only to Ulm Minster in the south of the country.

Cologne Cathedral was Germany’s most popular landmark, boasting twenty thousand visitors per day. During World War II, people had to be warned not to try to make pilgrimages after the United States took over that section of the city. Snipers still plagued the area even though the war was all but over.

“June?” Tommy said after a minute or two of waiting. “You okay?”

“Construction on that cathedral started in 1248. They didn’t finish it until 1880.”

That wasn’t an answer to Tommy’s question, but it was a start.

“What took them so long?” he asked.

She shrugged. “I don’t know. Probably resources. It was ongoing for about two hundred years until they stopped in the late 1400s. Then it just sat there for four hundred years until they started up again in the 1800s."

He reached out and put his arm around her shoulders, wary she might shrink away again.

She sniffled. "I'm fine. I just didn't think when I woke up this morning I'd have a gun pointed at me. Twice."

"I know. And I am so, so sorry. If I had known that might happen, I would have never involved you."

She forced a smile onto her face. "It's okay. Really. It's not your fault. You're here doing your thing. People get mugged all the time. It could have happened to anyone anywhere."

"Thank you," he said. "I just want you to be safe. Is there someone you can stay with for a few days until this blows over?"

"I have a friend in Dusseldorf. I can stay with her. I just hope the university understands. This will put me behind significantly."

"I feel horrible about it," Tommy said.

"Don't," she said and shook her head. "I'll be okay. I needed a little time off anyway. I'll tell them it's for a personal emergency or something. They'll be okay."

Sean steered the car into the left lane of the bridge crossing the Rhine River. "You know, you could hang out with us if you wanted to."

"I think I've had quite enough adventure for one day, Sean. Thank you, though. I appreciate the thought. After we take a look at this sculpture, I'll catch the train to Dusseldorf and meet up with my friend. It's not far, and she's got a spare room."

The car quieted down again as it left the bridge behind. The enormous church loomed on the horizon to the north.

"It really is an impressive structure," Tommy said. "So much bigger in real life. The pictures don't do it justice."

"Have you ever been inside?" June asked.

Tommy shook his head. "Nope. Not that one. Lots of others, but never Cologne Cathedral."

She grinned. "Maybe when you guys are done with your treasure hunt, I'll take you by there. That is, unless you'll be in a hurry to leave."

He shook his head. "No. I'll definitely be down for that."

"You'll need to turn right at the next street, then left, and then right again," Adriana said. "You'll see it on the left when we get close."

Sean nodded. "Got it."

He followed her directions, making their way through the crowded streets of downtown Cologne. The west side of the city was full of tourists and working folk alike, everyone in a hurry to get to their destinations. The hour was getting late, and that meant more people and cars would be injected onto the streets soon. Some of the citizenry had already found places to get an early dinner or a late-afternoon beer.

After parking the car and making their way through the cobblestone pedestrian streets, the group found themselves in front of the historic rathaus.

"It's kind of a hodgepodge of designs, isn't it?" Sean said as they stood near the building, looking up at the façade.

"That's because it was built piecemeal over time, like many of the older buildings in this country. The Cologne city hall is the oldest in the country. It has a documented history back to the eleventh century. There are four distinct influences of design that span that timeline."

"It's impressive," Tommy said.

"Indeed. Come on. I'll show you the way to the sculpture."

June led the group to the entrance and into the old building. Sean lingered behind, letting a little distance grow between him and Adriana and the other two. Adriana noticed him slowing down and matched his pace.

The interior was quiet, much like a church. The interior Gothic design with the dramatic high domes and seemingly endless rows of pillars was also reminiscent of some of the great cathedrals of the world. The cool air reeked of ancient stone, dust, and wood.

Adriana merged closer to Sean as the group walked through the foyer and into the giant main hall.

"I noticed," she whispered into his ear, "you didn't draw your weapon back there in the alley."

Sean wondered if she'd mention that. He was surprised Tommy didn't bring it up sooner.

"Heat of the moment," Sean said. "I didn't really think about it. I just reacted and went after that guy."

"Okay." Adriana accepted the explanation on the outside. Internally, however, she knew that wasn't the truth.

Sean was a well-trained agent. He'd been an operative for the American government for years before calling it quits. His instincts, his training, everything was hardwired into how he reacted to certain situations. That sort of thing didn't just go away. It took a conscious effort to push away those instincts.

She didn't push the issue. Adriana had a keen sense of when to try to get something out of him and when to let things go.

The group made their way through the main hall, past a small gathering of tourists, and into an adjacent building through a pair of large wooden doors. Entering the next chamber, they found it was sparsely decorated. A wooden desk sat flush against the wall on the left. There was a red velvet-upholstered chair pushed against the right-hand wall. The ceiling was lower than in the main hall but still had the dramatic swooping curve of a Gothic dome that led up to a single line running the length of the room.

At the other end, the sculpture of the Nine Worthies was embedded into the wall, high above the floor.

No one dared breathe for a moment as they took in the sight. Seeing the sculpture was like looking into the face of history. Sean and Tommy always held the deepest appreciation for historical works like these. They took in the scene with reverence while they stepped softly closer to the far wall.

"It's smaller than I thought it would be," Tommy said just above a whisper.

"Incredibly intricate," Sean said.

The group passed under a chandelier full of half-burned candles.

"I've only been in here twice," June said. "Not sure what you're looking for, but it's definitely an interesting piece. These men depict the standards of chivalry that came out of the Renaissance."

Tommy didn't mention they already knew that.

"It's amazing," Adriana said. "I don't mean to be a downer, but how does this thing help us?"

The other three turned to her with questioning expressions.

"I'm just saying, we already knew what it looked like and had analyzed every possible component. Did we really need to come to Cologne to see it personally?"

"Sometimes you can't see everything through a computer screen," Tommy said. "You have to get up close and feel it, see it with your own eyes, smell it."

She didn't argue the point further.

The four moved closer to the sculpture until they were standing right in front of it.

Tommy scratched his head.

"Notice anything?" Adriana asked in a cynical tone. "Smell anything?"

He cast a sidelong glance at her. “Just give me a minute.”

Sean rubbed his chin as he stared at the sculpture. “You know, part of the problem is that we know so little about some of these guys. Like Hector, for example. Pretty much a mythical character. As for Alexander the Great, no one knows where he’s buried. Same with Julius Caesar. In fact, we don’t know where most of these guys are buried.”

“The tomb of Joshua is in Palestine,” Tommy said. “Good luck visiting there.”

“Right. And the tomb of King David is still missing. I mean, people claim it’s in Jerusalem, but it’s never been proved.”

“So we’re looking for graves now?” Adriana asked.

“She makes a good point, boys,” June said. “Are you looking for graves, or are you looking for a sword?”

The two men turned to June with mouths agape.

“What?” she said. “I’m just saying, she’s right. Maybe you’re focusing on the wrong thing. You’re searching for a sword. So think about the sword instead of graves or something else.”

Sean and Tommy nodded, took a deep breath, and returned their gaze to the sculpture.

“Okay,” Sean said. “Every one of these guys has a sword.”

“Right,” Tommy agreed. “And they’re all identical. We knew that already.”

“You said that this sword was originally the sword of Peter?” Adriana asked.

Tommy shook his head. "No. The first one to carry it would have been Joshua. But it makes sense that Peter would have had it. That's the theory, anyway."

"So Peter had a sword...*the* sword," Adriana said. "And Jesus told him that anyone who raises the sword will also die by it."

"Right."

Adriana stepped nearer to the sculpture, so close she could touch it without extending her arm. She was staring at something. Sean could tell the gears were turning in her head.

"What is it?" he asked.

She reached out a finger and touched part of the sculpture the figure of David was standing on. "The rock," she said in an absent tone.

"What?" Tommy said.

"Peter was known as the rock. Jesus said to him at one point that He would build His church upon this rock. Some people believe that Jesus was talking about Himself. A more common belief is that He was telling Peter that the church would be built on him, that he was the cornerstone."

"Yeah...so where are you going with this?"

Sean picked up what she was saying. "No, she's right. Think about it. Each one of these guys is depicted standing on a rock." He turned to June. "Like you said, all nine of them represented what the Renaissance culture believed was chivalry. Those same noble characteristics would apply to Christianity."

June smiled. "I didn't think of it that way."

"Correct," Adriana said. "And take a look at these things below each pedestal."

"Those triangles represent churches," June said. "You see them in lots of places on these old buildings."

"Exactly."

"Okay, hold on," Tommy said. "Let's put all this together. Say we focus on Peter. So all these guys are standing on a rock, and that represents Peter. And all of them are above a church, which Jesus said would be built on Peter."

"Along with all the fundamentals of chivalry," June added.

"Right. So what does all that mean?"

His voice faded after a moment of echoing off the ancient stones, and the room fell silent once more.

Sean had been unusually quiet. He finally spoke up. "June, you said that there are lots of places with those church symbols."

"Yep," she said with a nod. "All over Europe."

"There wouldn't happen to be any more on this building, would there?"

She thought for a moment, and then her face brightened. "Oh yeah. I almost forgot. There's one outside over the cornerstone of this building." She paused.

"Can you show us?"

"Sure," June said. Then she paused. "Although you'll have to try to ignore the unusual base of that particular sculpture."

"Unusual base?" Tommy asked.

June raised an eyebrow. Her voice filled with mischief. “You’ll see. Come on. I’ll show you.”

Chapter 11
Cologne

"Yeah...that certainly is...um, unusual," Tommy said in an awkward voice.

"Kind of hard to not look at it," Sean said.

Adriana shook her head. "You boys and your sexual issues. Could you please try and focus on the sculpture above the base?"

"I was until you mentioned it again. I mean, it's a little person with their pants around their ankles flashing that entire part of the city."

Adriana and June both sighed. The latter had a playful smirk on her face.

"Who is this guy again?" Tommy asked. "The priest. Not the...you know, the one without pants."

"That would be Konrad von Hochstaden," June said. "There are about 130 dignitaries represented on the exterior of this building. Konrad was a bishop, though he had aims of being more than that. He was constantly involved in conflict and driven by what seemed to be greed."

"Greed?"

June nodded. "He took bribes to give his blessing to men who would be king. In effect, that made him more powerful than the kings themselves. When kings died, he took over temporarily and even waged war like a military leader."

"Hardly seems fitting of a man of the church," Sean said.

"Indeed. So this representation of him is one of contradictions. The pantsless figure below was sort of the people's way of memorializing how embattled the man was, and how much trouble he caused for the country. At least that's what one local told me."

"Yet he's the one who laid the cornerstone of this building, the oldest city hall in Germany?" Adriana asked.

"That is correct. It was pretty much his idea. At least he took credit for it. He laid the cornerstone in 1248 and died thirteen years later."

"He only missed the completion by six or seven centuries," Tommy joked.

"This rock..." Sean said to himself.

"What?"

The other three turned to him.

Sean was staring up at the sculpture. "Peter. Jesus said to Peter, 'Upon this rock I will build my church.' The cornerstone of a building is a rock."

"Yeah," Tommy said, "but this isn't a church."

"No, but that is," Sean said, pointing up at the triangle below the bishop's figure. "Or at least it's the symbol of one."

"Right. Now how does that help us?"

"Look at the design just below the pinnacle of the triangle. What does that look like to you?"

Tommy and the others thought for a moment before he responded. "The three interlocking circles? Looks like some sort of ancient symbol from..." Then it hit him. "Britannia."

"There you go," Sean said. "And where did King Arthur come from?"

"Great Britain," June answered, suddenly mesmerized by the idea.

"Come back to Peter for a second," Sean said. "What is the connection to all of this?"

"The sword," Tommy said in an absent tone. "The legend suggests that when Peter was executed by Nero, his sword was taken to Britain by Joseph of Arimathea."

"The one who gave his grave to Jesus," Adriana said.

"The very same. There are other legends, too. One says that he took the Holy Grail to Britain to be its guardian. Another suggests that he was the one who brought Christianity to the isles and became the first abbot of Britain, founding the first abbey."

"Wait," Sean said, holding up his palm. "If he founded the first church of Britain, maybe that's where we're supposed to look next."

Tommy looked as if he was going into a trance. "As the story goes, Joseph took the sword of Peter and the Holy Grail to Britain and founded the abbey at Glastonbury. I can't believe I didn't make that connection before now."

"What connection?" June asked.

"Glastonbury Abbey…it's where King Arthur and Queen Guinevere are buried."

"You mean supposedly buried," Sean said.

"Right. But come on. It can't be a coincidence. Can it?"

"And I thought you said we're not looking for the grail," Adriana added.

Frustrated with all the comments, Tommy held up both hands. "Okay, hold on. Nobody said anything about looking for the grail. I'm just putting it all out there. At this point, we don't know what is right or wrong."

"Sounds like we need to pay Helen and Mac a visit in France," Sean said.

"Good idea," Tommy agreed. "Right now we're grasping at straws. That codex might hold the key to figuring out this whole thing."

"Unfortunately, Mr. Schultz, your friends won't be in possession of the codex much longer," a new voice said from behind. It was oddly familiar.

The four spun around simultaneously and were met by the man who'd accosted them in Aachen, the one who'd posed as a waiter. He was standing several feet away with both hands tucked inside his jacket pockets.

Tommy took a step toward him.

"You should know every one of you has a gun aimed at your head right now," the man said. "I would prefer not to spill your blood."

"He's bluffing," Tommy said.

"Am I?"

Tommy and the others glanced around at each other. Red dots danced on their foreheads.

Sean scanned the buildings across the street for the shooters but couldn't immediately see any of them. He doubted they'd be in buildings with closed windows. More likely, they were hiding in some of the trees or bushes.

"Leave the McElroys out of this. They're just doing their jobs," Sean said. "They don't know what that codex means." He didn't let on that none of them really knew. Not yet, at least.

"Whether they know or not doesn't matter to me. You are involved with something more powerful than you could ever imagine. We cannot allow that."

"I'm sorry," Sean said, "but you know our names. We still haven't caught yours. I mean, don't get me wrong, we know something about you. Just not who you are. You look like a Billy." Sean turned to Tommy. "Wouldn't you say that's about right, Schultzie? Billy. Or maybe Steve?"

"I don't know, Sean. He strikes me as one of those with a gender-neutral name like Chris or Kelly."

"Your sense of humor won't get you out of this. This is your last chance to walk away."

"Wait," Adriana interrupted. "You just want us to walk away?"

"We are not here to kill you," the blond man said.

"Sorry if I'm a little skeptical of that statement seeing as you have guns pointed at our heads," Sean said.

"Consider this your last warning, Mr. Wyatt. Leave this place. Let go of this quest. It will only end in death."

"And our friends in France? I guess you're going to let them off with a warning, too?"

"Your excavation site, along with the artifacts, will be destroyed. Your friends will be unharmed, provided they do as we say."

"So what happens if we leave and then decide to come back around?"

The blond took his hands out of his pockets and crossed his arms. "Then we won't be so forgiving."

Sean noticed the spotter loitering by a black sedan on the other side of the street. The man had a bandage wrapped around his head.

"Is that your friend over there? Last time I saw him he was out cold on his back." Sean waved emphatically to the guy. "Hey over there! How's the head?"

The man shifted uncomfortably and then stiffened, visibly irritated.

Sean turned his attention back to the blond. "He always this friendly?"

"Leave Germany, now, Mr. Wyatt."

"Yeah, you keep saying that, but I'm not sure we're going anywhere. We're here on vacation, and there's nothing you can do about that. Besides, we kicked your tail before. We can do it again. And just like before, you and your men in the trees and bushes aren't going to kill four Americans in public. Well, I mean she's a dual citizen," he pointed at Adriana. "But you probably knew that. Anyway, there are too many witnesses here. Seriously, you really need to pick better spots to threaten us. Maybe somewhere isolated. I don't know, like a wooded meadow out in the country or something?"

The man started to respond, but Sean cut him off.

"And I have to ask, how did you guys get hooked up with the North Koreans? You don't really look like Dear Leader's type. I mean, maybe that's your thing."

The puzzled expression on the man's face told Sean all he needed to know. These guys weren't working with the North Koreans. They knew about the murder, surely. And they were well aware of the folder containing the DNA testing results. But they had no idea who was behind the murder of the research scientist.

"He has no idea what you're talking about," Tommy said. "You know, for a group of bullies with matching tattoos, you guys aren't very good at whatever it is you're supposed to be doing."

Before the blond could retort, four figures appeared behind the Americans. Their sunglasses concealed their eyes. Their hair was black and short, all cut in a similar fashion.

Sean felt the men approach from behind and immediately sensed the danger. The blond's expression changed to one of immediate concern.

The way Sean saw it, there was only one way to play this rock-and-a-hard-place situation. "They're standing right behind us, aren't they?"

One of the men reached out and grabbed June by the arms. She shrieked, and the result was a gloved hand clapped across her mouth.

Tommy spun around to defend her, but another man leveled a gun at his chest and waved a warning finger.

One of the four North Koreans stepped forward. He was slightly taller than the others, with broad, strong shoulders and a thick neck. "Give us the medallion," he said in an even tone.

"Funny you should ask for that," Sean said. "We actually left it in our hotel room. If you'll wait here, I can run back and get it real quick. Won't take long."

"You don't have a hotel room," the man said. "We followed you here from Aachen. This was the first place you came. Now, medallion." He held out his palm. "Or we shoot her in the head right here in front of you."

His English was good, good enough that Sean wondered if he'd been educated somewhere in the States.

"No," Tommy started to step forward, but the man aiming a gun at him brandished it menacingly.

"Take it easy, buddy," Sean said. "Fight another day."

Sean reached in his pocket and produced the medallion.

"It's okay," Sean went on. "These idiots don't know what to do with it."

"You're interfering with something you cannot comprehend," the blond said to the North Koreans. "Leave here now, or we will be forced to take you down."

Sean gave a nod of the head toward the blond. "He likes to talk about their little group. Honestly, I'd listen to him. They've got guns pointed at all of us at this very moment."

The leader of the North Koreans glanced down at his jacket and saw the red laser dot flickering on his chest. He looked back up with only a mild twinge of concern in his eyes.

"It would appear we are in a stalemate," he said.

"Sure would," Sean said. "So if you guys want to walk out of here in one piece, put down your weapons and play nice."

"Please," Tommy said with more desperation in his voice. "Do what he says. Let's talk about this."

Sean knew better. There would be no talking it out with the North Koreans. They were here to get what they wanted or die trying. It was the way they worked. He'd seen it once on a mission for Axis. They were relentless. If these four died, they'd be replaced by eight more the next day.

The only question was, why were they here and what did they want with the sword of Peter?

No one said a word for nearly a minute. Eyes flashed from one person to another. Tommy looked around nervously. Sean and Adriana kept their cool, sizing up the closest man to them in case things went hand to hand.

June didn't struggle much, but Sean could see the desperation in her eyes. At least he thought it was desperation.

A bicycle bell rang from across the plaza. The noise caused the man with the gun to waver momentarily, his gaze shifting ever so slightly.

June saw the movement and seized the opportunity. She opened her mouth and bit down on her captor's hand. He screamed as her teeth sank through the leather glove, gnashing all the way to bone.

The gunman spun around to face her.

She jerked her elbow back into the man's face, crushing his nose, and then dropped to the ground as the guy with the gun fired. The bullet smashed into the rathaus wall, missing her by inches. Tommy charged forward and clotheslined the shooter with his forearm. The force of the attack was so strong, it took the gunman's feet off the ground and flipped him over, sending him crashing face-first into the floor.

The leader and the other North Koreans leaped into action.

The latter rushed at Adriana, who matched the man's attack with equal speed. He jumped, leading with his left boot, which she deflected easily to the side. Using his momentum against him, Adriana twisted her body and swung her elbow into his midsection as he was still flying through the air.

The man grunted and rolled on the ground several feet away.

Meanwhile, Sean dealt with the leader.

He opened the battle with a series of quick jabs that the North Korean blocked easily. The man countered with a roundhouse that caught Sean on the cheek and sent him retreating one step backward.

"Good one," he said, rubbing the wound with the back of his hand. "Whoever you are."

He rushed at the man again, taking two steps and firing a left foot at the guy's knee.

The opponent chopped down on Sean's leg and swung the bridge of his other hand at Sean's throat to end the fight right then and there. Sean anticipated the counter and ducked to the side as the hand zipped just by his neck. He bounced back up and retaliated with a chop of his own to the man's temple.

The blow was devastating. The leader stumbled to the side for a moment, disoriented. Sean stalked toward him and snapped a sharp kick up into the man's abdomen. The leader dropped to his knees, and Sean drove a hammer fist down onto the man's face.

Bleeding and dizzy, the leader wavered, barely able to keep his balance in a kneeling position.

Sean stood over him and grabbed the back of his hair. He tugged on the fistful of hair, forcing the man to look him in the eyes.

"What is your name?" Sean said through clenched teeth.

The man resisted, so Sean pulled harder on his hair. "Tell me your name."

The man sniffled and spat. "Han-Jae. And you'd better kill me now. Or I will kill you and all your friends. You have no idea who you are dealing with."

"You know, Han, I've been hearing that a lot lately. And you know what, I'm not worried about it."

Sean raised his palm above his shoulder, ready to deliver the killing blow. "When your nose is driven into your brain, they say death is almost instantaneous, Han."

He brought the bridge of his hand down hard and stopped it right in front of the man's flaring nostrils, mere centimeters away. Then he formed a fist and rubbed the man's head hard and shoved him over.

Sirens blared suddenly from all corners of the plaza. Police rushed into the area with weapons drawn. They shouted orders in German for everyone to get down on the ground.

The Americans complied, getting down on their knees with their hands over their heads. The North Koreans struggled to obey, having been beaten down in the fighting.

As a cop with a handlebar mustache wrapped handcuffs around Sean and forced his face into the cobblestone, Sean looked around for the blond guy.

He and his bandaged friend were nowhere to be seen.

Chapter 12
Cologne

Han-Jae and one of his men were shoved into the back of a squad car. The German cops said something to them that neither man understood. Not that it mattered.

There was no way Han-Jae was going to let the police take them in. If that happened, there'd be no getting back to Pyongyang. It was understood that if he or any of his men were captured at any point, the general would disavow any knowledge of anything surrounding their mission.

Not that any of the European authorities would be able to connect them to Pyongyang. Han-Jae and his men had fail-safes in place to not only protect their identities but also their country of origin. If any investigator searched too deep, all they would find would be some ordinary guys from South Korea.

In this instance, the charges would be troublesome. They'd been caught with weapons and in the middle of a fight with some Americans.

Then there was the matter of the other man at the scene—the blond man who seemed to have a quarrel with the Americans. Han-Jae watched as the driver of their car finished giving instructions to the other driver from the car behind them. Right now wasn't the time to figure out who the blond man was or what his connection to the others might be.

All that mattered for the moment was escaping.

Han-Jae had learned many useful tricks growing up in the slums of Pyongyang. He'd become an expert at unlocking doors without keys. While he'd never been arrested in North Korea—which might as well have been a death sentence—Han-Jae took a keen interest in learning how to pick many kinds of locks. He spent countless hours breaking into safes, unlocking multi-pin vaults, and even handcuffs.

The general encouraged all of these practices because he knew that a spy who could access high-security locations without a key was an incredibly useful asset.

As a safety precaution, Han-Jae always carried a small tool—no larger than a paper clip—built into his watch. It looked like an ordinary watch stem, like a million others. This stem was far from ordinary.

Before their car's driver got in, he'd already started removing the stem with a quick push and twist with his fingers. Ever so carefully, he slid the stem out of its housing, revealing a short pin attached to the knob.

His partner glanced over at him. He barely noticed the subtle movement of Han-Jae's wrists as he worked the pin into the handcuffs.

Han-Jae's focus was intense. He stared straight ahead as the cop finished his conversation with the other driver and walked over to the open driver's side door. He got in and slammed the door shut. A quick glance in the rearview mirror told him his prisoners were still there and keeping quiet, though for one uncomfortable second he locked eyes with Han-Jae's cold, vapid stare.

The cop started the car and eased it out onto the street, followed immediately by the second car holding Han-Jae's other two men.

Han-Jae felt the cuffs go limp against his wrists. He lowered them to the seat without making a sound. The cop flashed another quick look into the back. The prisoners remained perfectly still.

Next, Han-Jae reached down slowly to his shoe. With his fingernail, he pressed in on the raised heel of his boot. The button built into the heel was almost invisible, it had been so well concealed.

The button popped out revealing a small, razor-sharp knife. He grasped it in his fingers and returned his hands to their previous position.

As they started crossing a bridge, the cop looked back into the mirror again. This time he saw Han-Jae flashing a toothy grin.

Suddenly the prisoner twisted his body, laying his torso across his partner's lap. The cop's eyes widened as Han-Jae kicked out with both feet, smashing his boots into the window.

On the first kick, the window didn't give. On the second, it shook. The third kick burst the reinforced glass out of its rails and onto the road outside. Fresh air blew in through the window, but it only lasted a second.

The cop spun the steering wheel and pulled the car over onto the side of the bridge. The other car slowed to a stop behind them as Han-Jae's driver angrily shifted into park and got out.

He was shouting something in German as he stepped around and opened the door. The next move he made would be fatal. The cop reached in to grab Han-Jae by the collar, but the prisoner's hand moved out from behind him in a quick slashing motion. The cop's wrist sliced open in an instant. Before he could even scream, Han-Jae reached out and grabbed the cop's shirt, yanked him close, and shoved the blade tip into the man's throat.

Horror filled the cop's eyes as he immediately started grasping at the mortal wound. Han-Jae pulled the knife out of his victim's throat and in a deft move unlatched the dying man's weapon from its holster.

Han-Jae twisted and kicked the man out onto the road as blood seeped through the cop's fingers.

With no time to waste, Han-Jae slid out of the car and stepped toward the one behind him carrying his other two men. The cop inside scrambled to open his door. Han-Jae raised the weapon and fired several shots through the windshield. They ripped holes in the glass, some catching the cop in the vest and two tearing through his neck. Han-Jae moved fast, stalking around the open door and firing one more round, this one into the side of the cop's head.

Cars slammed on their brakes at the horrific scene taking place right in front of them.

Han-Jae opened the back door of the second car and ushered his men to the lead vehicle. He waved the gun around at some of the cars stopped on the bridge and then fired a shot into the front tires of the two holding up traffic.

People screamed. Some got out of their cars and took off running in the other direction. A woman scrambled into the backseat of her car to protect her child.

When the other two men had packed into the squad car, Han-Jae turned and jogged back to the open driver's side door.

The cop he'd stabbed in the neck was lying completely still on the road several feet away, covered in thick crimson liquid.

Han-Jae ran over and grabbed the cuff keys off the dead man's belt then scurried back to the car.

He tossed the keys into the back and then hopped in the front, shifted into drive, and sped away. They would need to find a safe house. Preferably somewhere out of the country.

With the blood of two cops on their hands, everyone in Germany would be looking for them.

Chapter 13
Cologne

Sean stared at the cinder block wall from the narrow bench in the middle of the room. Tommy had been pacing around for the better part of the last hour. There was no way to know exactly how much time had passed since they'd arrived in the holding tank. A clock on the wall just outside the cell was just beyond their field of vision.

Not that it mattered. The North Koreans had been apprehended, which was definitely a good thing. The only question rattling around in Sean's mind was how in the world the other two guys had disappeared.

They'd each been allowed to make a phone call. Sean used his to call Emily. She had a useful way of getting him out of trouble like this from time to time. He hoped she wouldn't be upset. Then again, if she was, she'd get over it. She always did.

"I hope the girls are okay," Tommy said for the fifth time in twenty minutes.

The women had been taken to a different holding area, as was protocol.

"I'm sure they're fine. Speaking of, what was that from your girl? Did you see how she handled herself?"

Tommy nodded. "Yeah, I don't know where that came from."

"You don't sound happy about it."

He shrugged and continued gazing at the floor with his elbows on his knees and his hands folded.

"It just means there's something weird about her. For once, I'd just like to meet a normal girl. You know?"

"Something weird about her?"

"I mean she's probably a member of a gang or a spy or something else. You remember the Japanese girl, don't you?"

"How could I forget?"

Tommy had met a girl he believed was interested while they were on a mission in Japan. She'd turned out to be the leader of the Yakuza, an underworld crime syndicate that had spread across the country.

"Look, Schultzie," Sean said, "you need to realize something very important about women."

"They're all crazy?"

Sean guffawed at the comment. "No, although some definitely are. What I mean is, there is no such thing as normal. Everyone's got a little weirdness to them. That's just the result of life. After all, life isn't normal."

"I hope you're not saying I should have still gone after the Japanese chick."

Sean smirked. "No, you were right to let that one go. Pretty sure she's in a supermax security prison somewhere. But June seems like a nice person. And honestly, it doesn't hurt to have a woman who can kick a little butt on your side. Adriana's bailed me out lots of times."

Tommy relented with a nod. "That's true."

"Yeah. I mean, maybe June's taken some kickboxing classes or something. Women have to be able to defend themselves these days. Heck, if I had a daughter, I'd teach her everything I know."

"I guess."

Footsteps clicked on the floor in the hall outside the cell.

"Wyatt and Schultz," a man's voice said in a thick German accent. A second later, a rotund cop appeared with a ring of keys dangling off his belt. "You have a car waiting for you outside. Try not to cause any more trouble while you're here in Germany."

The door unlocked automatically and slid to the left.

Sean and Tommy thanked the cop and walked by, heading down the hall the way they'd been brought before. Sean kept his eyes forward as he spoke. "If the door opens automatically, I wonder what all those keys are for."

"Just shut up, and keep walking unless you want to get thrown back in there."

"Roger that."

They made their way through the maze of corridors until they reached another set of bars. Once more, something buzzed inside the walls, and a moment later the barred door slid to the side.

When they were on the steps of the jail, the two Americans took a deep breath and exhaled. A black Mercedes sat on the street right beneath the steps. A man in sunglasses and black jacket and pants was standing next to the rear door with hands folded.

He reached over and opened the back door, motioning for the two to get in.

"Looks like Emily hooked us up this time," Tommy said.

Sean smiled, albeit suspiciously. "Yeah. I'll be sure to send her a thank-you bouquet."

As the two friends neared the bottom step, Sean paused. "Where are the girls?" he asked the driver.

The tall man answered by pointing at a similar car at the end of the street.

"So I guess we're going to follow them?"

The man nodded. "That's what I was told," he said in a heavy accent.

"Great," Tommy said. "Where we going? Hotel?"

"Arrangements have been made for your accommodations. That's all I know for now."

The two Americans accepted the answer and slid into the car's backseat. The driver closed the door behind them and hurried around to the driver's side.

"He looks a little like Lurch, doesn't he?" Tommy whispered before the driver got in.

"Shh. Be nice. Just be grateful we're out of jail. We owe Emily big time."

"You can say that again. She even hooked us up with a place to stay. Talk about going above and beyond."

The driver got in the car and pulled out onto the street. The two passengers didn't think much of the locks automatically engaging since so many models across so many brands had the same feature.

Both Americans watched the people and buildings go by as the drive steered the car through the streets and eventually away from downtown and across the Rhine, back toward the heart of Germany.

"We're not staying in town?" Tommy asked.

"You are, but Cologne has some nicer places on the other side of the river. We'll be there shortly."

Once more, the passengers accepted the explanation.

Sean wondered why the girls couldn't have ridden with them. It would have been a little cramped, but not bad.

Out of the main part of the city, the driver took the second exit and continued driving another ten minutes until they reached an industrial area. Hollowed-out steel mills, decrepit warehouses, and decaying factories littered the landscape. A few abandoned houses lay scattered around the perimeter. Some of the buildings looked like they'd been bombed. Given the location, that was entirely possible. Many German buildings were never repaired after World War II.

"We making a stop on the way or something?" Sean asked.

The car in front of them stopped abruptly in front of an old church. The bell tower had a hole in the side, and parts of the roof were also missing.

The driver halted the car behind the other and then spun around quickly, pointing a pistol into the back seat. He moved the weapon from one man to the other until both doors opened.

"Seems a little over the top, even for Emily," Tommy said.

"Emily wasn't the one who bailed us out," Sean said.

"Yeah, I know. I was kidding. The question is, who did?"

They got their answer momentarily.

"Out of the car," a voice said from outside Sean's side.

Sean obeyed and eased out of his seat slowly. He planted his feet on the asphalt and looked around, taking quick inventory of his surroundings and the men who'd taken him and the others captive.

He saw Adriana and June getting out of the other car. They appeared to be fine, though it was hard to tell in the weak moonlight.

The blond man from before appeared in the doorway of the church, along with his bandaged companion.

"Oh hey. It's you again. So nice to see a friendly face. Thank you so much for bailing us out of jail. I really appreciate it." Sean's sarcasm didn't sit well with the blond, but the guy let it go.

Instead, he ordered the others to take them inside. "Make sure you don't take your eyes off of them," he added.

Sean counted nine men. *Coincidence?* he thought.

"June, you okay?" Tommy asked as he was being ushered into the old stone building.

She nodded, though she was clearly not happy.

The two women were taken in right behind the men, separated by some of the blond's crew.

Once inside, the last man slammed the heavy wooden door shut.

The Americans were taken through the foyer and into the main sanctuary. They made their way down the nave and hung a left, moving into an antechamber where an open door led down a flight of stairs into the basement. The building smelled like rusty metal, old wood, and damp stone. It couldn't have been used in more than a decade or two, a relic from a time long ago.

"They have power in here?" Tommy asked as they reached the bottom of the stairs lit by small candle-shaped bulbs fixed to the walls.

"If I had to guess, we're about to see what this place really is," Sean said.

"Quiet," the man directly behind them ordered.

They reached another metal door, this one painted black with rivets around the edge. A single light hung from the low ceiling.

The man in front flipped open a steel panel to the left of the door, revealing a fingerprint scanner. He pressed his thumb to the screen and the device lit up bright blue. A line passed over the thumb going up and then down again. Then a green light on the side blinked. A second later, an unseen mechanism clicked inside the door, and it swung open.

"Pretty high-tech stuff for an abandoned church," Sean said.

"I told you to be quiet," the same guy from before snapped.

He shoved Sean through the door. Tommy was pushed in next. They were more courteous to the women, allowing them to walk through the opening voluntarily, albeit with a sense of urgency.

Inside, the next room was like walking into a million-dollar government bunker. High-definition flatscreens hung from the walls. Half a dozen computers were busily downloading information at workstations in various places. A glass window in the back that stretched from one side of the room to the other protected what looked like a conference room on the other side, accessible through a glass door at the other end.

Another door on the far side was the only other way in or out. From the looks of it, Sean guessed it led to the bathroom or a kitchen area.

“Nice digs,” Sean said as he finished taking in the scene.

The man behind him shoved him forward toward a chair. “Sit down.”

Sean didn’t wait to be told twice. In spite of the guns being pointed at them by seven of the men, he still didn’t get the sense that he and his friends were going to be executed. If these guys—whoever they were—wanted the Americans dead, they could have done it long ago.

Tommy found an empty chair close to June and sat down. Adriana did the same, sitting close to Sean.

“One big happy family,” Adriana said.

“Good to see some things don’t change,” Sean quipped.

“I have to say,” the blond started, “you certainly don’t seem to respect the trouble you’ve gotten yourselves into.”

Sean rolled his shoulders. “I’ve seen worse. But I meant what I said.”

“Which was?”

“This place is nice. Seriously, who funds this? Are those computers pulling intel from rotating floating proxies?”

“Mr. Wyatt, you have no idea who we are. Do you?”

Sean’s head moved slowly back and forth. “You finally gonna tell us or just keep playing Mr. Secret?”

“We are the Brotherhood of the Sword. For thousands of years we have protected what it is you seek. So you can see why I would be somewhat irritated at your recent actions.”

“Oh, so you’re some kind of secret society. Okay, well, that makes sense.”

“A secret society seeks to gain an advantage over others in some way. We seek only to protect something of great power, something that you would expose to the world. That, Mr. Wyatt, we cannot abide.”

“You know what, I’m gonna go ahead and hit the pause button right there, friend. First off, you can call me Sean. This whole Mr. Wyatt thing is a little worn. Usually, it’s the bad guys that say stuff like that. Super cheesy when they do, by the way. And while maybe you’re just trying to be respectful, I’d appreciate it if you didn’t call me by my dad’s moniker.”

"Very well, Sean. Since I'm certain you can't appreciate the gravity of what we're dealing with here, I'm going to fill you in."

"This should be good," Tommy said.

The man behind him shoved him in the back, catching Tommy off guard. He snapped his head around threateningly but said nothing.

The blond went on. "We have been protecting this secret for a thousand years, and we cannot have you four—"

"I'm sorry," Sean interrupted. "We didn't catch your name."

The irritation on the man's reddened face couldn't have been more obvious. "Who I am doesn't matter."

"Well, it's just that I like to know who's lecturing me, that's all. Or would you just like me to call you professor."

"Baldwin. My name is Baldwin."

Tommy's eyes narrowed. "That's no relation to the Baldwins of Jerusalem, is it?" he joked.

Baldwin's face remained stoic. "I'm a direct descendant of the kings of Jerusalem."

Tommy's playful smirk disappeared as he realized the man was serious.

"Whoa, seriously?" Sean said, raising both eyebrows. "I thought that lineage was gone a long time ago."

Baldwin shook his head slowly. "We have remained in the shadows, watching over the sword of my forefathers for generations."

"Okay, so let me get this straight," Tommy said. "You guys are a secret society, protecting Excalibur from the world. And you, the leader, are a direct descendant of the Crusader kings of Jerusalem?"

Baldwin responded with a slow nod.

"Wow! I mean, that is heavy!"

"Yeah, no kidding," Sean agreed. "How do you deal with that kind of pressure? Seriously. That's gotta be tough."

"Yes. It is. And thanks to you two, there are a group of North Koreans on the sword's trail."

Adriana frowned. "Wait a minute. The North Koreans were arrested, same as us. I saw the police taking them away."

"Yes," Baldwin said. "They were arrested. And subsequently they escaped. They never reached the station. Two cops were killed in the process."

"What?" Sean said. The mood in the room turned serious all of a sudden. "How is that possible?"

"We're not sure. But just in case you think I'm lying, here's the headline."

He pressed a button on a small remote in his hand, and the biggest screen on the back wall switched to a local newspaper. The headline corroborated Baldwin's story: *Two dead in escape plot*.

"How is that possible?" June asked.

"You four need to understand something. The Brotherhood represents good in this world. We are protectors of a powerful relic that, if in the wrong hands, could bring about the end of the world."

Sean was dubious. “I’m sorry, man. But I have trouble believing one sword could cause that much trouble in a world of air forces and tanks and navies. Not to mention the armed public, in America of course.”

“You really don’t understand what you’re looking for. Do you?”

“I guess not. I thought we were looking for the sword of King Arthur.”

Baldwin shook his head. “Arthur was only one of many who held the sword.”

“Yes, we know that,” Tommy cut in. “There were eight others.”

“No. There were more than that. Many more.”

The puzzled looks on the faces of the four Americans told the blond man to keep talking.

Baldwin stepped around behind one of the workstations in the center of the room, putting the large screen directly behind him. “Long ago, our world was hit with a barrage of meteors. Many burned up in the atmosphere. One, however, made it through our planet’s natural shield and struck the Earth. Hundreds of years passed before anyone found it.”

“Joshua,” Tommy said in a reverent tone.

“Very good,” Baldwin said. “Moses led the Israelites out of Egypt and all the way to the border of Canaan. But he was not allowed to lead the people into the promised land. That task was passed to his apprentice, Joshua.”

“Sinai,” Sean said. “Moses found the stone on Mount Sinai.”

"I can see your intuition is strong, Sean. The stone found by Moses emitted a powerful form of radiation. It made the one who possessed it extremely powerful, but it also had consequences."

"Consequences?" Adriana asked.

"Yes. While this type of radiation wasn't immediately harmful, it effectively caused genetic disorders that eventually resulted in death."

"He who raises the sword will die by it," Sean quoted the text from Matthew.

"Precisely. For a short time, the sword will give incredible power to the one who wields it. However, if it is not surrendered, it will cause death."

Tommy shook his head. "I'm sorry, I don't understand. You were talking about a meteor. Now it's a sword. Which is it?"

"The story about the sword in the stone is allegorical. In truth, Excalibur was forged by combining metal of Earth and metal from the meteor. It was the ultimate weapon, a sword of God."

"And whoever took it into battle couldn't lose," Tommy whispered.

Baldwin went on. "Now, the forces of evil seek the sword. If they succeed in locating it, the North Koreans will be unstoppable. I don't believe I need to tell you what that would look like for humanity."

He was right. Everyone knew about the massacres in North Korea, the corruption, the people starving to death every day. If they were able to take over, their way of doing things would spread like a pestilence.

"Still hard to believe that a single sword could cause that much trouble. Like we said, in an age of planes and bombs and such, what harm could it cause?" Tommy asked.

"If the sword is found, they could use it to alter their own genetics." Baldwin paused for a moment to let the implications set in. "They could create a race of super soldiers."

Everyone in the room fell silent for a long minute.

"Okay," Tommy said. "We get it. Sword in wrong hands, bad. So let's just go get it and move it to another location. That way, they can never find it."

Baldwin's statuesque expression flinched. He glanced over at the man with the bandage on his head.

"Wait a minute," Sean said. "You've gotta be kidding me."

"What?" Adriana asked, turning to Sean.

He shook his head. "They have no idea where it is. Do you?"

Baldwin drew in a deep breath. He finally shook his head as he exhaled. "No."

Chapter 14
Cologne

"Hold on," Tommy said. "You guys are protecting this thing, but you have no idea where it is? Doesn't sound like you're very good at what you do."

Baldwin crossed his arms. "We monitor everything," he said. "When someone finds something related to the sword, we intervene."

"And scare them off the trail," Sean said.

"I wouldn't put it that way, but yes. We deter people from searching further."

"I have to ask," June said, emboldened, "how is all of this funded?" She waved a hand at the tech gadgets surrounding them. "This kind of operation can't be cheap."

"We're a special order of the church. This is our monastery."

"Wow," Sean gasped. "So you guys are like warrior monks?"

"We are ordained by the church, yes. So technically, we're priests assigned to protecting the sword at all costs."

"A sword you still can't find," Tommy added.

"Mr....Tommy, we believe it is safer if no one knows the true location of the sword to better protect it and the world from its power. That means no one in the Brotherhood can know its location either."

It was an old trick. Sean had heard of that sort of thing before. Better no one know where the treasure is. That way, no one would be tempted to go take it. In this case, the treasure was a radioactive sword.

"So this sword, if found, could be manipulated to genetically alter human beings?" Sean asked. "Sorry, but that sounds a little too much like science fiction."

"Look at the facts, Sean," Baldwin leveled his gaze with the American's. "The nine men you know of were incredible warriors. They never really suffered defeat."

"There. You said it again."

"Said what?"

"You said the nine men we know of. Earlier, you said something similar to that. Are you saying there are others?" Sean raised an eyebrow.

Baldwin drew another long breath in through his nose. "The history of Excalibur is a sordid one. It was held—for a time—in Ireland. It was called Caladbolg then. Some of Ireland's greatest heroes wielded it in battle and, as a result, enjoyed incredible military success. Songs were sung about their exploits. But nothing lasts forever. Those who raised the sword died by it, and it disappeared once more."

The room fell silent again as the visitors processed the information. Sean considered the story, though there were still some missing pieces.

"Who else had the sword? Were there others besides the Irish?"

"Of course. Excalibur turned the tide of the Trojan War. Troy was wiped from the face of the

Earth, never to be seen again—much like Jericho when Joshua and the Israelites invaded Canaan."

Tommy nodded. "The *Bible* says the entire city was wiped out. I thought the Ark of the Covenant did that."

Baldwin's lips creased slightly. "The Ark was a powerful weapon in its own right. When combined with the sword, the Israelites were almost invincible."

"Almost?" Adriana asked.

"They became consumed with being more like their neighbors. As you Americans say, keeping up with the Joneses. Greed, lust, and other temptations took hold of their nation. That's why the Brotherhood was formed. Since the time of Joshua, we have protected it. When a worthy warrior reveals himself, only then did we remove it from its hiding place."

Sean was confused. "So wait a minute. You guys knew where it was and were responsible for giving it to people you deemed worthy throughout history."

"Only when it was needed," Baldwin interrupted.

"Right. Fine. So what happened? Did someone misplace it along the line or what? Seems like an awfully important relic to lose."

Baldwin pushed back his irritation. "No. One of our forefathers returned it to its resting place and hid it so that it couldn't be used for evil."

"But you said that part of what you guys do is bring it out in times of need, to give it to a worthy warrior. Seems like if you're supposed to do that, it might be handy to know where it is."

Baldwin realized Sean made a good point, one for which he didn't have an answer. He looked down at the floor for a moment, perplexed by the issue. "Thank you for pointing that out. Our orders now are that we do not allow anyone to find it. That is our creed and will continue to be until the end of time."

Sean thought about pointing out their blind obedience, but he decided he'd asked enough questions on that issue.

"What about the North Koreans?" Adriana asked. "You said they want to engineer some kind of super soldiers. How do you know that? And what happened to the guys who escaped earlier?"

"We have reason to believe that one of the Chairman's generals is going to try to overthrow the government and seize control of the country. While most of the military is loyal to the leader, if the general were to acquire the sword, his coup would be virtually guaranteed a victory."

"So why not send a message to Dear Leader? Tell him that he's got a rebellious general in his midst. Let him take care of the problem." Tommy brought up a good point. Sean knew the answer, but he let Baldwin give it.

"The Chairman does not take well to messages from the outside world. I'm not sure if you've noticed, but he tends to be a bit paranoid when it comes to that sort of thing."

Was that sarcasm? Sean wondered. Up until that point, he was fairly certain Baldwin was a robot with no emotions, feelings, or a sense of humor.

"Were we to send him a message, he would simply ignore it," Baldwin finished his thought.

"He's right," Sean agreed. "They look at anything coming in from the outside as propaganda. Wouldn't believe it for a second."

"So what do we do?" June asked.

"You," Baldwin said in a sharp tone, "will do nothing. You will let us do what we have been trained to do. We will eliminate the threat and keep the sword safe."

"Well, you guys are doing a bang-up job right now," Sean said. "You've got a North Korean hit squad running loose in Europe right now."

"And if you'd stay out of our way, we could get back to taking care of them."

"Do you even know where they are, where they're going?"

"We'll know shortly."

"And how is that?"

"We have our methods." Baldwin snarled the last word.

The others in the room felt like they were watching two young rams butting heads.

"You still didn't answer my question," Adriana said. "How do you know about their plans for the super soldiers? And how did the North Koreans learn about the medallion and the other clues?"

Baldwin looked over at the man with the bandage on his head. The guy shrugged and then gave a nod.

"They had help."

"Help?" Tommy asked. "What kind of help?"

Baldwin shifted, clearly uncomfortable with either the question or the answer. No one in the room could figure out which.

“For the better part of two decades, they’ve been searching for Excalibur. Initially, it was the former Chairman’s idea. When he learned about it and the potential it held, he spent millions scouring the globe to find it. When he died, his son took over and scrapped the entire project. Said it was a foolish errand, a wild goose chase. He wanted to spend more money on nuclear warheads and less on trying to find a mythical sword with magical powers. The general, however, was less willing to let go.”

Baldwin turned to the big screen and pressed a button on his remote again. The image of a man in North Korean military garb appeared on the screen. He had an angry scowl on his face that looked like it might have been permanent.

“This is General Ku Min-Woo. He was behind the initial search. It was he who convinced the previous Chairman to search for the sword. When the son refused to continue looking, Min-Woo started formulating a plan to seize power. He has a loyal group of followers in the army. You met some of them today.”

“We actually met them before,” Sean said.

Adriana ignored the comment and pressed on. “You said they had help. Who would help the North Koreans? Chinese? The Russians?”

Baldwin shook his head slowly. “No. They are not involved. The Chinese know better than to mess with them. The Russians might have, but they didn't know anything about the sword."

"Who then?" Tommy asked.

Baldwin paused, contemplating how to answer. His eyes blinked rapidly. When he spoke, it was in a grave tone. "They had help from American archaeologists."

"What?" Tommy said. "Why would Americans help them? They're like the weakest enemy we have. Every American knows that. Why in the world would someone do anything that could help make North Korea more powerful?"

"They didn't do it willingly, Tommy. They were forced to."

"So they're prisoners?" Sean said.

Baldwin nodded, but for some reason he kept looking at Tommy. "Yes. They were captured almost twenty years ago. We believe the previous Chairman knew what they were looking for and tracked them. Once he had them...let's just say they have ways of getting what they want out of their captives."

"He tortured them," June said. "Ugh, that must have been awful. For twenty years, living like slaves? I can't imagine."

Baldwin's gaze never left Tommy.

It was clearly making Tommy uncomfortable. "Um, why do you keep looking at me like that? It's kind of weird. I get it. I'm an archaeologist; the Americans who helped the General tin-boo or whatever are archaeologists. You're creeping me out a little."

Sean's eyes widened as the realization hit him. He knew it before Baldwin opened his mouth to speak.

"Tommy," Baldwin said, "the people helping the North Koreans…they're your parents."

Chapter 15
Cologne

"What did you just say?" Tommy stared at the leader of the Brotherhood.

At first, the man's words barely seemed real. It took a minute before they set in. When that happened, Tommy's confusion turned to anger. His eyes blazed like bonfires, and his nose flared with every breath.

He stood up from his chair suddenly. The man behind him placed his hand on Tommy's shoulder to force him back down, but he may as well have been a fly buzzing around a bull. Tommy swatted his hand away and shoved the man in the chest with surprising force.

The guy started to step toward Tommy, but Baldwin held up a hand—a silent order to stand down.

"You got a lot of nerve bringing up my parents. What kind of sick joke is this?" Tommy's voice raged, booming off the walls like thunder.

Baldwin remained calm, keeping his voice low and even. "I know that it must be hard to hear. I can't imagine the tidal wave of emotions you must be feeling. But it's no lie. Your parents are alive, Tommy. They've been living in North Korea for the last two decades."

"Shut up! Stop it! Do you hear me? Stop it!" Tommy yelled. Tears welled in his eyes. His face burned red.

"As far as we know, they're okay. They've been living in a nice apartment under the careful supervision of General Min-Woo. Our operative said they have not been harmed, they're well fed, and well cared for."

"No," Tommy shook his head emphatically. "No. This can't be real." He lowered his voice and bit his lower lip. "They were killed in a plane crash."

Baldwin treaded carefully with the subject. "That's what you were told, Tommy. But the plane was never found. You know that. When search teams couldn't find it, they assumed it was lost at sea. It wasn't."

Tommy started to jump over the counter to tackle Baldwin, but Sean sprang out of his chair and wrapped a strong arm around his friend's chest.

"Easy, buddy," Sean said, holding his friend back. "Take it easy." Sean turned to one of the other guys. "Can you get him a bottle of water or something?"

One of the men nodded and disappeared through the door at the other end of the room.

Tommy choked. Sean felt him go limp as he held him, so he eased his friend back into his seat. Tommy collapsed, putting his head in his hands. He could control the tears no longer, and the dam holding them back burst, letting them flood down both cheeks and through his fingers.

Sean looked up at Baldwin. "For your sake, I hope you're not making this up. Because if you are, I'll kill you myself. Do you have any idea what he's been through over the years?"

"I can only guess," Baldwin said. "I'm not lying, though. Have a look for yourself." He pressed the button again, and the screen behind him changed.

It was a black-and-white image of a window, taken from a considerable distance. There was no mistaking the faces in the glass. Tommy's mother and father were sitting at a table. They were surrounded by papers. His father held a pen in one hand. His mother was looking at a stack of files.

Sean couldn't believe his eyes, and a moment later a tear streaked down his cheek.

He put his hand on Tommy's shoulder.

Tommy hadn't looked up yet, but when he felt his friend's strong grip, he picked up his head and stared with unbelieving eyes at the screen.

"This was taken last week," Baldwin said.

Tommy swallowed. His head twisted back and forth. "No. It can't be."

"They're alive, Tommy. Until now, we still haven't figured out a way to get them out safely. For the moment, they're okay. We know that much. The general won't do anything to his golden geese as long as they keep getting him leads."

"Those leads will eventually run out, though, won't they?" Adriana asked.

Baldwin nodded. "Yes. And I don't need to tell you the methods the North Koreans use on people who cease to be useful to them."

"What are you saying?" Sean said.

"I'm saying we know where his parents are. If you want to see them alive again, you'll do what we say. Do that, and you may have a chance to save them."

Tommy wiped his face and peered through eyelids that were little more than slits. “What do you want?” he asked through clenched teeth.

“Walk away from this crusade. Leave Excalibur to the mists of legends and folklore. Forget everything you’ve seen and learned. Do this, and we will give you the exact location of your parents.”

“That’s a fine offer,” Sean said. “Except there’s one huge problem. Even if we do what you say and you tell us where we can find his folks, there’s still the little issue of how we get them out of North Korea. It’s not like we can just waltz in there, knock on a door, and drive them to the airport.”

“It’s the best we can do for you,” Baldwin said. “You have connections, Sean. You can figure something out.”

Tommy slowed his breathing. He sniffled a few times before speaking again. “Why did you send someone to North Korea?”

“We received an encrypted message from your parents, though we’re not sure how they found us or how they got it out of the country without any of the North Korean authorities catching it. They warned us as to what was going on. They also told us that if we found you to let you know that they’re alive and well.”

Tommy continued shaking his head. “Sent you a message? How did they know you would find it? How did they even know you exist?”

“Your parents are…resourceful, Tommy. They took a big risk attempting to contact us. We have operated in secret for thousands of years. You could imagine our surprise when someone got our attention with a direct message."

Sean stared at the image on the screen. Even with the resolution not being optimal, there was no question it was Tommy's parents.

"So you just want us to walk away, and you'll tell us where his parents are?" Sean asked.

"That's the deal," Baldwin gave a nod.

"And if we don't?"

"Then we will return you to the police, tell them you were responsible for a terrorist plot, and you'll be put away in a German prison for a very, very long time."

"Oof. Tough decision," Sean joked. "You know what, my friends and I are going to need a minute to talk this over. Would you mind giving us a little privacy?"

"Certainly."

Baldwin motioned for his men to follow him back to the conference room door. One man stepped through the door they'd come through on the way in, presumably to guard it from the outside.

Tommy was still staring at the screen, visibly shaken by the revelation. He kept shaking his head and biting his nails, rocking back and forth.

Sean gave him a moment and then beckoned the two women closer.

"There's nothing to discuss. We have to take the deal he's offering," Sean said. "If we have a chance to get your parents back, at least it's something. Who cares about the sword at this point?"

"We don't even know if that's really them," Tommy said. He still couldn't wrap his head around it. "What if it's people in disguises? Huh? What if this is all some kind of sick ploy?"

Sean put his hand on Tommy's shoulder. "It looks legit enough to try," Sean said. "If they give us the location of your parents, maybe I can put something together with Emily to get them out."

"Maybe?" Tommy asked. "Look, even if that is my parents, they're in North Korea, Sean. There's no way we can get them out. Not even you could put something like that together. Once they run out of leads to feed the North Koreans, they're as good as dead anyway."

The room dipped into silence once more. June reached out and touched Tommy's hand gently with her fingers. He didn't react, just continued staring forward at the big screen.

"There's another way," Tommy whispered after thinking on the issue for a minute. "Tell them we'll take it. We want as much detail as they can give us on my parents' location. And we'll drop the Excalibur case."

Sean's lips pinched together, and he gave an acknowledging nod. He turned to the window and motioned for Baldwin and his crew to come back in.

Tommy waited to speak until all the men were back in the room save the one guarding the door outside. "Tell us everything you know about my parents," he said in an icy tone. "We'll drop the Excalibur investigation."

"We can go a step further than telling you where they are," Baldwin said. "We can tell you how to get them out."

He put his hand out toward the man with the bandaged head. The wounded guy passed him a black folder, which Baldwin relayed to Tommy.

Tommy opened it to find pictures, building schematics, and topographical maps with certain areas circled.

"Are those drop zones?" Sean asked, pointing at the maps.

"That file contains everything you'll need to get a team in and out of North Korea, including your best options for point of entry and preferred extraction zones. Feel free to double check our work, but it's thorough."

Sean sifted through the file. "How did you guys pull these satellite images?"

Baldwin crossed his arms. "We have our resources, Sean. An operation like ours doesn't exist without considerable...support."

Adriana still had something on her mind. She'd been holding it back during the course of the discussion. "What about the North Koreans that are here looking for the sword? Are you going to stop them?"

"We are monitoring their movement now. It appears they are lying low. When they pop their heads up to take a look around, we'll take care of them."

"You going to offer them a deal, too?" Tommy asked. He didn't try to hide his cynicism.

“The only deal we have for them is death,” Baldwin answered. “Do not mistake our mercy toward you as weakness. We are soldiers, Tommy. We do what soldiers do. Sometimes that means doing what is necessary.”

An awkward silence slipped back into the room. For a moment, the only noise came from the humming machines running their processes.

Tommy looked over the information in the folder as Sean passed piece after piece to him. When he was done, he looked up into Baldwin’s steel-blue eyes. “Okay. We’ll get out of your way. Just make sure you take care of those North Koreans.”

“That’s what we do,” Baldwin said. “Karl will take you back to the cars.” He motioned to the bandaged man, who still had an irritated look on his face. “The cars will take you wherever you need to go. I would suggest leaving Cologne immediately.”

“I think we can both agree on that,” Tommy said.

Chapter 16
Brussels, Belgium

Han-Jae looked out the window of their room. Most of the buildings within view were old, showing off the rich history of the city. Dramatic church spires and domes sprang up in the distance, contrasted by intermittent modern buildings made mostly of glass and steel.

Belgium was a center of culture and diversity, which made it an easy place for Han-Jae and his crew to blend in.

They'd managed to escape the German police, though at great cost. He didn't care about the cops they'd killed to get away. The real cost to Han-Jae was that now Interpol would be watching for them.

He'd spent a good amount of time putting this operation together. Getting their false papers and identifications was no easy task, not originally anyway. Now Han-Jae had a network throughout the criminal underground. Brussels was one such place where his connections thrived.

Going to Prague had been a consideration. He had plenty of reach there as well. Something in his gut told him to stay closer to the United Kingdom. That meant Brussels.

A knock came at the door and startled the four men in the room. Kin Pak—the one who'd injured his head previously—was sitting on the chair next to the door with a pistol across his lap.

Their weapons had been taken by the German police. The gun Kin held was the one he'd taken from the German cop he'd killed during their escape.

Han-Jae motioned to one of the other men to open the door while Kin stood back with his weapon pointed at the doorway. When Han-Jae was happy with Kin's position, he gave a nod to the man holding the doorknob.

The guy twisted it and eased it open.

A skinny, pale figure stood in the doorway wearing a hoodie and torn blue jeans.

"What's with the gun?" the man asked in a scratchy voice. "You know I don't like guns."

"Excuse our caution," Han-Jae said. "We had some trouble in Germany."

"Yeah, no kidding." The figure stepped into the room and pulled back his hood, revealing his stubbly face. "I saw you killed some cops over there. They tend not to like it when you do things like that." His sharp English accent belied the part of London where he'd grown up.

Two large-gauge earrings dangled from sagging lobes. A miniature black spike stuck through his nose. Matching dagger tattoos ran up either side of his neck, pointing toward his ears.

The guy at the door closed it quickly behind him and remained at full attention.

Kin lowered his weapon but kept a ready finger on the trigger.

The guy with the tattoos went by the name Raven. Han-Jae didn't know his real name, and that didn't matter. All that mattered was that the guy delivered.

Raven stepped over to the bed and plopped a duffel bag down on the edge. He unzipped it and reached inside.

"Four 9mm pistols," he said, setting the weapons on the bed next to the bag. Then he placed several passports down by the guns. "Passports, driver's licenses, visas, etc. Brought you some spare magazines, too. You'll probably be needing them. They're in the bag."

"Rounds?"

"Boxes of them in the bag. Check for yourself. You've got enough ammo in there to start a small revolution, though if that's what you're looking to do you might want bigger guns."

Han-Jae shook his head. "This will work."

Raven drew in a breath and sighed. "Good. I thought it might. I also brought you some silencers for the pistols, as requested."

Han-Jae rummaged through the bag and found the sound suppressors. He did a quick eyeball test, making sure the cylinders were clean and free from damage. Underworld types like Raven were often guilty of delivering faulty product. It wasn't necessarily intentional. Sometimes they had to deal with what they received. In this case, the weapons and their accessories were high quality.

Raven stood by a few feet away as his buyer finished going through the goods. He patted his palms against the outside of his thighs, clearly anxious about the whole deal. He knew better than to ask too many questions, especially from guys like the ones in the room. He had a partner at one point, a guy who had a nervous habit of talking way too much, asking more questions than he should have, and all in all just being annoying.

During a deal with some Russians for some microchips and AK-47s, he ended up getting shot in the back of the head and dumped in a river.

Killed selling Russian guns to a Russian crime syndicate. The irony wasn't lost on Raven, and he constantly reminded himself to keep his mouth shut during a deal.

Han-Jae flicked his head up at one of his men. "Give him the money."

Raven didn't dare breathe a sigh of relief. His motto was: Act like things are always going according to plan. That kept him calm, or at least made him appear calm on the outside.

The man closest to the door walked over to a duffel bag on the floor near the bathroom. He picked it up and tossed it to Raven, who caught it with a grunt. It was heavier than he'd expected.

"Thank you," Raven said.

He pulled back the zipper and thumbed through a few stacks of tightly packed euros.

"Ten thousand," Han-Jae said.

Raven gave a nod and clutched the money bag tight. "Thank you for your business. Please let me know if you ever need anything else in the future. I'll be happy to—"

"We know where to find you," Han-Jae cut him off. "Leave us."

Raven nodded emphatically, even bowed a few times as he backed toward the door. "Right."

He reached the door and spun around to find one of the other men blocking his path.

"Excuse me, sorry," he said.

The man wouldn't budge.

"I'll just slip by you and be on my way," Raven said, his voice becoming more insistent.

He heard the sound of metal threads squeaking against another metal adapter. Raven swallowed and twisted his head to look over his shoulder. Han-Jae was standing there with one of the pistols he'd just bought, now with a suppressor attached to the muzzle.

"You know, Raven, I've been thinking. We could just kill you right here, take our money and all the goods you've brought us. I doubt anyone would miss someone like you."

Han-Jae raised his weapon and pointed it at Raven's chest.

Raven's breath quickened. He felt his heart pounding inside his ribcage. Panic rushed into his mind. It was all he could do not to turn around and try to barge his way through the man guarding the door.

"Yes...that...that's true," Raven stammered. "You could do that. But...but then who would you call when you need something in the future? Right? I mean, don't kill the golden goose. I'm your guy here in Western Europe. We've got a good thing going here. I don't know your names, you don't know my real name. It's great for business, for both parties."

He was rambling now, desperate to say or do anything to keep from being a headline on tomorrow's front page.

Han-Jae cocked his head to the side as if deciding to shoot an animal. His eyebrows closed the gap above his nose. "I'm sure there are many others out there who will be happy to fill the void you leave behind."

Raven shook his head violently now. "Fine, you know what, keep the money. I don't need it anyway. Been a good year for me up to this point. I can take a loss on this one. It's fine."

Han-Jae's finger tightened on the trigger. "You think we need the money?"

Raven shrugged. "I don't know. I mean, obviously not. If you can afford...listen, please, just let me go." He started sounding pitiful.

"If there's one thing I detest, it's someone who can't die with honor," Han-Jae said. "At least learn how to die like a man."

He pulled the trigger, and the weapon clicked.

Raven winced, tightening his shoulders and nearly every other muscle in his body. After a second of waiting for the pop followed by a bullet tearing through his flesh, he opened one eye and saw Han-Jae standing with the weapon still aimed.

"I didn't load it," Han-Jae said. "Did you really think I was going to kill my best connection in Europe?"

He started laughing. The other three men started laughing, too, all the while watching their guest for a reaction.

Raven swallowed hard and then forced a smile. He chuckled even though he didn't find anything funny.

"Good one, sir. Good one. Okay, thank you. I'll just be on my way."

He turned around, and the man in front of the door stepped to the side. As Raven reached out to grasp the doorknob, he heard the familiar sound of a magazine clicking into place.

Had his customer changed his mind? He didn't dare turn around to find out. He pulled the door open and took a step across the threshold, expecting the weapon to fire at any second.

He kept walking, one foot after the other until he heard the door mercifully close behind him. Only then did he turn around and look back to make sure no one was following him.

The door was closed, and no one else was in the hall. He took in a deep breath and sighed. His body still shook from fear.

Raven hurried down the hall and around the corner to the elevator, unable to get away fast enough to calm his nerves. As the elevator door closed, he shook his head and rubbed his face.

"I've got to get into another line of work."

Back up in the hotel room, Han-Jae handed out the passports and weapons to his men.

First thing they'd done when they arrived in Brussels was send one of the men into a market to buy a few hygiene products. Now every man's hair looked different. One had shaved his head completely. The other three changed their style as well to better conceal their identities.

"We're going to have to travel separately from now on," Han-Jae said after he finished handing out the supplies. "The authorities will be on the lookout for the four of us."

The others nodded that they understood.

"Fortunately, we know where we're going next. The Americans got a call from Bellevaux about something they discovered at the dig site in France. That's where we will rendezvous."

The guy with the shaved head raised an eyebrow and a question. "What do we do if one of us doesn't make it?"

"Complete the mission," Han-Jae said without hesitation. "Even if I don't show up, finish what we have started. According to the email, the excavation revealed something else that might help us find the sword. There are two Americans in charge of securing the artifacts. They are staying at this hotel in a town not far from the dig site."

He handed out three pieces of paper he'd scribbled an address on previously.

"Be at this hotel at nine o'clock tomorrow night. There's a bookstore across the street that closes at seven. Next to it is an alley. That is where we'll meet. If I'm not there by nine, go to the room number on the paper, apprehend the two Americans, and find out what they know or where this new artifact is."

"What if they won't give us what we want?" one of the others asked.

"From what I understand, they are a husband-and-wife team. To get the husband to talk, torture the wife."

Chapter 17
Cologne

Sean and the others stood inside one of two hotel rooms they'd rented for the night. As promised, Baldwin's men had taken them where they requested. The hotel, while clean and modern, was not as upscale as some of the places Sean and Tommy had stayed through the years. Not that that mattered. Nicer places simply had better food, at least in their experience.

Baldwin's men had been kind enough to return all their things, too. Phones and clothes were stuffed into the Americans' gear bags. No guns, though. Those had been confiscated by Baldwin's Brotherhood.

Sean knew better than to think the blond would let them keep their weapons. That didn't keep him from checking.

"They kept our guns," Sean said.

"You didn't think they'd give them back to us, did you?" Tommy asked.

"No, but hope springs eternal. Not that we need them right now anyway. We've got to put a plan together to get your parents back. Figuring out how to get in and out of North Korea will be no easy task no matter how thorough Baldwin's research might be."

Tommy went silent for a moment. He looked down at the floor and then back to his friend. "Sean, we're not going to North Korea. Not yet."

Sean's forehead wrinkled as he frowned. "What do you mean? We have to get your parents out, like yesterday. Who knows how much time they have left?"

Tommy nodded absently. "I know. You're right. And no one wants to get them out safely more than me. Maybe a part of me doesn't really believe it's them. I mean...it's been twenty years, Sean." He clenched his jaw to fight back the tears.

Sean stepped a little closer. "I know, buddy. But you saw the pictures. I think Baldwin is telling the truth. Let me call Emily. She can help me put something together—"

"No," Tommy said, shaking his head. "We're going to get my parents out my way."

"Okay..."

"All the plans and maps in the world won't help us if we get caught inside North Korea. And just a heads-up, we will stick out like a crocodile at an alligator party."

Adriana raised both eyebrows at the metaphor. "Okay, so what's the plan?"

"Simple," Tommy said. "We find the sword and use it as a bargaining chip for my parents."

"Um, I don't mean to tell you what to do in regards to your parents," June said, "but if what that guy said was true about the sword, are you sure you really want to give it to an evil dictator?"

"We're not going to give it to him. I just said we'll use it as a bargaining chip."

"So we're going to just walk into North Korea with a big sword and say, 'Hey everyone, we got your leader a present'?" Sean asked.

"Look, I don't have it all planned out. But you know as well as I do that it never hurts to have a little insurance. If we can find that sword, it might be the safety net we need."

Sean couldn't disagree with the assessment. That still didn't make it easier to accept the plan. He knew his friend wanted to see his parents again more than anything. If they'd survived this long, though, maybe they could make it just a little longer. From the images Baldwin showed, they looked to be in good health. The leader of the Brotherhood even said that they'd not been tortured. Still, after twenty years of leading the North Koreans down a twisty path of misinformation, time had to be running out.

"Fine," Sean said finally. "Where do we start?"

"Remember that call I got from Mac and Helen?"

Sean thought for a second and then gave a nod. "Oh right. I almost forgot. They said they found something that might help us."

"Maybe it's time to make a little trip to see what they're up to."

"I'm coming with you," June blurted.

"No, absolutely not," Tommy said, his voice insistent.

"You've dragged me into this," June said. Her tone was every bit as stubborn as Tommy's.

"I can't let you come with us. It's too dangerous."

"I can handle myself."

Sean and Adriana exchanged a sidelong glance. "She really is perfect for him," Sean whispered.

"Remind me to never let them decide on where we meet for dinner."

"Or which movie to see."

"I saw how you handled yourself," Tommy said. "And while I'm impressed, I don't want anything bad to happen to you. I...it's just that...I like you...and..."

June blushed. "That is very sweet of you. And I appreciate your concern. I really do. But at this point, I'm not going back. Not until all of this is done and over with."

"But what about your friend, the one you were going to stay with?"

"I'll visit her some other time."

Sean and Adriana kept their lips sealed as they watched Tommy struggle.

"Okay," he said. "Fine. If you won't take no for an answer."

"I won't." Her lips curled into a smirk.

"What's the plan, chief?" Sean asked after he figured the discussion was over.

Tommy thought for a second and then crossed his arms. "Well, I'm sure Baldwin has assigned one of his goons to watch us to make sure we stay out of his way."

Sean nodded in agreement. "Probably."

"So we will need to figure out a way to sneak out without him knowing."

"And how will we do that?" Adriana asked.

"I'll tell you first thing in the morning," Tommy said. He turned to Sean. "Got any connections in Europe that could hook us up with some weapons?"

"I'm not going to call Emily for that one. But I do have a guy I've used before. He's a little...how should I say...eccentric?"

"So he's an arms dealer."

"Arms, drugs, counterfeit ID. You name it; he's got it. Let's just say he has a diverse portfolio of products and services he offers."

"Sounds like some of the people I associate with," Adriana said.

"This guy got a name?" Tommy asked.

"I don't know his real name. He just goes by Raven."

Chapter 18
Frankfurt, Germany

Cars passed by on the street outside the coffee shop. Sean sat alone, watching the pedestrian traffic rushing around to get to work. A window-cleaning crew busily washed the seventh-floor windows on a building across the road.

Sean took a sip of his cappuccino as he stared at the workers. “No way in the world I would do that,” he said to himself. “They couldn’t pay me enough.”

He’d often wondered how people could force themselves to work in the extreme conditions at incredible heights on those moving platforms. He recalled a video he’d seen online that showed men swinging back and forth out of control on one of those window-cleaning platforms. The platform had been a terrifying ninety-one stories up on China’s second-tallest building. Fortunately, the men aboard the swinging platform survived the ordeal, walking away with only minor injuries, though Sean figured it would be a while before they did that job again. According to the story he’d read, the wild ride ended when the platform crashed into the windows and broke the glass.

Sean preferred to not even be inside a ninety-one-story building, much less outside.

He chuckled and took another sip of coffee. Some people would say the line of work he got into was more dangerous than cleaning windows. Maybe, but it’s a funny thing how what you don’t know can sometimes be comforting. In the secret agent world, he was constantly in the dark on things. For whatever reason, that made certain tasks easier.

His eyes shifted from the street to his watch. It was almost nine in the morning, local time. Raven wasn't usually late. If he was this time, Sean would give him a pass. Raven claimed he was leaving Belgium, heading south toward Geneva. Sean promised that if he'd make a short detour east, he'd make it worth the while.

Having enjoyed Sean's generosity before, it was too good for Raven to pass up. Only problem was getting what Sean needed on such short notice would be difficult. And costly. Fortunately, money wasn't a problem.

Sean put the cup to his lips again and heard the door open on the other side of the cafe. He smiled and kept the cup close to his face, waiting for Raven to approach. When Sean could smell the cheap body spray the young man always wore, he set the cup down.

"I was starting to think you'd be late," he said and spun around in his chair.

Raven looked like he'd been awake for three days. His ratty hair was disheveled, his clothes worn down. Dark circles hung under his bloodshot eyes.

"First of all, I wish you wouldn't do that. It's creepy. I mean, how on earth did you know it was me coming?"

Sean rolled his shoulders. "Call it a sixth sense." He didn't tell the younger man that his body spray gave at least an eight-foot warning radius. Plus,

Raven wasn't exactly a quiet walker. His feet shuffled along the floor every time Sean met him.

"Fine, whatever. Second, do you have any bleedin' idea how hard it is to find guns in a"—he looked at his watch—"twelve-hour window? Much less get them across the German border?"

"I got you a latte," Sean said, ignoring his guest's irritation. "Pumpkin spice. Your favorite."

The aggravation melted slightly, but not all the way. Raven took a wary step toward the table and eased into the seat. "It's not fall. How'd you get a pumpkin spice?"

Sean put his palms up. "You're not the only one who knows how to get things. Oh, and do me a favor. If you're going to bring up guns, lower your voice. I'd rather the other good people in this coffee shop not know I'm buying illegal arms from you."

Raven gave a sheepish nod. "Yeah, sorry."

"So what's in the bag?" Sean asked with a cheery smile. He found that approaching these types with less intimidation and a more casual demeanor helped them relax. That was especially true in Raven's case.

The younger man set a blue duffel bag on the table and nudged it a few inches. "Hard to get you everything on your Christmas list with the small amount of time and minimal resources I had on me. But I managed to get you a few good pieces. There's a Walther in there, a couple of Smiths."

"Springfield?" Sean asked.

Raven shook his head. “No. Sorry, mate. Beggars can’t be choosers. Did get you a nice Glock, though. That’ll have to do.”

Sean peeked into the bag for a few seconds and then zipped it shut. “Extra mags, rounds—”

“Yeah, yeah. It’s all there. I gotta say, I don’t know what’s with you guys and the little wars you’re trying to start.”

Sean drew in a long breath and sighed. “No wars here. Just making sure if we run into trouble we’re prepared.”

“We?” Raven drew a sip from his cup.

“My friends and I.”

“You tend to find a bit of trouble whenever you’re around, don’t you?”

Sean grinned. “Maybe trouble finds me.”

Raven slapped a hand on his thigh. “Well, either way, I just want to stay clear of any sort of trouble. Now if you don’t mind, I’m going to go find a bed somewhere and crash. Haven’t slept in over twenty-four hours, no thanks to you.”

“No sleep in twenty-four hours? Sounds like you’ve been busy.”

Raven offered a short laugh. “Yeah, well, let’s just say you’re not the only one who needed to start a small war this week.”

Sean’s eyebrows shot up. “Oh really? Other customers?” He took another drink from his cup.

“You could say that. Although they aren’t as nice as you.” Raven slid back into his seat like a snake. “At least with you, I know you’re not going to point a gun at me or try to short me on money." He lowered his voice so no one else could hear.

"Not my style," Sean said.

"Yeah, well, tell that to the four Asian guys I just sold a sack full of pistols to. I tell you, some people think fear and intimidation will get them whatever they want."

"Wait. What did you just say?"

Raven's face scrunched into a puzzled look. "Um, I said that some people think fear and intimidation—"

"No, not that. The other thing. You said you sold pistols to four Asian guys?"

"Oh, yeah. Right. Look, man, I try to keep everything confidential. If you're worried about me telling anyone about our little arrangement, I haven't. Honest."

Sean shook his head and waved a hand, dismissing Raven's concern. "No. I know you wouldn't. These four Asian guys, they didn't happen to be Korean, did they?"

Raven thought hard for a minute. "I think so. I mean, I've done deals with Yakuza, Triads, even some of the Korean gangs. If I had to guess, I'd say they were Korean. I heard one of them say something that definitely wasn't Japanese or Chinese. I speak a little of those two languages, so I'd know."

"Did they say anything about why they wanted the guns?"

"No one ever tells me what they're going to do with weapons I sell them. And to be perfectly honest, I'd rather not know. I have a hard enough time sleeping at night."

Right. Stupid question, Sean thought. He should have known better.

Raven eyed a brown paper bag on the table. "My money in there?"

"Yep," Sean said and leaned back in his chair. "For a second I thought you might walk off and forget it."

"Thanks. Like I said, I'm exhausted. Not exactly 100 percent in my mind right now." He snatched the bag off the table. "Pleasure doing business with you, as always. Do me a favor. Don't call for at least two days. I'm gonna take a nap."

Raven spun around to leave, but Sean stopped him.

"Of course, if you'd like to make a little extra cash, you could stay for one more minute."

Raven paused, looked up at the ceiling, and then let his head droop. He turned back around and put his hands out. "How much for one minute?"

"Five grand."

The gun dealer's face shrank back, causing the skin on his neck and jaw to merge like a pug. He spun the chair around backward and slumped into it. "Five grand? For one minute of my time?"

"If you talk faster, it might be less than a minute. Ever made five grand for a minute of work before?"

Raven thought about it for a moment. "I guess that depends."

"You haven't," Sean said. "Otherwise, you wouldn't be sitting here talking to me right now. So, you want it or not?"

"Where's the money?" Raven asked, suspicious.

Sean's face remained like stone. "It's already in the bag."

"It's in the bag?"

"Mmmhmm."

"So you were gonna just let me leave with an extra five thousand?"

"Raven, or whatever your real name is—not important—I believe in taking care of the people who take care of me. You have helped me out in the past. And you've helped me out today, with very short notice."

"Very short."

"So, if you get up and walk away, you can keep that extra money. I won't try to stop you. I believe, though, you'll give me my one extra minute."

Raven considered what Sean said. "I like your style, Agent Zero, or whatever your real name is. Okay, I'll give you your minute. What else you want to know?"

Sean raised his cup and held it in front of his mouth. "Where were the four Koreans when you met them?"

Raven eyed Sean with suspicion. He took another drink from his latte and then licked his lips. "Okay, I'll tell you, even though I don't normally do this. And it's not just for the money."

"How noble."

"No, you don't understand. These guys are different. They're worse than the normal scum I deal with. I don't know what it was about them."

"Korean gang?" Sean asked, putting the feeler out there.

"Nah," Raven shook his head. "Not these guys. They didn't have all the tats most of those gangbangers are sporting. In fact, I didn't notice any tattoos."

"So who are they?"

"No idea. I got a call from a guy asking me if I wanted to make a quick ten grand. I said sure. Last time I do a deal like that with people I don't know. They pointed one of the guns at me as I walked out of their hotel room. The one in charge...he pulled the trigger. I nearly pissed myself."

"Their hotel, Raven. Where was it?"

The gun dealer looked around the room, nervous that someone might be watching or listening. He glanced out the window to make sure there was no one across the street who looked suspicious keeping an eye on him.

"Brussels," he said after a long hesitation. "I met them in Brussels."

"I suppose you sold them the usual: passports, weapons, etc."

"Careful, mate," Raven wagged a finger. "Infringing on the confidential thing again."

"Five grand in that bag says you tell me."

The scruffy younger man looked up at the ceiling as if the tiles and lights above would give him an answer. Then he put his gaze on Sean. "Yeah, that's what they wanted. Probably in trouble with the law or something. None of my business. Well, actually, it kind of is my business."

"Literally."

Raven stood up to leave. "Thanks for the extra money, mate. Remember—"

"Don't worry. I'm not telling anyone what you told me. I thought you knew me better than that."

"Do yourself a favor, mate," Raven said as he turned halfway around. "Steer clear of those guys if you're thinking about starting a fight with them. There was something evil about them. I don't know what they're up to, but it can't be good."

He took a look around and then walked to the door, gave another cautionary peek out the windows, and stepped outside.

"So the North Koreans ran to Belgium," Sean said to himself. "I wonder where..." His voice trailed off. The epiphany hit him like a sack of rocks. "Oh no."

Chapter 19
Bellevaux

Han-Jae stepped behind the counter in the hotel lobby and smiled politely at the innkeeper.

"I'm sorry," the old woman said in French. "You can't come back here."

Han-Jae didn't understand what she was saying. He didn't care, either. What was a stern expression on the woman's face quickly turned to fear as he pulled the pistol out of his jacket and smacked her on the back of the head with the bottom of the grip.

The heavy woman wavered for a moment and then fell over with a thud. Her big dress spread out on the floor like a blanket. Han-Jae stepped over the unconscious woman and over to the computer. One of his men stood guard at the door while the other two hurried behind the counter and dragged the woman back into a closet next to the office. They stuffed her inside and shut the door, breaking off the knob with a quick kick from the one with a shaved head.

A notepad sat on the counter next to the computer. It contained a list of all the inn's occupants and their room numbers.

That certainly made things considerably easier for Han-Jae and his crew. In hindsight, knocking out the old woman might have caused an issue had they needed a password to access the computer. Fortunately, that wasn't the case. The notebook contained everything he needed. And the computer was already logged in.

Han-Jae motioned to one of the other men. “Get on this computer and program a key card when I give you the room number.”

The man with a buzzed haircut gave a curt nod and ran around to the keyboard. He stopped there and awaited further instruction.

Han-Jae ran his finger down the lines on the notebook but didn’t see the name he wanted. Flipping the page back, he scanned the next one and finally stopped near the bottom.

“McElroy,” he said, tapping the paper. “Room 311.”

The guy at the keyboard typed quickly, entering the information to program a new key. When he was done, a device near his knees beeped. He reached down and picked up a card with a magnetic strip on it.

“Let’s go,” Han-Jae ordered.

The man at the door joined the rest of them as they rushed down the hallway, bypassing an antique-looking elevator. They pushed through a door on the left with a stairway sign on the wall and ran two steps at a time up the stairwell.

When they reached the third floor, their pace had slowed considerably. The four men panted for air but pressed on. Each was in peak physical condition, having gone through an extraordinarily intense training prior to working for the general.

The guy with the shaved head opened the door leading into the third-floor hallway and poked his head out. He checked both directions. “All clear,” he said and motioned for the others to go ahead.

The other three moved one at a time into the corridor. One took a position on his knees across the hall. The other two spread out, moving several feet down in either direction. The fourth took one last look down the stairwell and then tiptoed into the hallway, easing the door shut quietly.

Han-Jae inspected the signs next to the hotel room doors. Noting the numbers were moving in ascending order to the left, he pointed for the others to move that way. They obeyed immediately and hurried down the hall, moving as silently as possible. The only noise they made was the occasional swishing of their pant legs, a sound that would be nearly impossible to hear through a wall.

The four men reached room 311 and stopped, crouching around it. Han-Jae took the key from Buzz-Cut and carefully slid it into the slot. He pulled it out and waited. Nothing happened.

He pressed down on the latch, but the door was still locked.

Han-Jae frowned and tried the card again. This time he left it in a second longer than before. When he pulled it out, still nothing happened. He looked back at Buzz-Cut, wondering if his assistant had made a mistake.

The guy shrugged and displayed his best *Don't look at me* face.

Buzz-Cut pointed at the card and made a motion that Han-Jae needed to turn it around, suggesting he was doing it backward.

Han-Jae nodded and twisted the card the other way. Sure enough, now he could see little arrows printed on the plastic pointing the direction in which the card should be inserted.

He slipped the card back into the reader, and instantly the green light on the side blinked. They heard the door lock click. Han-Jae didn't wait for it to relock. He grabbed the latch and pulled down gently, careful to make sure he didn't make any sudden noises that would wake the people inside.

When the latch would move no farther, he pushed the door softly and eased his way through the narrow opening—stopping only to make sure the door chain wasn't engaged. He was glad to see it wasn't, even though he knew how to foil that primitive security.

The lights in the hallway would wake any light sleepers in the room, so they'd need to work fast. He drew his pistol and continued through the doorway into the darkened hotel room.

The air conditioning unit on the wall was blowing loudly, flooding the room with icy cool air. Whoever these people were, they liked their temperatures chilly while sleeping. In a minute, their bodies would start to cool permanently.

Han-Jae gave one more twist of his sound suppressor as he stepped around the bathroom corner and into the main sleeping area. The room was faintly lit by a crack in the curtains, which let in a narrow stream of moonlight: a pale line ran across the sheets and comforter on the queen-size bed.

Two of the others followed Han-Jae into the room, stopping a few inches behind him.

The plan was to wake the two Americans and then search the room for whatever they'd found at the dig site. They'd considered executing the archaeologists, but then getting answers might be difficult to come by.

Han-Jae tapped Buzz-Cut on the shoulder, his cue to turn on the lights. The man obeyed, moving back toward the door and feeling his way along the wall until he found the light switch. When he did, he flicked it up.

A single light in the foyer came on overhead, brightening the room but leaving shadows in the far corners. Still, it was enough light for them to see the bed and its occupants.

Han-Jae's head twisted slightly as he gazed upon the sheets and comforter. It was made to look like two people were sleeping under the covers. In reality, it was just pillows stuffed underneath the blankets.

Fury boiled up in Han-Jae's mind. He stepped over to the bed and jerked the covers back. Sure enough, nothing but pillows. His nostrils flared as he spun around in a circle, looking all over the room.

"Where are they?" he snarled. "They are supposed to be here."

Tires screeched in the parking lot below. Han-Jae rushed to the window and shoved the curtains aside. A four-door hatchback whipped out onto the road and sped away heading east.

In a rage, Han-Jae yanked the curtains down. Two of his men joined him at the window in time to see the car disappear around the next corner.

"Someone told them we were coming," he said. "Someone warned them."

"Who?" Buzz-Cut asked.

"No time to think about that. We have to follow them. Go. Now!"

The other three ran back into the hallway and turned right.

They didn't expect to find eight men waiting in the corridor—all wearing the same black outfits, all holding weapons. Four were to the right and four to the left.

Han-Jae and his men were surrounded and outnumbered. He recognized the blond man to the right. He was the one with the Americans in Cologne.

"Put down your weapons, and we will let you live," the blond said.

Han-Jae couldn't place his accent. It sounded English, but not quite so refined.

The leader of the North Korean group had no intention of putting his gun down or leaving peaceably.

His hand shot up in a flash, and he fired. The round sailed by the blond guy and struck one of his compatriots in the shoulder, dropping him to the ground.

The second Han-Jae pulled the trigger, the other seven men in the hall dove for cover. There weren't many places to hide from bullets, so they had to make do with shallow recesses next to door frames. Two of his men retreated down the other side of the hall, finding protection behind pillars built into the walls. The blond motioned to the two remaining guys on his side to do the same.

Han-Jae and his four men ducked back inside the hotel room. While they had no immediate way to escape, at least they were protected…for the moment. That wouldn't last, though, and Han-Jae knew it. Sooner or later the authorities would arrive, and there would be no getting out.

He peeked around the corner of the door and fired another shot to the left. The round sank harmlessly into the wall but caused the four men on that side to stay pinned back.

An older man, probably in his late seventies, poked his head out of a door close to the blond guy. The second he saw the bleeding man writhing on the ground and the other men with guns, his eyes opened wide and he scurried back into his room. The sound of a chain sliding in its receiver sounded faintly in the immediate area.

Han-Jae stuck the long barrel of his weapon around the edge of the door again, but this time it was greeted by a series of muffled pops from both directions. He dove back inside, narrowly dodging a barrage of hot metal from the men outside.

The one with the shaved head looked into his eyes. "There's only one way out, sir."

Han-Jae misread the intent in the man's eyes. "If we have to go, we go out shooting."

The henchman shook his head. “No, sir. I mean out the window.”

“It’s too far down. We’ll break our legs, or worse.”

“It’s only three stories. We can use the blankets and sheets to lower ourselves down to a safe drop. Only problem is getting out the window.”

Han-Jae stared at the wide piece of glass. Outside, the dark outline of jagged mountains stood against the sparkling sky. “Give me some cover fire,” he said. “Conserve your ammo. Just shoot enough to keep them back.”

The man nodded and scooted over to the door. Buzz-Cut joined him on the other side to provide crossfire.

Han-Jae rushed to the window and tapped it with the suppressor. “Perfect.” He took a step back, looked over his shoulder, and nodded at the two by the door. “Cover fire.”

The two men poked their weapons through the opening and squeezed off three shots each. Simultaneously, Han-Jae and Shaved Head pointed their guns at the window and unleashed half the contents of their magazines, making a huge square of holes in the glass. Spiderweb cracks slivered the window in all directions.

Han-Jae motioned to a club chair next to the bed. He and Shaved Head moved fast, picked up the chair, and stepped close to the window. They swung it back and forth until their momentum was what they believed was strong enough to break through.

“Fire again,” Han-Jae told the other two.

They did as told, taking three more shots apiece at the attackers in the corridor. This time, the other men returned fire, sending Han-Jae's men retreating farther into the room as drywall, wood, and wallpaper exploded all around them from the onslaught of bullets.

"Now!" Han-Jae said to his partner holding the leather chair.

Both men released the chair at once. It seemed to float for a second in the air until the side struck the weakened glass, bursting through it easily and shattering the window into millions of pieces.

They didn't watch the chair fall. They had to move quickly if they wanted to get out alive. Han-Jae grabbed the comforter first and wound it into a kind of rope. Then he took the top sheet and tied off the strongest knot he could muster. Shaved Head worked on the other end, using the main bed sheet and the extra blanket that hotels always seemed to provide.

Once their makeshift rope was done, Han-Jae motioned to one of the men at the door to help them. "Fire again," he said to the last guy.

With a nod, the remaining man shot two more rounds into the hall in both directions before ducking for cover again.

The other three positioned themselves on separate corners of the bed, and when Han-Jae gave the signal, they all heaved, shoving the bed across the floor to the shattered window. The men grunted as the bed slid reluctantly. When the foot butted against the wall beneath the window, Han-Jae hurriedly tied off one end of the blankets to one of the bed's legs. He gave it a tug and—satisfied it was secure—tossed the bulk of the sheets and blanket rope out the window.

"Go," he said to Shaved Head first.

The man didn't hesitate. He grabbed onto the rope, climbed out the window, and started lowering himself down.

"You're next," Han-Jae said to Buzz-Cut.

"You're our leader," the man said. "You should go. I'll stay here and cover."

Han-Jae shook his head. "That's an order."

Buzz-Cut didn't argue further. He watched as the first guy reached the end of their rope and dropped the remaining eight feet to the ground. The landing wasn't pretty, but he rolled out of the way and stood back on his feet.

As soon as Buzz-Cut disappeared out the window, Han-Jae stalked over to the doorway and tapped his guard on the shoulder. The guy looked up at him.

Han-Jae jerked his thumb at the window. "When he's down, you go."

"But—" the guy started to give the same protest. He was the youngest of the group. His hair was cropped to the side as was popular in the 1950s.

"Go," Han-Jae said again.

The young man didn't need to be told a third time. He got up off the ground and ran over to the window in time to see Buzz-Cut drop clumsily to the sidewalk. Sirens echoed through the city, and the sound filtered into the hotel room.

Han-Jae heard the noise as he saw the third man go out the window and over the edge. Han-Jae gave the guy a few seconds for a head start and then stuck his gun out the door. He fired several shots to the right and then emptied the magazine's contents to the left. A quick press of the button released the magazine. He caught it, shoved it into a cargo pocket, and pulled a full one out of his belt. It took less than four seconds for him to reload the weapon and pull the slide to chamber a new round.

More shots came from the silenced weapons in the hall. The doorframe and surrounding walls were destroyed. The hallway light streaked through multiple holes in the wall.

Han-Jae darted back to the window and looked out. All three men were safely on the ground. Two of them were keeping watch. The third was looking up, an anxious expression on his face.

With no time to waste, Han-Jae shoved the weapon into his belt and grabbed the rope. He climbed over the ledge and pressed his feet against the outside wall, then hand over hand began repelling down the side. He reached the top of the second floor, and suddenly his right foot slipped from its hold. Han-Jae's other foot slipped, too, and he swung out away from the wall. He looked up to the window and saw more lights flicker on.

The attackers were entering the room. He didn't have time to do a controlled drop. His fingers ached from holding onto the sheets. Rapidly, he put one hand below the other until he reached the bottom of the second floor. There was still rope to use, but he had to hurry. Any second, the men above would be at the window with easy targets below.

Han-Jae let go of the sheets and fell the last ten feet. He struck the ground with a heavy thud and did his best to absorb the drop by rolling to the side.

The impact sent a sudden pain through his right foot, but he pushed himself off the ground and took off down the sidewalk. His three men followed, disappearing into the shadows around the corner just as one of the men in the room arrived at the window. He had a flashlight attached to his weapon and flashed it around on the ground, looking for the escapees.

They'd vanished.

Chapter 20
Thonon-les-Bains, France

Joe McElroy—affectionately known as Mac to his friends—waited nervously next to the water's edge of Lac Léman. In the day, the crystal-clear water allowed an observer to see several feet down. It was one of the few places on Earth where pollution—it seemed—hadn't penetrated.

A chilly breeze rolled in across the water, sending rippling waves crashing against the rocks at Mac's feet. The cool air brushed through his thick brown-and-gray beard. He ran a hand through his matching hair and felt a tingle shoot through his spine from the sudden burst of wind. He pulled his jacket zipper up a couple of inches to keep warm.

"Do you usually walk alone by the lake at midnight?" a familiar voice asked from a cluster of trees fifteen yards away.

Startled, Mac spun around in the direction he'd heard the voice. A pistol in his right hand stayed by his hip. He didn't need to raise it. No threat came with the sound of that voice.

"Not a good idea to scare a man with a gun in his hand, Sean," Maç said, narrowing his beady eyes.

Sean stepped out of the shadows and had a quick look around. "I thought it might be better to get your attention while I had some cover, you know, in case your trigger finger was a little itchy."

Mac stuffed the weapon into his belt and tugged the jacket over to conceal it. He shook his head dramatically as Sean approached. He put his arms out wide and enveloped his friend with a big hug. After slapping him on the back twice, Mac let go and shook Sean by the shoulder.

"I gotta say, Sean, you sure are a sight for sore eyes."

"You, too, Mac. It's good to see you. Although I'm sorry for the trouble."

"Pfft. Trouble?" Mac blew it off. "I appreciate the warning, but it's probably best those guys who came after us didn't come toe to toe with the missus. She's got a mean streak in her, and that government training of hers makes her a killer."

"I know a thing or two about that," Sean said.

"The training or her mean streak?"

Sean chuckled. "Both." He looked around, still uneasy about the setting.

"Relax," Mac said. "Helen and I already scoped it out. Plus, she's on a rooftop somewhere watching us. She'll keep an eye on things."

"That makes me feel a little better. You're sure you weren't followed?"

"Pretty sure. One of the nice things about that hotel in Bellevaux was there was only one parking lot and one way in at night. We watched them approach from a second-floor room we rented under a fake name, thinking they would look us up in the registry. Once they were in the building, we waited by the stairwell and listened for them to pass, figuring they'd take the stairs as opposed to the elevators.

"Sure enough, they ran by in a hurry and once we heard the door above close, we snuck out down the stairs, made it to our car, and got the heck out of there."

"Impressive," Sean said. "I was worried you might not get the message. Still, cutting it a little close, weren't you?"

"We didn't have cell service out there at the dig site. When we got back from the day's activities, the first thing we did was take a shower and get into some clean clothes. Didn't check our messages until after."

"Lucky you did."

Mac snorted. "You got that right. And lucky you warned us. You saved our skin, Sean. Thanks."

Sean rolled his shoulders. "Don't mention it. So tell me more about this thing you found at the dig site."

"In good time, my friend. Where's your crew?"

Sean's lips creased on one corner. "Not far. They're waiting in the car about a block from here."

"Perfect. Come back to our place and we'll show you what we've got."

Sean led the way back to the car where Tommy and the other two were anxiously waiting. When Tommy saw Sean and Mac approaching, he got out and greeted his bearded friend with a big hug.

Adriana walked around the front of the car and stood next to Sean while June took a position next to Tommy.

"Adriana Villa," Mac said with a broad smile. "It sure is nice to see you again." He stepped over and gave her a hug, then a kiss on both cheeks as was customary in some Spanish cultures.

"It's good to see you, too, Mac," she said. Her eyes gleamed, matching the grin on her face.

Mac turned to June and embraced her tightly. "You must be June Holiday," Mac said.

June returned the hug and put on her happiest expression. "And you must be Mac," she said.

Mac let her go and took a step back, putting his hands on his hips. "I gotta say, Tommy sure has told me a lot about you."

Sean and Adriana glanced at each other with the same questioning look.

"But he couldn't do you justice. You're prettier than he said, and he said a lot." Mac chuckled.

"So you told Mac about June, but not us?" Sean said, pretending to be offended.

"I couldn't help it. Helen bugged me so long about..." He let his voice trail off.

"About what?" June said, her bright blue eyes staring right through him.

"Nothing. Say, it would probably be best if we get out of plain sight here."

"Good idea," Mac agreed before June could continue her pursuit of the previous conversation. "Our place isn't far from here. Just a short drive. We rented a chalet on the side of the mountain over there." He pointed off toward a dark shadow a mile away. "If anyone decides to join us, we'll see them coming."

———

Fifteen minutes later, the group walked into the chalet. Mac closed and locked the door behind them while his guests set their bags down on the round wooden table near the entrance.

The chalet's interior was almost entirely made from wood, designed to look more like a log cabin. The walls and floor were constructed out of a yellowish-amber variety, while the kitchen cabinets were deep red with gray granite countertops. The front of the chalet featured three massive central windows with one more on either side, angling out to the flat façade. The lights of the city burned in the valley below, and the moonlight rippled on the surface of the lake. Big leather couches occupied the sitting area. A fireplace crackled off to the left.

"Figured the fire would be a nice touch," Mac said. "I know it's not winter, but a fire in the hearth always makes things feel a little better."

"Where's Helen?" Tommy asked. "I thought she was going to meet us here."

"Somebody had to watch over the lot of you while you were down in the valley." The woman's voice came from one of the hallways that ran to the back of the chalet.

A second later, a middle-aged woman with deep auburn hair and a tanned, freckled face appeared in the doorway next to the stairs.

"There she is!" Sean exclaimed.

"Almost feels like a family reunion in here," she said with a thick Southern twang.

Helen and Joe had been living about forty minutes north of Atlanta in the small town of Cartersville. Joe worked as a park ranger for years until he and Helen joined up with Tommy's IAA.

Helen's past was still mired in secrecy. All anyone knew was that she worked for the government—and in a similar capacity to Sean's job with Axis.

No one bothered her about it, figuring some things were better left secret.

After another round of hugs and introductions, Helen stood with her hands on her hips, staring at June. "I have to say, Tommy, she sure is pretty. And I love those freckles on your nose and cheeks."

June blushed. "Thanks."

Sean saved June further embarrassment by getting the group on task quickly. "So where's this codex you guys found at the dig site?" he asked. "I'm interested to see what's on it."

Mac's eyes squinted. He saw Sean was trying to bail the new girl out. "Okay, Sean. Okay. We've got it tucked away in a safe place. Give me a minute, and I'll bring it out."

Mac disappeared up the staircase to a loft and into one of two bedrooms on the upper level.

"Would y'all like something to drink?" Helen asked. "We have some Cokes and bottles of water."

"Water would be great," Tommy said. "You want one?" he asked June.

"Sure."

Helen got four bottles out of the refrigerator and set them on the counter.

Tommy took one and handed it to June.

Mac's boots clomped on the steps and he descended, carrying a rolled-up piece of plastic.

"We went ahead and sealed this so it wouldn't take any more moisture or air damage," he explained. “This thing is definitely old, one of the older vellum pieces I’ve seen.”

He laid the rolled-up plastic out onto the table and flattened it, holding it down on four corners with books he’d left nearby.

“You laminated it?” June asked.

Mac grinned. “No, ma’am. You don’t want to do that with something like this. No, we heat sealed it around the edges of the plastic, but kept the heat away from the vellum. That way we don’t hurt it. The trick is making sure you get all the air out of the plastic before you seal it. That takes a bit of work.”

“Nearly drove him crazy doing it,” Helen remarked from behind the kitchen counter.

“It’s a painstaking task, okay. And I’m not the most patient person in the world.”

“You can say that again.”

“Anyway,” Mac got back on topic, “this piece is really interesting. You can see these designs are definitely from the medieval period.” He hovered his finger over a flower, a cross, and three intertwined circles like the ones Sean and his companions had seen in Cologne. “I think they were added later. Everything about this document suggests it’s older than the medieval era.”

“See that, Schultzie?” Sean asked.

“Yep. Exactly like what we saw at the Cologne rathaus.”

Mac nodded even though he wasn’t sure what they were talking about. “What’s really fascinating, though, is what’s written here.”

“Latin,” Adriana said.

"Indeed," Mac confirmed. He leaned over the sheet and ran his finger along the plastic surface. "It says here that whoever seeks the keys to the kingdom must first seek the symbols in the land where Arthur sleeps."

Sean and Tommy exchanged a knowing glance.

"Glastonbury Abbey," Tommy said.

Mac nodded. "Possibly. It goes on to say that he who seeks the keys and finds the symbols the lady hides on high will uncover the trophies of the fallen that illuminate the way to the sword bearer's altar."

"Trophies of the fallen?" June asked. "What's that mean?"

"We have no idea," Helen said. "Been trying to figure that out."

"Trophies of the fallen," Sean repeated. "I wonder if that means some kind of loot that was taken after a war."

"To the victors go the spoils," Tommy said. "It's one of the oldest traditions in history. Winning armies take all kinds of plunder with them when they conquer another country."

"Yeah, but which army and which country?"

"Maybe we have to visit Glastonbury to figure that out," Adriana offered. "It sure seems like the riddle is left for the next piece of the journey."

"Right," Mac said. "Problem is, Glastonbury is one possible place where King Arthur is buried. It's possible his tomb is at Tintagel."

"True," Tommy said. "He makes a good point. It's long been believed that what may have been the birthplace of Arthur is also where he's buried."

"Except for the fact that—according to legend—Tintagel has no connection to the sword."

Mac stood up straight and ran a thumb and forefinger through his beard. "I still can't believe y'all are looking for Excalibur. I mean, it's an ambitious thing to take on. That's for sure. Just not sure how much of this stuff you can take as legend and how much is real, concrete evidence."

The four guests fell silent for a long moment, causing Mac to feel like he'd said something inappropriate. "I'm sorry. I didn't mean to offend. It's just that the whole King Arthur thing, Excalibur, the Camelot story...seems like it's half history and half fairy tale."

"The North Koreans don't seem to think so," Sean said. "That's who came after you earlier tonight. They're trying to find the sword, too."

Helen padded around the counter and leaned up against it with her side, placing an elbow on top. "North Korea? What do they want with that sword? And since when did they take an interest in historical artifacts?"

"I asked the same exact question," Tommy said. His voice drifted, like he was floating in a void. "It seems that they have some prisoners who know about the sword. Those prisoners have been feeding them information for the last few decades, giving them leads, always keeping away the most vital of details."

"Prisoners?" Mac said. "How'd you know about that?"

"It's a long story. But we have strong reason to believe that they are holding...that my parents are in North Korea."

He may as well have hit Mac and Helen upside the head with an iron skillet.

"What?" Mac said in disbelief. "Your parents?"

Tommy nodded slowly. "Seems that way."

"How did you find this out?" Helen asked.

"We were apprehended by a secret society who call themselves the Brotherhood of the Sword. They believe it's their mission to protect the location of the sword and keep it secret for all time."

"And this...Brotherhood," Mac said, "they told you the North Koreans had your parents?"

"Yeah. They showed us pictures. Said my parents contacted them through an encrypted message."

No one said anything for a long minute. Tommy stared at the vellum sheet spread out on the table. "You know, this hunt for the sword was just another adventure to find the hidden treasure, to bring something of historical importance back to humanity. Now, though, it's personal." He locked eyes with Mac. "We have to go to Glastonbury and find the symbols this codex mentioned. It's the only chance I have of saving my parents."

"And these men...this Brotherhood," Helen interrupted, "you think you can trust them?"

"They're well funded," Sean said. "Said they're actually priests trained in the arts of hand-to-hand combat, among other things, I'm sure. If they wanted us dead, they'd have done it already. I think they're going after the North Koreans. The enemy of my enemy is my friend."

Mac and Helen exchanged a knowing glance.

"What can we do to help?" she asked.

Sean crossed his arms. He had a mischievous look on his face, the one he had when he was up to something. "I don't know how they're doing it, but the Brotherhood has been keeping tabs on us. It's a good bet that they'll have tracked you guys here, to Thonon-les-Bains. Unless I miss my guess, they're probably headed here as we speak."

"So you want us to throw them off course, tell them you went to South America or something?"

"Their deal with us," Tommy cut in, "was that we drop the pursuit of Excalibur and leave."

"Leave?" Mac said. "You mean, like leave and never come back?"

"No, nothing like that. They just wanted us out of the way for the time being."

"Okay, so we tell them you were never here."

Sean shook his head. "Actually, no."

"No?"

Sean and Tommy flashed a quick look at each other.

"No. We want you to tell them exactly where we're going."

Chapter 21
Thonon-les-Bains

Helen and Mac sat next to the fireplace, sipping hot toddies as the flames licked the bottom of the hearth. Occasionally, a piece of wood crackled or popped, sending sparks flashing into the protective screen.

They heard the footsteps outside on the wraparound porch before the door opened. Sean and the others had suggested the men in the Brotherhood were dangerous, but in a strange way allies. They wouldn't hurt the two Americans, at least that was Sean's read on the situation.

Of course, he'd been wrong before, which was why Mac and Helen both had their sidearms concealed under the blanket.

"They're not very quiet, are they?" Helen whispered into her husband's ear, pretending to nuzzle him for show.

"Like a greased pig in Mama's kitchen."

"Did you just make that one up?" Impressed, she pulled back and looked at him.

"Probably the toddy talking," he said with a wink and took another sip from the steaming cup.

A draft of cool air wafted through the living room, causing the hairs on Mac's neck to stand up.

Mac turned around and found four men standing in the doorway. They were all dressed in black cargo pants and snug-fitting black jackets. The one in front—a tall blond with a strong jaw—was the one Sean had mentioned before leaving.

"You must be Baldwin," Mac said, turning back around to face the fire. "Come on in and have a drink. Plenty of tea left over there in the kettle. And if you want to give it a little kick, the whiskey is in the pantry by the fridge."

The man closest to the door slammed it shut, startling the couple.

"Easy," Helen said. "You don't have to go around slamming doors like that. Startles people."

"Please forgive the intrusion," Baldwin said. "We're not here to drink. And we'd prefer to not have any trouble."

"Oh, good," Mac said. "We don't want any trouble either. We're here on vacation. Pretty country they got here by the lake. I gotta say, I love the South, but this is one nice spot."

Baldwin took a step forward, keeping the menacing expression on his face.

"You and I both know you're not here on vacation, Joe. You work for Tommy Schultz. Tommy said you found something, something that we need."

"Oh, you guys know Tommy?" Mac turned slung one arm over the back of the couch, careful to keep his weapon in his lap. "How long you known him?"

"Don't play coy with me, Joe. Where is the codex? And where are Tommy Schultz and Sean Wyatt?"

"Coy? That's a tad insulting."

Baldwin stopped short of the couch and crossed his arms. "We know they were here. Where are they now?"

"First of all," Helen said, "I don't care much for your tone, young man. You need to treat your elders with respect. Second, if you're so good at tracking Sean and them, how come you need us to tell you where they went? Sounds to me like you put some kind of tracking beacon on them and now you've lost it."

Baldwin's right eye twitched. She'd hit the chink in his armor. "So your friends found the homing device we planted. I see. Well, that would explain why the signal is still here."

He pivoted to the right and walked casually over to the big front window. Looking out over the scene below, he paused for a moment to consider his next move.

Mac and Helen waited patiently. Up until now, the script had gone according to Sean's plan.

"Perhaps Sean told you that we aren't dangerous, that we won't do terrible things to people like you to get what we want."

"And what is it you want?" Mac asked in as innocent a tone as he could muster.

"Tell us where they went. I'm warning you. Don't try to lie to us. Because if you do, we will find you."

"Well now, seems like finding people is the very problem you're having right now. So I'm sorry if we don't appear threatened by that little warning," Helen said.

Mac nearly did a spit take with his toddy, forcing his lips to stay closed to keep the liquid in his mouth.

Baldwin reached into his jacket and produced a pistol. The two Americans immediately recognized the suppressor on the end.

Helen clenched her pistol under the blanket. Mac had turned around to keep an eye on the blond guy, and as he did, slipped his hand back under the covers as well to get hold of his weapon.

"You know, up here we're so far away from everyone, you probably don't need that thing on the end. No sense in losing accuracy to keep something quiet when there's no one to hear it."

"Thank you for the advice," Baldwin sneered. Drops of spit shot out of his mouth. "Now tell me where they went."

"Okay, okay. Hold your horses," Mac said. He slid his pistol over into Helen's lap and got up from the couch, holding his cup and his free hand in the air to show the intruders he meant no harm. "Sean said you'd be coming by. Told me to give you something."

Baldwin's anger turned to curiosity. "Give me something?"

"Yeah," Mac said as he wandered over to the kitchen counter. "Wrote down some nonsense from the codex we found. Sorry, but they took it with them. Said if you wanted it, you could come get it."

He picked up a piece of paper from the counter and set it on the opposite counter above the island sink. "Here you go."

Baldwin motioned to a guy with a bandage on his head, who immediately stepped over to the island and picked up the paper. He took it over to Baldwin.

"What happened to your head?" Mac asked, with a slight slur.

The man's eyes narrowed, full of malice, but he said nothing.

"Just asking."

Baldwin finished reading the note and then crumpled it. “This says they’re going to Glastonbury Abbey in England. You think I’m going to believe that?”

Mac shrugged. “Honestly, son, I don’t care what you believe. I don’t know if that’s where they went or not. That’s just what they told me to give you. They said that nine of you would be coming by shortly and to give you that note.” He did a quick count. “Although there’s only four of you. Anyway, Sean said you wouldn’t believe it. Not sure why.”

“Why?” Baldwin snarled. “Do you honestly think that if there were any clues as to the whereabouts of the sword, our ancestors would have been so foolish as to leave them at the abbey where Arthur was buried?”

“Don’t tell me you buy into that whole King Arthur and Knights of the Round Table fairy tale. It’s just a story.”

Baldwin remained silent, perhaps feeling as though he’d already said too much.

A calm silence washed over the room. Helen pursed her lips after a moment. “You know, sometimes the best place to keep a secret is right where everyone can see it.”

“What do you mean by that?” Baldwin asked.

“What do you think I meant? If you say that Glastonbury Abbey is where King Arthur is buried, it seems like a far too obvious place to hide something. Surely all the grail and Excalibur experts in the world wouldn’t miss a clue right there in front of them. Would they?”

Her remark gave Baldwin something to think about.

"She's right," Mac added. "We find things like that all the time. People tend to miss the stuff that's right in front of them. You ever open the refrigerator looking for the milk carton and you can't see it, only to close the door, open it again, and it was right there the whole time?"

Baldwin said nothing, still considering their thoughts.

"Just saying, if you've been there before, maybe you missed something that was in plain sight. I'll tell you one thing, though. Sean Wyatt may be a lot of things, but he's not dishonest. If he said he's going to Glastonbury, that's where he's headed."

"We had a deal," Baldwin said. "They were to drop this quest immediately and leave Europe. They've broken their end of the bargain."

Helen cocked her head to the side, letting her auburn hair cascade down past her shoulder. "Sometimes deals have to be broken, if it's for the right reasons."

"Your friends have been warned. We will go to England. If your friends are there, we will let you go. If they aren't, we will use you as bait."

"Sorry," Mac said. "But we're on vacation. Don't have time to take in England on this trip."

A sinister grin crept across Baldwin's lips. "It wasn't a question. You'll be coming with us. And you'll come peaceably. And if you think those guns you have under that blanket are going to save you, you are sadly mistaken."

He raised his right hand and snapped his fingers.

Instantly, two red dots appeared on Helen's and Mac's chests.

Mac swallowed back the fear that welled in his mind. “You know, I was wondering where the other five were. Smart to put them outside like that. I don't know about you, Helen, but I like this guy's style.” He tried to remain calm, appearing cool on the outside.

“Yeah,” she said. “Pretty clever. Well, honey, I guess we're going to England after all.”

Baldwin motioned to his men, and they moved toward the Americans. “Hand over your weapons to them. We leave for Glastonbury immediately.” He turned to make his way back to the door and stopped abruptly. He twisted his head around and looked at the couple as they peacefully surrendered to his men. “By the way, there are only eight of us now.”

He walked out of the chalet, leaving everyone inside with the somber thought. When he was outside, he looked down at the crumpled paper in his hand. It would make sense for Sean and his companions to mislead the Brotherhood. But what if he wasn't lying? Why would Wyatt want Baldwin and his men to find them, especially after they'd immediately broken their bargain?

Baldwin didn't know why, but something in his head told him Sean and the McElroys weren't lying.

Chapter 22
Geneva, Switzerland

"How did they know we were coming?" Han-Jae asked his three men. "The Americans knew we would be there, and when. Someone must have warned them."

"Wyatt or Schultz?"

Those were the first names Han-Jae had considered, but there was no way to know for sure. They'd dropped off the grid after being arrested. Han-Jae called in an extra asset to watch the jail in Cologne. His man reported seeing the Americans escorted out of the building and put into two cars. He followed them to an old church on the other side of town in a quiet area full of rundown buildings.

After they were taken into the abandoned church, he didn't see them again. If they left the building, they went out a different way than they went in. What was more troubling was the men who'd taken them from the jail.

Han-Jae's tail reported that the man who appeared to be in charge had short blond hair and matched the description of the guy he'd seen talking to the Americans outside the Cologne city hall. The same guy who'd showed up at the hotel with eight other armed men.

He shook his head. "It doesn't matter anyway," Han-Jae said after a long moment of reflection. "What's done is done. We were lucky to get out alive. Now we have to figure out our next move."

"Which is?" Shaved Head asked.

"The McElroys said they had something important, something that might help Wyatt and his friends figure out the location of the sword."

"Yes, but we don't know where the McElroys went. Or Wyatt, for that matter."

It was their biggest, really their only, problem at the moment. Sure, they were wanted men, and every cop in the country would be looking for them. Except they weren't in France anymore.

After dropping down from the hotel window, the four men made a mad dash back to their car. They were barely able to get away before the police arrived and swept the area.

Roadblocks were set up mere minutes after they escaped Bellevaux. As Han-Jae and his crew sped toward the Swiss border, they knew they were racing against time. Heading to Switzerland was a gamble. While most of the borders were open and easily crossed, occasionally security would be tightened. That sort of thing usually happened when there were terrorists or criminals involved.

Fortunately, when they arrived at the border, the four men had no trouble getting across. Word about the hotel shootout had, apparently, not spread quickly enough.

Stuffing two of the men in the trunk may have also helped, since any reports would have suggested there were four men on the run. It was also to the North Koreans' benefit that France and Switzerland weren't big fans of profiling. Sometimes it seemed they'd rather let a murderer go free than arrest someone because they looked like the suspect.

Han-Jae rubbed his eyes. He was exhausted and could see the fatigue on his men's faces. They needed to rest. He glanced down at his watch. Local time was 2:27 in the morning.

They'd found an old convenience store that had long been closed for business and broken in through one of the back doors. There were no usable supplies inside, but it gave them a place to regroup and get some rest. Han-Jae hadn't been willing to risk getting a room anywhere. Even with their new passports, four Asian guys matching the description from a shootout in France would raise even the least suspecting person's suspicions.

After rummaging through the office in the back and the former storage closet, they found a few jackets, packets of toilet paper, and even a tattered blanket, all things that could be used as pillows.

It wasn't first class, but it would do. Han-Jae knew his men were hearty enough to endure far worse conditions. They'd been forced to sleep in muddy ditches during their training as soldiers. Their spy training had been even more rigorous, forcing them to go days with mere minutes of sleep. That intense training was a huge part of why any of them were still functioning.

"That's it," the youngest of the group said, breaking the long silence.

Han-Jae's eyes perked slightly. "What's it?"

"Cologne city hall."

"What about it?" Buzz-Cut asked.

"When we were there, I heard the Americans talking about a symbol on the side of the building, the one where the priest was atop that...strange pedestal."

"I remember which one you're talking about," Han-Jae said. "They said something about a church."

"Yes. An abbey in England that Joseph of Arimathea supposedly founded. They said something about King Arthur."

"He's right," Shaved Head agreed. "I heard the same thing, but I didn't hear the exact location. There must be thousands of old churches in England."

"It could be any one of them," Han-Jae said.

"Not necessarily," the youngest insisted.

He pulled out his phone and checked the battery life. The device still had 30 percent left before it needed a charge. He typed in a few words and then hit the search button. A moment later, the screen changed and displayed several results. He tapped the first one and scrolled down until he found what he was looking for, then turned the phone around so the other three could see it.

"Glastonbury," he said. "This is where they claim King Arthur is buried."

"Very good," Han-Jae said. "But that doesn't mean the sword is there. And the codex the McElroys had is long gone."

"Maybe," the young man said. "But if Wyatt and Schultz were able to get away from those other men, this would be the first place they would go. It's the next logical step."

“Okay. I see where you’re going with this, but if the Americans went there, they’d be long gone by now,” Buzz-Cut argued.

“True. But it’s worth a shot. If they haven’t yet been there, we might still have a chance to catch up to them. And even if they aren’t at the abbey, it’s possible we can figure out what they were looking for and determine their next destination.”

Han-Jae considered the option for a long moment. “It’s our best lead at the moment. I haven’t heard anything else out of Schultz’s parents. The general has relayed no new information. That means we’ll have to take our chances on the abbey.” He leaned his head back against the glass of an old refrigerator, the white racks within long empty of the soft drinks and juices that were previously sold there. “Get some rest. I’ll take first watch. We sleep four hours, rotating a man each hour. That will give us three hours of sleep. First thing in the morning, we head for England.”

Chapter 23
Glastonbury, England

Sean got out of the car and stretched his legs, working them back and forth to get the blood circulating again. Then he reached his arms to the sky to stretch them out. The other three exited the car and went through a similar ritual.

The flight from Frankfurt to London hadn't taken long. It was a trip Sean and Tommy had made several times throughout the years. The drive from Bellevaux back to Frankfurt in the early hours of the morning, however, had been exhausting.

By the time they boarded the IAA private jet, all four were ready to collapse on anything that would make do as a bed. Even a carpeted floor would have been acceptable. Luckily for them, the seats on the plane reclined and provided a comfortable place to sleep on the short flight to England.

They didn't wake up until the wheels touched down at Heathrow, and even then June and Tommy went back to sleep for a few extra minutes while the plane taxied to the private hangar where their car was waiting.

The sun still hadn't come up over London when the Americans arrived. The lights of the city twinkled in the distance as some of the earlier risers began waking for their day.

After leaving the plane, their driver took them to a hotel where they got another two hours of sleep before leaving for Glastonbury in Somerset. Now they stood outside the abbey grounds, staring at the ruins beyond the perfectly manicured grass surrounding the edifices.

The sun was blunted by a constant haze of gray clouds blanketing the sky above. An occasional raindrop splattered the hood and windshield of the car, which reminded Sean and the others to make sure they had their waterproof jackets with them.

After zipping up their outerwear, the group made their way up a path toward the remnants of the ancient church.

The main structure was like something out of a fairy tale, especially with the early morning mists still lingering around the old stonework and trees. On the far end, two giant structures rose into the sky, both with dramatic sloping sides where time had worn down what was once a glorious entryway into the church. The Gothic frames where windows once hung were still there, giving a sense of what people of medieval Somerset might have once seen when they came to worship.

The Americans approached the entrance to the section of the abbey known as the Lady Chapel. Its structure was in far better shape than the rest. The walls, while worn down, were still mostly complete. The big stones used to tile the floors were still in place. Sean wondered whose feet might have touched those tiles over the years.

The four companions passed through an archway and stopped by a railing overlooking the long, narrow remains of the sanctuary. Steps led down into the bowels of the chapel on either side. The original floor of the main sanctuary was completely gone, allowing visitors to see a stripped-down version of the building.

"Pretty amazing how this part of the abbey has stayed in such good shape," Tommy remarked.

"Especially when you consider that it and thousands of others like it were effectively shut down hundreds of years ago," Adriana added.

"Shut down?" June asked.

"Yes. The Dissolution of Monasteries was a major event in the mid-1500s. The king at the time, Henry VIII, essentially disbanded all Catholic religious houses in the country. The government confiscated property, buildings, and money. He used much of it to fund his military campaigns. After that happened, most of the monasteries and abbeys fell into disrepair. This one suffered tremendously. I'm surprised it has remained in such good condition."

"It doesn't hurt that they claim it's the location of Arthur's tomb," Sean said.

"Speaking of which," Tommy said, pointing through an opening in the side of the building, "I think that's it over there."

The four wandered through the chapel and back out onto the grass, making their way toward a brown sign propped up on a metal rod. On the other side, they were able to read the words on the placard.

Site of King Arthur's tomb.

In the year 1191, the bodies of King Arthur and his Queen were said to have been found on the south side of the Lady Chapel. On 19th April 1278 their remains were removed in the presence of

King Edward I and Queen Eleanor to a black marble tomb on this site. This tomb survived until the dissolution of the abbey in 1539.

"That's an interesting bit of history," Tommy said. "But it doesn't really help us with the symbols we're looking for."

"No. No it doesn't," Sean agreed. "Remember what the codex said. In the land where Arthur sleeps."

"Check," Tommy interrupted, pointing at the rectangle graveside cut into the grass.

"Right. Then it says whoever seeks the keys and finds the symbols the lady hides will discover the trophies that illuminate the way to the sword bearer's altar."

June raised both eyebrows. "You remembered all of that from looking at that codex one time?"

"Don't get me started," Tommy answered before Sean could. "He's some kind of freak when it comes to that stuff. He killed it on tests when we were younger. Most of the kids in our classes always tried to cheat off his paper because they knew he had a ridiculous memory."

"No, it's not eidetic," Sean said, sensing that would be her next question. "I'm just able to paraphrase things really well. Getting exact details is more difficult."

"He's being modest. I think he remembers the first twenty-seven digits of pi."

"Sorry to break up this little Sean-worship session," Adriana interrupted, "but we should probably get moving. The clue says to find the symbol the lady hides on high. If that's the Lady Chapel, maybe the codex is talking about that."

"Good idea," Sean said.

Back inside the chapel, the four made their way around the interior, scouring the walls for the symbols described in the codex.

Unfortunately, there weren't any symbols that were out of the ordinary. A few crosses and occasional triads of circles representing the Trinity were all they found.

"How are we supposed to know which symbols are the ones we're looking for?" Tommy asked.

"I'm inclined to think that these symbols aren't the ones we're searching for," Sean said. "Remember, the codex said that we have to find the ones the lady hides. These don't seem like they're hidden."

"Yes, these are very typical of monasteries from that era, and they're out in the open," Adriana said. She crossed her arms and spun around, taking in the entire structure. "Far too obvious to be the ones we're trying to find."

"She's right. Let's split up and check all the alcoves. Maybe there's something in one of them that will point us in the right direction. Tommy, you and June check out over there. We'll take this side."

Tommy nodded. He and June took off toward the front corner of the building while Sean and Adriana went to the opposite corner and began investigating every recess and alcove along the chapel's bottom floor. They moved in and out of the shallow cavities, making their way toward the grand entrance of the main sanctuary. After several minutes of thorough searching, the four met in the middle at the other end of the basement floor.

"Nothing," Sean said. "You guys find anything?"

Tommy shook his head. "Nothing out of the ordinary. I don't understand. Those symbols should be here."

Sean frowned and walked up a set of steps, leaving his friends for a moment to get a better view from above. He scanned the stone façade of the walls, columns, and openings, but nothing stood out. He spun around and stared at the two big structures that formed the entrance to the main sanctuary. Most of its walls had long since been destroyed, the floor of the nave replaced by the same green grass that pervaded most of the grounds.

The other three joined him at the top of the stairs, hoping he'd seen something of note.

"The codex said the lady hides the symbols on high. So maybe the basement wasn't the right place to start," Sean said.

"You think they may be up closer to the roof?" Tommy asked.

Sean leaned his head to the side for a second. "I hope not. The roof was destroyed a long time ago, along with the upper walls. If the symbols were that high up, we might never find them. They'd be long gone by now."

"What about over there?" June asked, pointing at the two opposing edifices across the way.

"That's the main sanctuary," Sean said. "But it's worth a look."

The four made their way across the lush grass and onto the walkway that led to the crumbling ruins of the old basilica. Time, it seemed, had been far crueler to it than the Lady Chapel. The walls were completely gone in some places, collapsed or torn down long ago.

The group wandered around the interior where the nave used to be. Sean imagined what it must have looked like long ago with dramatic flying buttresses, high ceilings, stained glass windows, and gold adornments sparkling in the rays of sunlight streaking throughout. Now it was a shadow of its former glory.

After wandering around for several minutes, they still didn't see any symbols that were out of the ordinary.

Sean wandered out the side of the structure and looked to a building a few hundred feet away. It had an odd shape, much like a six-sided pyramid atop a square base.

A man with white hair and a wrinkled face approached. He wore a green sweater and tanned corduroy pants. A name tag on his sweater claimed his name was Robert.

He smiled politely at Sean and waved as he drew near. "Enjoying your visit to Glastonbury?" Robert asked in a smooth accent.

"Yes, sir," Sean answered. "Just having a look around the abbey. Fascinating history here."

"Oh, to be sure. Lots of interesting stories about this place."

"So we've heard."

Robert followed Sean's gaze to the odd building across the way. "That there is the abbey kitchen," he said. "It's the only building on the grounds that remains undamaged."

"You work here?" Sean asked.

"Yes, going on about ten years now."

"Maybe you could answer a question."

"I'll do my best. You'd be hard pressed to find someone who knows more about this place than me. Lived here in Somerset my whole life, mostly in Glastonbury."

Tommy and the two women walked around the corner to find Sean talking to the older man. They stopped short and listened in to the conversation.

"I'm wondering if there are any ancient symbols on some of these structures. I'm not talking about the usual ones you'd find in a church. We're trying to link the history of the abbey to pre-Christian times. Might there be some sort of Celtic runes or something of that nature?"

Robert thought hard for a moment, staring off into the little forest on the edge of the property. Intermittent drops of rain splattered on his sweater, seemingly having no effect on the man's disposition.

"I don't recall seeing anything like that in this abbey. Although it was a Catholic monastery for a long time. Most of the symbols in here were Christian in nature."

"Well, I appreciate your help nonetheless," Sean said. "You probably want to get in out of the rain. Nobody likes to walk around soaking wet."

"Ah, this is nothing. Been through far rainier days than this. I'm sure I will in the future, too. Sorry I couldn't be more help. That's an interesting project you're working on. You from the States?"

"Yes, sir," Sean said. "My friends and I came over just this morning. We've been working on this for a while, but it looks like maybe we've reached a dead end. I don't suppose there's anything worth looking at in the abbey kitchen?"

Robert's wrinkled face scrunched as he considered. "Maybe. But I doubt it. Only interesting thing over there is a well...wait a minute."

The four visitors' curiosity rose a notch.

"The well. Oh, goodness me. I can't believe I forgot about that. Had a few too many pints last night, I suppose."

"Well?" Sean asked. "What well?"

"The well over by Glastonbury Tor. It's between that and Chalice Hill. There's a cover on it with all kinds of interesting symbols. Originally, it was the well that was supposedly used by Queen Guinevere when she would take long walks around the area. When she needed a drink, she'd walk over to the well and help herself. According to the story, that was one of the places Lancelot first noticed her."

Tommy stepped forward. "Sorry, Robert, is it? My name is Tommy Schultz. I'm a friend of Sean's. You said there are symbols on the well's cover?"

"Sure. Lots of 'em. Although the original well cover has been replaced by a replica. The old one was made of wrought iron and wood. It rotted away long ago. The new one isn't an exact match, though."

"Would you mind showing us?" Sean asked.

Robert's face brightened. "I'd be happy to. Don't get many Americans asking unique questions. Except that it's not on this property. It's not far away, though. You could walk there in no time."

Robert proceeded to tell the group how to get to Chalice Well. When he was done with the directions, he asked if they had any other questions.

"Just one," Tommy spoke up. "You said some of the symbols from the original well cover were no longer there."

"Yep. That thing has been gone for a while now."

"Do you happen to remember what they were?"

"The symbols? Hmm. Seems like I saw pictures of it at one point. I never actually saw it in person. They took it away before I got here. I do remember a few of the symbols, though. There were some stars and lions. Other than that, I don't really recall anything else."

"Stars and lions," Adriana said, contemplating the answer. She turned to Sean. "England is usually symbolized as the lion."

"Three lions, actually," Robert chimed in.

Adriana smiled at him. "Right. Three lions."

"Yeah," Tommy said. "That would make sense, especially if it's a reference to the early kingdom, maybe even the Arthur story."

"But what about the stars?" June asked. "How do those figure in?"

No one answered immediately.

"Maybe that's one we need to ask the kids," Sean said.

Robert drew his head back. "Kids?"

"We have some younger folks who do a bit of online research for us," Tommy said.

"Oh." Robert nodded his head but clearly didn't understand.

"Thanks for your help," Sean said. "We should get going."

He shook Robert's hand, as did Tommy and the other two before they turned and started walking back toward the parking area.

"He was nice," June said as they strolled down the narrow path leading to the Lady Chapel.

"Lucky that we bumped into him," Tommy said. "Guy just saved us a ton of time we would have wasted looking around."

"Maybe," Adriana said.

"Maybe? You heard him. He saw the symbols."

"Yes, but we still don't know what they mean for certain. And he said there were more that he couldn't remember."

"There's something else, too," Sean said. "The clue says that the symbols were hidden on high. How is a well cover on high?"

No one answered right away as they turned into the chapel and walked out the other side.

"I guess it's a matter of perspective," June said after realizing no one else had an answer. "If you're down in a hole—surrounded by darkness and cold—getting to the light would be high."

Tommy stared at her, full of admiration. "I have to say, I would have never thought about that. I think you might be right."

"It's a good explanation," Sean agreed. "We'll see what the kids have to say about those symbols. That is, if they can find any information on the original well cover."

He looked up from the path and down toward the parking area. He froze and put his arm out to stop the others. "Wait," he said.

"What?" June asked.

Tommy saw the look of concern on Sean's face and instantly knew there was trouble.

"Get back in the chapel," Tommy said. "Now." He grabbed June by the shoulder and spun her around, ushering her back inside the stone building.

Sean and Adriana were right behind them. Once all four were back in the chapel, June searched the other three faces for an answer.

"What is going on?"

"He's like Lassie with a sense for trouble," Tommy said. "Whenever he gets that look on his face, I know I should have probably stayed at home."

Sean ignored the comment. "We have trouble. Two black sedans in the parking lot."

"Brotherhood?"

"Probably. Remember, that was part of the plan. They're not who I'm worried about."

Tommy peeked around the corner of the building at the cars. One of the North Koreans exited a silver

SUV, which had also just pulled up. He was followed closely by another member of his gang.

Tommy retreated into the chapel. “Looks like a party. Brotherhood, the North Koreans.”

“Should make for an interesting dance,” Sean said.

“Yeah, but I don’t like this song.”

“Me, either. Which is why we’re going to sit this one out and let them dance alone.” He looked toward the back of the chapel at the ruins of the main sanctuary. “Time to run.”

Chapter 24
Glastonbury

Tommy panted as he and the others sprinted down the path toward the opening in the ruins of the main sanctuary. Sean looked back to make sure no one was behind them. Surprisingly, the only people he saw were a few early-bird tourists who'd decided to come out and see the sights before the crowds arrived.

They cut in around the wall to the right and took shelter for the moment, trying to stay out of sight.

Tommy leaned against the wall and looked up to the sky as if that would somehow ease his breathing.

Sean poked his head around the corner but didn't see anyone chasing them.

He darted across the aisle to the far wall and moved over to one of the window openings.

For a second, Tommy forgot about his need for air. "Sean," he hissed, "what are you doing?"

Sean waved a dismissive hand at his friend. It was an impolite but effective way to get him to shut up.

Sean leaned out the window just enough to see beyond the chapel. From that vantage point he could see the North Koreans stalking their way to where the Americans had been just moments before. They stopped suddenly and turned around. Sean frowned at the odd behavior.

Then he saw what halted them. Seven men—plus Baldwin—sauntered toward the group of North Koreans. The faces of the Brotherhood were full of righteous anger, probably at having previously lost one of their own.

Sean looked over at his companions. "Cavalry is here."

"Cavalry?" Tommy asked. "I know you don't mean—"

"Yes, the Brotherhood."

He dashed back to the other side of the nave and nodded his head to the left. "Come on, we're going to double back."

"Double back?" June asked. "No offense, but I don't feel like getting shot at again."

"You won't," Sean said. "They're going to have their hands full with each other."

"Clever," she said, realizing the plan was working exactly as Sean hoped.

He motioned for them to run toward the back of the sanctuary ruins and then out to the right. "Go around that last corner, turn right, and head for the abbey kitchen," he said.

"Won't they see us?" Adriana asked. "We'll be out in the open."

"No," Tommy said. "He's right. The angle should put the Lady Chapel right between us and the two groups. Let's just hope they're too busy fighting each other to notice us."

June didn't wait for more instructions. She took off at a dead sprint, running through the grass to the other end of the structure in remarkably quick time. Even in blue jeans and boots, she moved fast. Adriana followed close behind her.

Sean's eyebrows pressed together as he looked at his friend. "I think she's faster than you."

Tommy sighed and took a deep breath. "Who isn't?"

He gave Sean no time to respond, instead lumbering across the grass, careful to keep close to the wall in case any of their foes might have an opportunity to see in. Sean ran right behind him, bringing up the rear to cover the other three.

When he reached the back corner, the other three were crouching behind the column, looking around it to make certain the coast was clear. Nothing was there except wide swaths of green grass all the way to the chapel and over to the kitchen.

"No time like the present," Sean said. "We all go at once. I'll cover the rear. Okay?"

The other three nodded.

"Good. Go!"

The four took off, running as fast as they could while keeping an eye toward the Lady Chapel. The huge stone building blocked their view to the parking area, just as Sean had predicted.

A sudden pop startled them, nearly causing June to stop in her tracks.

"That wasn't aimed at us," Sean said. "Keep going. We're almost there."

More muffled pops sounded from beyond the front of the chapel.

Thirty more feet, and the Americans would be temporarily safe behind the abbey kitchen. They heard yelling now but still didn't see anyone.

With ten feet to go before they reached the abbey kitchen, Baldwin and his men came into view around the front left corner of the chapel.

"Cut to the left," Sean said as they made it to the kitchen's closest corner. "Stay close to the wall to keep out of sight."

The other three scurried around to the left, making their way to the backside of the kitchen. Sean stayed at the front corner, just beyond the line of sight with the men involved in the firefight. He poked his head around and watched the battle play out.

Baldwin's men had gotten the drop on the North Koreans, but they blew the element of surprise by getting out of their cars too soon. Approaching the North Koreans in the open presented a ton of problems. They had no cover, so unless they were planning on taking the men out right away, the North Koreans would have a chance to fend them off.

That's exactly what happened.

Sean didn't see the beginning of the firefight. He only heard the first gunshot. Since shooting someone in the back didn't seem like Baldwin's style, Sean figured it was the North Koreans who shot first.

Now Baldwin's men were scrambling to protect themselves. One was lying on the ground, not moving. Sean shook his head. The guy was probably shot down before he could defend himself.

Baldwin stood his ground—out in the open—firing on the four Koreans as they retreated toward the entrance to the chapel. The first man made it to the doorway, then the second. The Brotherhood poured a barrage of rounds at the running targets. Pieces of the chapel wall exploded into hundreds of tiny fragments and clouds of dust over and over again. One bullet struck the third man in the back of the leg just before he made it around the entrance corner to safety.

Sean saw his head rock back as he screamed in pain, immediately grabbing his hamstring before falling into the chapel and disappearing from view. Their leader was the last into the building, narrowly missing dozens of bullets by mere inches.

With the North Koreans in the chapel, they now had the advantage of shooting from cover.

To counter that problem, Baldwin motioned to his men to fan out and flank both sides of the building. Two went around to the right, and the other two disappeared around the left side. He stayed and one other remained in the middle, approaching the chapel head on. It was by far the more dangerous option of the three. Sean admired the move by the leader of the Brotherhood even though it seemed a foolhardy move.

Shots fired from inside the chapel as the North Koreans defended their position. The two men on the left were just outside of Sean's view, but he could see the men on the right pushing fast toward the outer wall. He assumed the men on the other side were doing the same thing.

Baldwin squeezed off his last round, firing on the entrance to the chapel. He deftly slid the empty magazine out of the pistol, grabbed a full one from his cargo pants, and slammed it into place. He took three quick steps forward, sliding at an angle to the right as he moved toward the building.

Sean had seen enough. He hurried around to the back of the kitchen where his companions waited. Tommy was peeking around the corner when Sean arrived.

"What's going on?" he whispered.

"Just what I hoped. They're shooting at each other. One of Baldwin's men is down, and I think one of the North Koreans took a round to the leg."

"That should slow them down."

"Yeah."

"What now?" Tommy asked.

Sean faltered for a second. "Um, I actually hadn't thought that far ahead yet."

Tommy's eyes widened. "Seriously?"

Adriana cut in. "Hey, boys. If we go through the woods over here, we should be able to circle around and get back to the car." She pointed at the small forest next to the kitchen building.

"See?" Sean said. "Everything works out."

Tommy's head went back and forth. "You're lucky you've got her around to bail you out."

"Boys, do you mind?" June said. "We should probably get moving. You two can start celebrating when we're on our way back to London."

Sean and Tommy twisted their heads to look at her then back to each other. They both shrugged and shared a knowing glance.

"Lead the way," Sean said to Adriana.

She was already crouching at the kitchen's back corner next to a large oval-shaped stone.

"What's that thing?" Sean asked as he crept up behind her and readied himself for a sprint into the woods.

"Omphalos stone," she answered. "They used to put them in the naves of churches. Stones like this were considered the navel of a sanctuary. Seems like I read that it was originally a Greek tradition."

She abruptly stopped talking and darted into the woods, jumping over a small tree like a hurdler as she swiped limbs out of the way.

Sean watched her for a second, looked down at the odd stone, and then waved Tommy and June ahead.

As soon as they were into the forest, he crept back to the other corner and took one more look over at the chapel.

Baldwin's men had encircled the ruins and were pressing forward. The two men on Sean's right took up positions on opposite sides of a window near the front of the building. They operated with military precision, causing him to wonder if any of them had been through some kind of training.

A shot came from the back end of the chapel, and Sean saw one of the North Koreans crouching at the corner. He leaned out and took another potshot at the two exposed men near the window.

Sean thought the North Koreans' next move would be retreating farther toward the back of the chapel, but he hadn't anticipated them counterattacking around the side. It was a smart move.

Speaking of smart moves, Sean decided he needed to move. His friends already had a head start, and he didn't want them to wait.

He turned and took off, rushing into the woods and leaping over the same small tree Adriana had jumped a moment before. Tommy and June were a good forty feet ahead with Adriana a few dozen feet in front of them, hacking her way through the forest undergrowth.

She moved like a professional running back, cutting around one oak then another, dipping her head under a tree limb, and then swiping another one away just before it smacked her in the face.

June, too, moved deftly through the woods. She was slightly less graceful than Adriana but had no trouble keeping pace.

Tommy's progress, however, was a comedy of errors. He tripped over a tree root, smacked into a tree trunk, got slapped multiple times by small branches, and looked more like a tank driving through a tea shop. He lumbered forward as fast as he could, only able to keep up with the two women through sheer willpower.

Adriana stopped when she reached a chain-link fence that stretched all the way from one end of the forest to the other. Fortunately, the barbs on the top were pointed straight up, which would make it easier to get over. Had it been one with the inward- or outward-facing barbed wire tops, they might have had issues.

She started climbing and in mere seconds had crested the fence and dropped down to the other side, easily landing on her feet.

June climbed the fence like a monkey. Her lithe body was perfectly suited for climbing, and she went over the top without issue.

Tommy ran headlong into the fence, his weight causing the waves to ripple down the fence line. He grabbed onto the fencing and started climbing. When he was a few feet off the ground, his right foot slipped, and he fell back down. He started again, getting a hand on the top bar before his foot slipped again. This time, Sean was there to stop his fall.

Sean caught his friend's foot and hoisted him higher until Tommy was almost straddling the fence top.

"I wouldn't sit on that if I were you," Sean said, looking at the sharp points right at Tommy's undercarriage.

"Don't think I didn't already take that into consideration."

He forced most of his weight onto his hands as he lifted his right leg over the fence and then the left. When both feet were on the other side he started to lower himself down but lost his grip and fell to the ground. He rolled clumsily in the wet leaves for a second and then stopped in a sitting position. He breathed heavily, but got himself together and brushed the dirt and leaves off his pants.

Sean shook his head and leaped onto the fence, grasping the top with both hands and vaulting over it with one swift movement.

He landed next to Tommy and patted his friend on the back. "You okay?"

"Just...don't, okay?"

"Keep moving," Adriana ordered. She turned and started running again, this time bending her direction slightly to head back to the parking lot.

By now, the sounds of the gunfight were all but gone. The sound suppressors both groups were using kept it from sounding like what it was—an all-out war.

Through the branches and bushes in the woods ahead, the four companions could see the cars. As they drew closer, the distant sounds of the muffled pops could be heard, but thankfully no one was around the parking lot except for a few scared tourists crouching next to their vehicles.

Adriana burst out of the forest first. Her feet pounded the asphalt, moving even faster. Tommy, June, and Sean were twenty feet behind her but moving quickly.

Sean took the key fob out of his pocket the second his shoes touched the pavement. He pressed the unlock button as Adriana arrived and opened one of the back doors.

She stood next to it, waving her hand, urging Tommy and June to hurry. June made it to the car next and slid into the back seat. As she did, a door opened on a sedan parked just a few spots away.

Sean watched as the man got out, looking right at his three friends. It was one of Baldwin's men. Then he saw another guy get out of the passenger side.

A sinking feeling shot through Sean's gut. He knew immediately what happened. Like a good chess player, Baldwin had anticipated Sean's move and set up a safety net to make sure the Americans couldn't get away if they tried to make an escape.

Sean bent his run to the left and charged the man closest to his friends.

The guy was raising a pistol when Sean's shoulder plowed into his ribs.

The gunman grunted loudly from the impact, and then again as the two hit the ground. He maintained a grip on his weapon and tried to overpower Sean to take aim at his chest.

Sean grabbed the guy's wrist and started smacking it against the ground until the pistol rattled out of the man's hand.

Meanwhile, the other gunman saw what happened to his partner and hurried around the front end of the sedan to assist.

Tommy had started to get into the rental car when he saw Sean take down the gunman. Out of breath, fatigued, and hampered by burning muscles, Tommy pushed all those factors out of the way and ran as fast as he could around the cars separating him and the two struggling men on the ground.

He and the second shooter saw each other at the same time. The guy brandished his weapon. His finger tensed on the trigger for a second, and Tommy thought he was certainly going to get off a shot. Suddenly, his hand holding the weapon flailed skyward as his knee buckled.

Sean had seen what was about to happen and for one second took his focus off the man he was fighting and punched the side of the other gunman's knee. Sean's reward was a set of strong fingers wrapped around his throat as his opponent attempted to choke him out.

With the other shooter thrown off for a second, Tommy took advantage and launched foot first. Tommy was more of a brawler than a martial arts kind of guy, but his flying sidekick worked perfectly on an enemy who'd just been knocked off balance.

Tommy's shoe landed squarely in the guy's abdomen, the force sending the man sprawling over the hood of his car. Not used to landing a kick like that, Tommy stumbled forward and nearly landed on top of the guy.

His gunman used that to his advantage and grabbed Tommy by the shirt. He forced him onto his back and punched hard. Tommy reacted fast, putting up both hands to block the first punch and then the second, but the third sank into his gut. He felt the air fly from his lungs and suddenly found himself gasping for air. His guard went down, too, which opened up his face as an easy target. The guy landed a hard punch squarely on Tommy's cheek and then another on the other cheek.

On the ground, Sean clambered to get on top of his opponent. He straddled the guy's torso with both legs and squeezed. He cocked his fist to deliver a blow to the man's face, but the guy suddenly jerked one way then the other. The move was so powerful it tossed Sean to the side with such momentum that he couldn't balance himself fast enough before hitting the other car with the side of his head.

Dazed, Sean put out both hands to try to grab onto something to steady himself. His right hand found a rearview mirror, and he pulled himself up with it. The gunman swung a hard uppercut and landed it on Sean's jaw. The blow was glancing but didn't do anything to help the pain thumping on the side of his head and his blurred vision.

The guy stood up and stepped to Sean as he lay slumped against the car door. His opponent reared back, about to drive his knee into Sean's face, when he saw a sudden movement out of the corner of his eye.

Adriana slid over the car's hood. She reached the other side, planted her feet on the quarter panel, and used her momentum to launch at the attacker. She flew through the air with her right fist drawn and snapped it hard, driving her fist into the guy's temple. Her knees crashed into his chest, driving him back into the door of his own vehicle, where he dropped to the ground and fell over on his side.

Tommy desperately tried to throw a punch at his opponent, but the man had him pinned and had already delivered two heavily damaging punches. It wouldn't take many more before he lost consciousness.

A woman's voice yelled from off to the right, and he saw June run up behind the guy. She jumped in the air from the curb and raised her right elbow next to her head. Gravity pulled her toward her target just as the man turned to see what the noise was.

June's elbow sank deep into the base of his skull with a sickening thud.

The man wobbled for a few seconds after June landed with a spin move to keep her balance. He looked about to fall on top of Tommy, but she swept her foot around and caught the back of his heels, sending him toppling backward. His upper back hit the curb, which would have hurt had he been conscious.

June stood up and reached out a hand to Tommy. A few feet away, Adriana extended her hand down to Sean. The two men stood up simultaneously, both a little woozy.

Confused, they looked at the two women, then each other, then the two women again.

Sean gently felt the side of his head and winced. "Looks like we found a couple of keepers, eh, buddy?"

Tommy worked his jaw back and forth, trying to get the pain out. "Yeah. And I vote one of them drives us back to London."

Chapter 25
Glastonbury

Han-Jae crouched at the back of the chapel and pressed his back to the stone wall. One of his men was on the other side of the church, holding his position against the two gunmen attacking from that flank. Another was on the opposite corner, doing his best to fend off the two coming from the right.

He'd ordered his men to fall back in an attempt to lure the attackers into an ambush. When he initially got his men safely into the cover of the chapel, he cursed himself for allowing the blond and his men to catch them by surprise. The enemy leader had been foolish in thinking he could talk his way out of a fight.

The blond had ordered Han-Jae and his men to drop their weapons and hit the ground. Han-Jae's reaction had been immediate and deadly: he spun around and fired a shot, sending a bullet into the chest of the guy closest to the blond leader.

The mortal wound dropped the man instantly, and Han-Jae's comrades also opened fire as they retreated toward the ancient monastery amid a hailstorm of hot metal.

Han-Jae narrowly escaped the initial gun battle, along with two of his men. One however—the youngest—took a bullet to the back of his leg. Han-Jae draped the young man over his shoulder and dragged him to the back of the chapel where he lowered him to the ground behind the rear wall.

The man insisted he was fine, that he could take care of himself. Han-Jae knew better. He knew he was going to have to cut the dead weight. The injured man would only slow them down. That was something he could not abide.

For the moment, however, he still had some usefulness.

Han-Jae leaned around an opening in the stonework and fired a shot down the aisle toward the entrance. The blond had pursued up the middle while his other men tried to take the flanks. It was a fairly standard maneuver, at least for someone who understood tactics.

The bullet ricocheted off the façade at the other end, missing the blond by more than a few feet. It didn't matter if Han-Jae hit him or not. He just had to buy a little time. He ducked back behind the wall and looked down at the bleeding man.

"I need you to hold the center," Han-Jae said. "Can you do that?"

The younger man grimaced but nodded. "Yes, sir." He dragged himself up and propped his shoulder against the wall close to the opening.

"I'm going to give some support to the men on the side. Keep their leader from coming down the middle. We're going to get out of this."

Han-Jae had no intention of getting the injured man out alive. By taking a bullet to the leg, the guy had just become the sacrificial lamb. Han-Jae patted him on the shoulder and then ran around to the right side where Buzz-Cut was reloading a full magazine into his weapon.

“How many do you have left?” Han-Jae asked as he skidded to a stop.

“This is my last magazine.”

“I only have one left, too.”

“We need to find a way out of here.”

“Yes, but there’s only one way back to the car.”

Sirens whined in the distance, interrupting their conversation for the moment. “You’re thinking linearly. We can make it back if we loop around over here,” he pointed to the main sanctuary and then a forest running alongside both sections of the ruins.

“They’ll see us,” Buzz-Cut said.

“Not if they think we’re making a stand here.” Han-Jae stepped to the corner and stuck his weapon around the rock. He fired five successive shots at the approaching men and sent them scrambling to the front of the chapel for cover. He moved back behind the wall and looked at Buzz-Cut. “The only place they have for protection is the front wall. If they’re all hiding at the entrance, they’ll not see our retreat. Then we can lose them in the forest.”

“But if we run, they’ll pursue.”

Han-Jae shook his head. “Not if they think we’re still here.” He turned and looked at the wounded man by the wall holding his weapon at shoulder height, ready to fire.

“You’re going to leave him?” Buzz-Cut asked.

“We have no other choice.”

The two made their way back to the opening in the middle of the chapel and joined the younger man.

"We're going to have to make a stand," Han-Jae said. "Push hard up the middle. If they try to come through the door, kill them."

The injured man nodded.

"We're going to push around to this side over here," Han-Jae said, pointing to the right. "There should be enough stonework inside for you to stay safe while we flank the enemy."

He didn't wait for more confirmation from his injured comrade. Han-Jae ran quickly over to the other shooter and filled him in on the plan. He'd kept his side clear, forcing the blond's men to stay back at the front of the chapel.

"Understood," Shaved Head said. "Just give the word."

Han-Jae rushed back to the opening and nodded at the young guy. "Go."

He didn't question the order. He hobbled into the opening as fast as he could and crouched down behind a broken piece of wall. The blond poked his head around the entrance door again, and the young man fired two shots that ricocheted off the stone.

Han-Jae nodded at his other two men, who took off at top speed toward the main sanctuary. Han-Jae gave one last look at the injured man and then followed behind the other two.

He didn't dare look back, knowing any sort of slowdown could cost him. If the ambushers saw where he and his remaining two men were headed, they would then be able to cut off their exit, an issue that was growing more and more possible every second the police closed in.

He reached the stone edifice and cut behind it to the left, pausing for a second where his men awaited further instructions. Han-Jae looked out straight beyond the remnants of the nearest wall.

"Right through there."

The sirens grew louder for a moment and then started fading. At first, Han-Jae was confused. Then he realized no one had called the police here. They were going somewhere else.

He let out a short sigh of relief. "Follow me."

He sprinted out of the opening as he heard more gunshots from the chapel. Han-Jae slowed to let his two men run by and looked back for a second. Two of the attackers had circled around behind the chapel and were going in through the back. He saw them take aim but didn't watch as the men gunned down the injured comrade he'd left behind. He didn't have time to watch. Lingering would lead to his downfall.

It was regrettable, Han-Jae thought as he ran ahead and disappeared into the foliage. He didn't want to leave the young man behind, but he had no choice.

As he nimbly danced around trees, bushes, and large rocks, his mind drifted to his little brother.

Son Yoo had been a promising young soldier until he was taken down by a South Korean sniper. The bullet had pierced his heart and exited out his back. Death came so quickly; Son Yoo was gone before anyone could call for help.

There'd never been any report as to why the sniper had fired, or why he targeted Han-Jae's brother. All Han-Jae knew was that any allies of the south or of America were his enemies, and he would do anything to destroy them.

His mind snapped back to the present as he almost ran into a low-hanging branch. He ducked beneath it and kept running as the men in front started to loop back around to the cars.

Off to his left, he no longer heard the sound of gunfire. Han-Jae figured the blond and his men would pursue to the main sanctuary. It's what he would have done. The blond would find the area empty. Next, he would have his men fan out and search the property. By the time they got back to their vehicles, Han-Jae and his men would be long gone.

The only question was, where would they go next?

Chapter 26
London, England

Tommy's phone vibrated atop the table in the corner of the pub. Sean was watching the news with the television muted, trying to see if there was anything about the Glastonbury shootout in the headlines. June and Adriana were discussing Adriana's unusual hobby of tracking down stolen Nazi art.

Oddly, none of the television anchors said anything about the shootout.

"It's the kids," Tommy said after checking the caller ID.

Sean and the other two turned their attention away from the television.

"Hello," Tommy said after pressing the green button.

"Hey, Tommy," Alex said. "What's all that noise in the background? Sounds like you're at a bar."

"We are. It's a little pub in London. Figured a crowded place might be a good idea after the events of the morning. Luckily, it's not their peak hours, so it's not too loud. What did you guys figure out?"

In the car ride back to London, Tommy called his two research assistants in Atlanta and described the Chalice Well along with the problem they had in finding the original symbols.

It took a few hours for Alex and Tara to get back to their boss, but Tommy knew that was most likely because they were being thorough.

"It wasn't easy to find images of that well cover. There was nothing in the search engine databases except the new one you described."

"But..."

"But we were able to dig up some images from some of our other resources. Wasn't easy."

"What was it?" Tommy asked.

"I'm sending you the email right now. Several of the same images, plus a couple of different ones. Tara and I have no idea what they mean. Figuring that sort of thing out is your deal anyway."

It was true. While Tara and Alex were highly efficient in finding and delivering information, they weren't necessarily good puzzle solvers. Their skills, however, were a huge complement to what Tommy and the rest of his organization did.

The laptop on the table dinged, and a new message tab appeared in the top right corner. Tommy clicked it and a second later the email filled the screen.

Sean and the two women huddled a little closer in the booth to get a good look at the images on the monitor.

There were no photos, just drawings.

"We couldn't find any real images," Alex explained. "I guess that thing was removed before anyone thought to take a picture. Or maybe it was just so deteriorated that there was nothing left to get a good image."

"No, this works," Tommy said as he stared at the screen.

The circular well cover had the same two big circles coming together in a sort of Venn diagram in the middle. To the historical world, it was also known as *Vesica Piscis*, literally the bladder of the fish.

Outside it were several other symbols. Four lion heads were huddled together on one side. Eight stars surrounded the center where the two circles merged. Then there was a strange collection of what looked like two humps with one hump on top and off to the right. A big sphere was at the top of the well cover, with a smaller one at the bottom.

"What do you make of it?" Tommy asked out loud.

"You talking to me?" Alex asked when no one else responded.

"Oh, sorry, Alex. We'll take it from here. If we have any more questions, we'll let you know."

"No problem. Always happy to help. I will say before I go that we think the spheres on that thing represent the sun and the Earth. Not sure but just thought it might be of some help to you."

"Actually, that is helpful," Tommy said. "I'll be in touch. Thanks again, Alex. You and Tara are awesome."

After he ended the call, the four continued staring at the screen.

"Vesica Piscis is often used as a symbol for Jesus," Sean said. "Does that mean we're supposed to look somewhere in Jerusalem for this thing?"

Tommy wasn't so sure. "I would have thought there would be a little more detail than this. Kind of leaves things to interpretation, doesn't it?"

The other three nodded.

"So we think the lions represent England?" Adriana asked. "If so, why are there four instead of three?"

"It's a good question. It makes me think we possibly might be wrong on that. What is the significance of the sun and Earth, the stars? Where's the moon?"

"And what about those humps?" Sean asked.

June was biting the tip of her finger as the others discussed the questions. "Is it me, or does it seem like those stars are surrounding the shape in the center?"

The other three reexamined the image.

"Yep," Tommy said. "You think that has some kind of significance?"

"Maybe," she said. "What if this thing is a sort of map, and the Vesica Piscis is like the X that marks the spot?"

It was a slightly oversimplified explanation, but June wasn't completely off base.

"That's an interesting theory," Sean said. "That could mean these symbols are locations, right?"

"You mean like landmarks?" Adriana asked.

"Exactly. If those symbols are points of interest, landmarks like you said, they could help us pinpoint the location of the X, as June put it."

Tommy squinted one eye and tossed his head to one side. "An X that marks the spot? Not sure I've ever come across anything like that in the years I've been doing this sort of thing. I guess anything is possible."

"The only thing we have to figure out is what those symbols mean." Adriana said.

"Or where they are. Anyone have a clue what the stars symbolize in legends surrounding Excalibur?"

Everyone shook their heads.

"Me either," Tommy said with a shrug.

"The two spheres—if they're Earth and the sun—might have something to do with the connection between heaven and Earth, the people of Earth I mean." Sean tried to make sense of his own comment after he said it.

"So that would mean that what is between heaven and Earth is the sort of connection point?" June asked.

"Maybe. I'm just kind of thinking out loud right now. This is a tough one."

Adriana stared for a long, quiet moment. Her eyes opened a little wider as an epiphany hit her. "Wait," she said. "These symbols. I've seen them somewhere before."

"Stars and lions and planets?" Tommy asked. "Yeah, I'd say they're all pretty common."

"No," she insisted. "I've seen them all together before. I just can't remember where."

"So you've actually seen these things in real life?" June asked.

Adriana nodded. "Sean, what was the last riddle again, the one that said something about the symbols?"

"It said, 'for he who seeks the keys and finds the symbols, the trophies of the fallen will illuminate the way to the sword bearer's altar."

"Trophies of the fallen. That's what I was trying to remember. What are some of the greatest trophies a kingdom has ever brought back from war?"

The other three fell silent for a moment.

"That's a big question," Sean said finally. "Throughout the history of the world, there have been some incredible antiquities removed as a result of war."

"On the subject of a Judeo-Christian-based theme—like the one we seem to have with this investigation—I guess you'd have to say all the items taken from the Hebrew temple in Jerusalem," Tommy offered.

"Yes," Adriana said. "But are those out where anyone can see them?"

"No, but is that a prerequisite?"

"I think it might be."

"She's right," Sean said. "The clue says that the trophies will illuminate the way. That would insinuate that they're out in the open, possibly even in plain sight."

"Yeah, unless they're in a cave," Tommy said.

"Ugh, I hope not. Had enough caves to last me a lifetime."

"Right?"

"Boys," June said, "try to focus. What are some other famous spoils of war from history?"

"The Amber Room," Tommy said, "but that was from World War II. Probably doesn't apply here."

"What about the Greeks, the Persians, or the Babylonians? The Israelites had a ton of trouble with the Babylonians. Did they take something of value?" June asked.

"Yeah, there were many important relics lost during the Babylonian occupation. None that I can think of as being visible in public."

"What if it doesn't mean spoils of war?" Sean said. "It could just be trophies that were taken from a fallen civilization."

"Such as?"

"Think about every major civilization that has existed throughout history. Rome, Greece, Persia, Babylon..."

"The Ottomans," Tommy added.

"Byzantium." Adriana said.

"The great Chinese dynasties," June said.

Sean nodded. "All exceptional examples. But there's one that stands out above all others. It was one of the first empires in our Earth's history. It spanned thousands of years. Egypt."

"What about it?" Tommy asked. "What trophies did they bring back from war?"

Sean had a knowing twinkle in his eye. "I don't think they were the ones who brought any trophies back."

He grabbed Tommy's computer. His fingers flew across the keyboard. When the results came up, he clicked on the first one and then clicked the images tab.

The computer screen filled with pictures of Rome. The center of focus in all the images were Egyptian obelisks.

"Obelisks were brought to Rome by various emperors and leaders of the Roman Empire," Sean said. "There are more than a dozen obelisks in Rome."

"Only eight of them are from ancient Egypt, though. Still, what's your point?" Tommy pressed.

Sean clicked one of the images and zoomed in on it. "That's my point," he said, tapping the screen emphatically.

"It's an eight-pointed star with a cross on top of it."

"And it looks just like the stars on the well cover."

Adriana could barely contain her excitement as everything became clear. "That's it. That's where I've seen those before." She grabbed the computer and twisted it so the screen faced her more directly.

She scrolled down and clicked another image. "See that one?" she said, pointing at the monitor. "Those humps are the same as the ones in the picture of the well cover. They represent the city on seven hills. That's one of the monikers Rome has carried for thousands of years."

"It looks exactly like the one from the well cover," Tommy said in awe.

Adriana clicked on another image. This one featured an obelisk with four lions below a star. "There are the lions." She moved the mouse arrow again and clicked a third image. "And there is our sun atop the Solar Obelisk."

Sean tried to contain his excitement. No matter how many times he, Tommy, and Adriana had done this sort of thing, the thrill of piecing together clues never went away. Adriana showed them a globe atop one of the obelisks.

She clicked through seven obelisks in total, showing off the symbols above the point of each one. Then she came to the last one, the Vatican Obelisk. The bronze symbols above the giant monolith were a cross on top of another star. The star sat over the same hills they'd seen on a few other examples.

"The keys," Sean said. "The riddle says that he who seeks the keys. Saint Peter's Square is a giant keyhole."

"Everybody knows that," Tommy said.

"I didn't," June commented with fake irritation in her voice.

Before Tommy could apologize, Sean went on. "I'm saying that it's a big keyhole because it references the keys. That's it. The sword must be somewhere near the obelisk."

"Or in the obelisk?" Tommy offered.

"It all makes perfect sense," Adriana said. "We're looking for the sword that Peter carried the night Jesus was arrested. Sure, it belonged to Joshua, David, Judah Maccabee, the three pagans, the three Christians like Arthur, but the man who carried it while walking the earth with Jesus was Peter. Why wouldn't it be in Saint Peter's Square?"

Everyone stared at the screen with tempered excitement.

"That would also follow the Vesica Piscis theory," June said. "If that symbol was used for Christianity, it makes perfect sense."

"The sword of Peter would have been an extremely important relic in Christian history," Sean said. "And if the Catholic Church has a penchant for something, it's relics. Think about all the resources they've used since their beginning to acquire anything related to the apostles or Jesus Himself."

"It's a staggering amount, for sure," Tommy agreed. Something still didn't add up as far as the sword's hiding place. "So if the sword is there at Saint Peter's Square, what does that last part mean concerning the sword bearer's altar?"

The question spurred another thirty seconds of silence before Sean attempted an answer. "The square is the altar?" he offered.

"Could be. That entire plaza is dedicated to Saint Peter. So in a way, it's an altar to him."

"There's the basilica, too," Adriana said. "Saint Peter's Basilica is a tribute to him."

"Or it could be the literal altar inside the basilica," June added. "Can you look that up?"

Adriana was a step ahead, already typing the search keywords into the box. She entered the search and got a fresh set of results. She clicked on the first one, and they were taken to an online encyclopedia article about something called the baldachin. An image displayed a gargantuan canopy with twisted pillars and intricately carved reliefs of heavenly beings around the roof's edge. Unhappy with the result, Adriana clicked the back button and then clicked the images tab to get more visual results.

The images displayed on the page showed an incredible structure. Four gigantic Solomonic columns held up a high bronze canopy, sculpted in the Baroque style. Adriana clicked on one of the images that showed bright beams of sunlight streaking through windows on the other side of the building, shining down on the altar as if through some kind of divine design.

“Is that a person underneath that thing?” June asked, looking at the incredible imagery.

“Yeah,” Sean said. “That thing is mammoth. Gives you perspective on just how big the rest of the basilica is.”

Tommy stared at the pictures without saying a word for a moment. There was something turning in his mind, and he knew it was in the back of Sean’s head as well.

“So if the sword really is in the altar of Saint Peter—in the Vatican—how in the world are we going to get it out?”

Sean thought for a moment and then looked over at Adriana. They both had the same thought simultaneously.

“We steal it.”

Chapter 27
Glastonbury

Han-Jae held the phone against his ear as he waited patiently for his spotter—a bright young spy named Sun Pak—to answer.

He and the two surviving members of his team had narrowly escaped Glastonbury. When they got back to their cars, they found two of the blond's men unconscious on the pavement. The only explanation was that the Americans had somehow found a way back to their vehicle and managed to escape. If he'd been forced to guess, Han-Jae would have said that they looped around much the same way he and his men had.

Both of his remaining men wondered how they were going to find the Americans now that they'd let them slip through their fingers again. Han-Jae, however, had already taken care of that issue.

"I got 'em," the voice on the other end said as he answered the phone. "Been watching them ever since they left the abbey."

"Where are they now?" Han-Jae asked.

"They're in a pub here in London. You on your way back?"

"Yes. We should be there within the hour."

"Good, because you're going to need a plane, and I doubt there's any down there that flies where you'll be heading."

"Which is?"

Han-Jae had put the spotter on the Americans without telling his three men. Making sure he always had a backup plan in place may have seemed a little overly cautious to some, but that was one of the reasons the general trusted him. Things rarely went according to plan. So having something in place for just such a contingency not only took some stress off his mind, it allowed Han-Jae to focus on the things he could control.

The spotter had been there in the parking lot when the Americans made their getaway. He'd remained hidden in another vehicle, parked outside the main visitor's area, while Sean and the others went in and snooped around. He watched as the two male Americans fought off the men the blond had left behind to guard the exit. He was surprised when the two women came to their rescue and effectively saved the two men.

The odd twist caused him to wonder just how good the men really were. Based on what he'd seen, he also tried to understand how these Americans had been able to overtake Han-Jae and the others. That wasn't for him to question. His job was to report to Han-Jae on what he saw, not convey doubts about his leadership.

"Su Pak?" Han-Jae said, snapping the spotter back to the question at hand. "Where are they going?"

"Humble apologies, sir. They are flying to Italy. They believe the sword will be found at the Vatican, in Saint Peter's Square."

A short pause came from the other end of the line. "Of course," Han-Jae snarled. "That has to be the place. The great sword of Peter must be hidden in his square. Were you able to get more details?"

"No, sir. They are in a pub, and there's some ambient noise making things difficult to hear. That was all I could pick up with my equipment."

He'd been using a listening device to hear the conversation between the Americans at the pub. His equipment, however, was outdated like much of the gear the Chairman bestowed on his spies. Su Pak often wondered how they could keep up with the rest of the world if they didn't have money to spend on better weapons and equipment.

"That's good enough," Han-Jae said. "We know where they are going and, more specifically, where to set our trap." He thought for a moment and then changed subjects. "Have you ordered the package I requested from the general?"

"Yes, sir. Understandably, he was hesitant to send it."

"Of course he was. I would be. Where is it now?"

"I took the liberty of having it sent to Rome. It will be there with an armed escort when you arrive. The general sent two of his best men to make sure it was well protected."

"Excellent. Send me the exact details on where to pick it up. I trust you will also send me a report on Saint Peter's Square with the best tactical information."

"Sending it right now, sir. You will find it in your email within moments."

"Perfect. Meet us at the airport in fifty minutes. You're coming with us to Italy."

Sun Pak hesitated. He hadn't anticipated that. "Yes, sir. I'll be ready."

Han-Jae ended the call and looked out the window.

Rain had been falling consistently for the last twenty minutes. The roads were soaked, and traffic was starting to pick up as they drew closer to London.

The driver, Shaved Head, looked over at him. "What did he say?"

Han-Jae continued staring out the window. They passed a tour bus on the right, full of people who had no idea about the war going on around them. He wondered if he'd overplayed his hand, asking that the package be brought in, but desperate times called for such measures. It was too late to go back on the decision now.

"We're going to Rome."

Chapter 28
Rome, Italy

Tommy stared up at the obelisk in the middle of Saint Peter's Square.

The monolith rose to over seventy-five feet, and while it wasn't the tallest of the Egyptian obelisks, it towered over the square and dominated the immediate view before the visitor's eye was drawn to the incredible dome just beyond.

Sean's eyes weren't locked on the obelisk. He was more concerned with the surrounding area. Saint Peter's Square was a security nightmare. Tens of thousands of tourists poured through there every day. It was wide open in the middle with plenty of places to hide behind the columns that ran four deep along the colonnade. He put the bridge of his hand against his forehead and turned in every direction, examining the faces as they passed by.

Most people were there to take pictures or there on pilgrimage to visit the place they considered holy. Occasionally he'd see children running around playing tag or throwing water on each other from the fountain. After reconnoitering the plaza for more than ten minutes, though, he didn't see a threat.

That didn't mean there wasn't one.

Sean and his friends were most vulnerable to sniper attack from one of the thousands of windows in the buildings surrounding the area. A sharpshooter could easily pick them off one at a time. A good one could take out all four in less than eight seconds. His eyes shifted, looking once more at random windows to see if there was a menacing silhouette.

From his vantage point, Sean knew it was a fruitless endeavor. They were going to have to risk being exposed to have a closer look at the obelisk. That didn't mean he wasn't going to keep his eyes open.

"Look okay to you?" Tommy asked as he turned his head toward Sean.

They'd been standing in the shade of the colonnade, waiting for the last few minutes as Sean checked out the situation.

"I don't like it," Sean said. "Too many variables. And you'll be exposed. Out there in the middle of the plaza, you're a sitting duck. If we're going to take a look at this thing, we need to make sure we make it as difficult as possible for someone to ambush us."

"You think they're here?" June asked.

"I think we'd be stupid to say it's not a possibility. They've somehow managed to track us down everywhere we've gone. No reason to think they won't figure out where we are now."

"But we swept everything. There weren't any bugs in our stuff," Tommy said.

Sean had done a thorough check of every item in their bags. There was no sign of any kind of tracking device, which meant if the North Koreans were following them, they had to be using a tail.

"Even so, we need to be careful." Sean didn't sound convinced that this was a good idea, but his friend was insistent. "We'll stay here and keep watch while you go out there. If you see anything suspicious, get back over here as fast as you can. We'll make easy targets if all four of us go out there together."

"Targets?" June said.

"In case there's a shooter in place."

She was taken back by the comment, the situation suddenly becoming very real.

Tommy put his hand on her shoulder. "Listen, you don't have to do this. We can go back to that little cafe we passed on the way here."

June appreciated his sentiment, but she steeled her nerves and shook her head. "No. Let's do this. Just be careful. I don't like the idea of you going out there alone."

He raised both eyebrows and held his hands out to the side. Tommy wasn't going to argue with her no matter how worried he was deep down. June had a strong personality.

"I appreciate your concern. But if there is a clue to the sword or how we get it out of the basilica, it might be on that obelisk. I know Egyptian hieroglyphics better than the rest of you. And my Latin is strong, too. If there is something about the sword written on the obelisk, I have the best chance of interpreting it."

June acknowledged his explanation with a nod. "Okay, fine. But hurry back."

"I will. If something happens," Tommy said, "don't come after me. Let Sean take care of it."

He didn't wait for her to say anything, instead turning immediately and heading out into the square.

He walked along one of the long white lines set into the cobblestone, a feature added later on in the history of Saint Peter's. The lines were designed as part of a large-scale sundial that worked in tandem with the obelisk's shadow.

Tommy turned his head from side to side, scanning the surroundings for any signs of trouble. Thousands of nameless faces milled around the plaza. Some were taking pictures by the fountain; others were staring up at the statues guarding the entrance to the giant dome of the basilica. Hundreds more people were lined up around the ticket office, waiting patiently to get their tickets to see the basilica.

Fortunately, Tommy and the others had gotten in line earlier that morning before most of the sightseers and pilgrims had arrived. He knew what the lines could be like to get into what was one of the holiest sites in all of Christianity.

The night before, the group decided they would show up early at the square, get their tickets, and then drop back into the shadows to watch for trouble. They'd waited for any sign of the Brotherhood or the North Koreans, but the men never showed, not that the Americans noticed anyway. Like Sean said, there were a million places to hide.

Tommy was halfway across the square when he noticed a sudden movement out of his right eye. His head twitched that direction, fearful one of the North Koreans was rushing at him. It was just a young boy running to meet an older couple. He was followed by a younger couple, probably in their mid-forties. The kid was just rushing to see his grandparents. At least that's what it looked like.

Tommy shook off the momentary surge of fear and kept walking, picking up the pace of his stride as he neared the base of the giant obelisk.

He and the others figured they needed to examine the altar in Saint Peter's Basilica since that was what the clue suggested—based on their interpretation. Tommy, however, had insisted they get a closer look at the obelisk, just in case they'd missed something.

The huge plinth was a massive marker in the series of clues that had led Tommy and his friends down a bizarre path in the pursuit of Excalibur. Just thinking about that sent a fresh pang of doubt through Tommy's mind.

We're looking for a sword that is mostly a thing of myth, he thought. But his parents believed in the sword. And they'd reached out to the Brotherhood about it. That brought new questions to his mind, mixing with some others that he'd been considering for the last day or so.

Why hadn't his parents contacted him? Why did they reach out to a bunch of guys they'd never met? They should have found a way to message him. He could have used his connections with the government to negotiate a way to get them out.

Then he reminded himself that the government would most likely not be of any help in negotiating with North Korea. Plus, according to what the Brotherhood said, it wasn't the Chairman who was responsible for Tommy's parents' imprisonment. The leader might not even be aware that they were still being held.

The whole situation was wildly improbable, but he had to try. If there was any chance that his parents were still alive—no matter how remote—he had to try to get them back.

He stopped under the shadow of the obelisk and looked up at the dark side of it, his eyes searching the ancient hieroglyphs for anything about the sword. Then he examined some of the Latin engraved on the base and lower area of the gigantic stone. *Nothing there.*

Tommy shifted his stance to the next side of the obelisk and repeated the process, occasionally taking his eyes off the ancient monolith to have a fast look around. Sean's words lingered in his mind. Tommy learned a long time ago that his friend's instincts were usually dead on. Those instincts had saved their necks on numerous occasions before. No reason to stop trusting them now.

He didn't notice anything out of the ordinary. He pored over the engravings, still finding nothing that seemed helpful.

Tommy repeated the process two more times, checking all four sides of the obelisk thoroughly before deciding the whole exercise was futile. If the monolith contained information on the sword, he didn't see it.

He'd wasted enough time. They needed to get inside of the basilica and examine the altar. That was what the last clue had said. He should have trusted it.

Tommy looked out across the square and then casually at his friends hiding in the shadows among the rows of columns off to the side. He ticked his head toward the entrance of the basilica, signaling that they should get moving.

He didn't wait for confirmation that they'd gotten the signal. Tommy knew Sean and the other two were watching his every movement with focused intensity.

He meandered slowly through the growing crowds and found his way to the steps of the basilica. On the left side—close to where he stopped at the base of the stairs—stood a giant statue of Saint Peter. Tommy cocked his head to one shoulder as he stared at the sculpture.

Peter, with a flowing cloak and robes, gripped a key tightly in his right hand. A scroll dangled from the left.

Tommy scratched his head and looked across the way at the other sculpture guarding the entrance to the basilica. It was the image of Saint Paul. From this distance, Tommy couldn't make out all the details, but one was impossible to miss. Paul was holding a long sword.

"Whatcha doing?" Sean asked as the other three arrived at the base of the steps.

Tommy shook his head, snapping back to the mission at hand. "Sorry. I was just looking at these statues. We should probably get inside." Sean's warning about shooters and easy targets kept banging on the walls of his brain.

"Saint Peter," Adriana said. "Holding the keys to the kingdom of heaven."

Tommy frowned, suddenly remembering the key he'd found in the man's pocket. He searched his jacket and found the key still there. He took it out and held it up, examining the similarities between it and the one in the sculpture's hand. They were a spot-on match.

"The key I took off that guy in the alley back in Cologne," he said. "It looks just like the one in Peter's hand."

The other three looked between the keys, running the same silent comparison.

"You don't think this has something to do with the sword, do you?" he asked.

"Only one way to find out, buddy," Sean said, taking a cautious look around the area. "Let's get inside where we aren't so exposed."

Saint Peter's Basilica was considered by many to be one of the most important locations in the Christian religion. It was the supposed location of Peter's grave, along with an extensive Roman necropolis from the pagan era. Since one interpretation of Jesus's words about building His church upon this rock is that the rock was Peter, Constantine decided he would literally build his church on top of Peter's tomb.

Inside, the four companions stopped and looked around at the incredible scenery surrounding them.

The tallest corridors and naves Sean had ever seen stretched out in multiple directions. The high arched ceilings all connected at the dome hovering over the altar and Saint Peter's Baldachin.

Sculptures of saints, popes, and apostles adorned the various nooks along the walls. Multicolored frescoes displayed scenes from parts of the *Bible*. Some sections of the archways overhead were gilded in gold leaf.

"I have never seen anything so opulent in my life," Sean said as he stared with wide eyes and a wider mouth at the incredible interior.

"And likely never will," Tommy added.

"Over there," Adriana said, pointing at the altar and elaborate canopy. "Let's move."

If she seemed less impressed by the scenery, it wasn't because she didn't appreciate it. It was because Adriana didn't get distracted by shiny objects. She was here to do a job and get it done as fast as possible. She didn't need to remind the others of the potential danger lurking outside, or even possibly inside, the basilica. The others followed her lead as she stalked past a cluster of tourists readying their headsets for the guided audio tour of the building.

Voices echoed through the great halls, though none of the conversations could really be heard since all the sounds mixed together to form a sort of ambient noise. Their shoes clicked on the shiny floors underfoot, floors made from multiple colors of marble and inlaid with various designs—some with oddly pagan origins.

"This place must be something to see during mass," June said as she looked around at the giant naves.

The basilica was designed to be a cross, like the one on which Jesus and Peter were crucified. Saint Peter's Baldachin and altar were located at the heart of the cross—the intersecting point of all the naves where the pope conducted traditional ceremonies. On such occasions, each of the adjoining halls was packed with chairs and filled with thousands of people.

For the time being, in spite of the tourists, the place was relatively empty.

They approached the altar and slowed their speed, taking in the enormous canopy and spiraled pillars surrounding it. Massive paintings hung from the four corners supporting the dramatic dome above the canopy. Alcoves with more sculptures of saints and patriarchs dotted the walls surrounding the baldachin.

"That thing is even bigger when you get up close," Tommy said. "It's unreal."

"Yeah," Sean agreed. "Pretty awesome. Now the question is, if the sword is here, how do we get to it?"

Tommy shook his head. "I have no idea. The clue just leaves us hanging. It says we'll find it at the altar of the sword bearer, but doesn't say exactly where."

Velvet ropes marked off the area so visitors would stay back. While the ropes themselves provided little security for the altar and tombs below, the Swiss

Guard watching over it from one of the corners were more than enough to keep people in line.

The Swiss Guard had originally been mercenaries, brought in to protect the pope in the early sixteenth century. They'd done the job ever since with the sole purpose of watching over the safety of the pontiff. The men were extensively trained and excellent marksmen, more than enough to make someone think twice about doing anything stupid inside the walls of Vatican City. While their Renaissance-style uniforms might not be imposing, the colors were highly visible and reminded visitors that they were always watching.

There was no way Sean and his companions would be able to get close enough. He also knew there were cameras everywhere, hidden out of plain view. He imagined some might even be tucked away inside some of the statues or perhaps the gilded molding in the corners.

"We need to get closer," Tommy said, leaning as far over the velvet ropes as he felt was permissible.

Two sets of candles sat atop the white marble altar along with a golden cross in the center. Other than that, there wasn't anything that suggested there might be a way to get inside the altar. From the visitors' vantage point, it appeared to be a solid piece of stone.

Adriana noticed one of the Swiss Guards was keeping a watchful eye on them.

"Well, I don't think we're going to get closer," she said to Tommy. "That guard is watching our every move. Probably because we're not with a tour group."

June's gaze drifted behind the altar to where another huge piece of art hung on the back wall behind the presbytery. It was hard to tell what she was looking at. Golden sculptures of cherubim, angels, and other figures hovered around an ornate chair that almost appeared to be floating in the center.

"What's that?" she asked.

The other three looked over at the beautiful display.

"Saint Peter's chair," a new voice said in an Italian accent.

The four turned to find a priest standing just a few yards away with his hands folded in front of his flowing robes.

"Oh," she said. "Thank you."

The man bowed his head a few inches. He had a kind face with a few wrinkles stretching out from his eyes and on his forehead. His hair was gray almost to the point of being white. The black spectacles on his face gave him the look of someone who'd spent their whole life in deep study.

"Always happy to help people get a better understanding of this place," he said as he approached. His footsteps were so light, it almost appeared as if he were levitating. "Speaking of help, is there anything else I can do to help? You look as if you have some questions."

The guy was astute. Sean imagined it came with the job. Maybe this priest could be useful.

“We are doing some research about Peter,” Sean said. “We’re wondering if there are any relics kept inside the altar.”

The priest’s forehead scrunched. “Now that is a question I’ve never had before. I don’t get many firsts anymore, not after being here for forty years. The answer is no. The altar is a solid piece of marble. So it would be impossible for it to be a reliquary. If you are interested in seeing relics, I could refer you to the right place, though.”

Tommy didn’t want to blow off the guy’s generosity, but they weren’t there for relics. They were there for the sword of Peter. According to the priest, the altar contained nothing, which completely invalidated what the last clue suggested.

Now they were in the dark with no idea where to go next.

Chapter 29
Vatican City

"May I ask what your interest is in the holy relics?" the priest said.

Sean and Tommy did their best to hide the excruciating disappointment. The priest's revelation had gutted them, removing nearly all hope of finding the sword and getting Tommy's parents back.

"We work for the International Archaeological Agency," Sean answered. "My friend here is the founder."

Tommy forced a fake smile onto his face and shook the priest's hand. "Tommy Schultz. These are my friends Sean, June, and Adriana."

"It's a pleasure to meet all of you. My name is Father Giovani Totti." He looked at Tommy with a peculiar expression. "The International Archaeological Agency? I believe I've heard of that before. Have you ever done work in Italy?"

Tommy didn't think the priest would approve of some of the details revolving around their work, so he gave a simple answer. "Yes, sir. We've worked on several projects in Italy."

"Anything I might have heard of?"

Tommy struggled to come up with an honest answer. He felt awkward lying to a priest. Fortunately, Sean stepped in.

"Just a few minor excavations here and there. Nothing that the media would have covered. We do work all over the world. Perhaps you heard about our discovery in Japan?"

The priest looked up at the ceiling for a moment and then shook his head. "No, I don't believe I heard about that."

"Well, it was pretty amazing," Sean said, discarding all modesty. "We found one of the greatest swords of all time. It went missing in the 1940s, stolen by Allied forces when Japan was disarmed."

"That sounds wonderful. Was it difficult to track down?"

"You could say that."

"Well, congratulations on your discovery. I'm sure the nation of Japan was thrilled to get back one of their most prized historical possessions."

Sean was about to bid the priest farewell when the old man spoke up again.

"You know, if you're interested in swords, I'm sure you noticed the Tadolini on the way in." He held out his hand, pointing the way back to the entrance.

"Tadolini?" Adriana asked. She knew the artist well. Tadolini had been contracted to create new sculptures in the nineteenth century. These new works of art would replace the ones made by Bernini, whose figures adorned the interior and exterior of the basilica for centuries.

"Yes," the priest said with a smile. "Just outside the steps are two large statues. One is Saint Peter, holding the keys to heaven. Opposite of him, on the other side of the steps, is Saint Paul, holding a great sword."

"I noticed that on the way in," Tommy said. "Would you mind telling us what the significance of that sword is?"

Father Totti smiled. "Of course. The statues by Tadolini replaced the ones that were there before. The originals were created by Paolo di Mariano and much smaller than the current sculptures. The sword in Paul's hand represents the weapon with which he was martyred."

"That's right. He was beheaded."

Totti crossed himself and then nodded. "Correct. When the sculpture was first created, the sword was coated in gold. Through the years, the gold plate has worn off. There's no trace of it anymore, unfortunately.

"Saint Paul also has a book in his hand. It is inscribed with Philippians 4:13."

"I can do all things through God who strengthens me," Sean said.

Totti's face brightened. His eyes narrowed as his lips stretched into a broad smile.

"Very good, Sean. Are you a student of the scriptures?"

"I've done a bit of studying, yes."

"Wonderful," Totti said. "It's rare to find laypeople these days with a good knowledge of the scriptures."

Sean blushed. "Well, my parents had a big hand in that. I used to memorize *Bible* verses when I was a kid. They even made me get up in front of church once to recite a really long one. Looking back, it was a traumatic moment since I was terrified of being in front of a lot of people. I think it was a good experience, though."

"I'm sorry to interrupt," Tommy said. "But would you mind showing us this statue?"

At first, the priest seemed puzzled by the request. "Well, I don't normally go outside during visiting hours, but I don't see what it could hurt. Come. Follow me."

The priest held out his hand and led the way back through the basilica to the front entrance. More people had gathered just inside the giant entryway, eager to get a peek at the magnificent interior.

Totti nodded at one of the security guards as he stepped through the doorway and out onto the landing. He paused for a moment to allow the four visitors to catch up before he continued down the center of the steps. At the bottom, he turned left on the cobblestone and made his way through a collection of tourists busily taking pictures in front of the basilica. He reached the large base of the sculpture, stopped, and turned around.

"You can see that because of its size, this sculpture and the one of Peter across the way were not placed inside the basilica." He pointed at Peter on the other side of the steps.

The four Americans looked up at the imposing statue.

The apostle Paul held a sword in one hand that was nearly three yards long. Just as the priest described, he had a book in the other hand with Philippians 4:13 written on the surface.

The huge base featured the papal coat of arms. Just above it, wrapping around the base just below Saint Paul's feet, was something written in Latin.

Adriana read the inscription out loud. "The Pontiff ordered the images themselves here, in a suitable place, equal to the size of the temple of Peter, prince of the Apostles. In the year 1847, the first of his pontificate, while he was curator of the Vatican Works, Lorenzo Lucidi."

"Very good," Totti said, clearly impressed with her abilities. "Most people don't read Latin."

"When you do the kind of work we do, it's kind of a necessity."

"Ah. Well, I hope that I've been of service to you. I should probably get back inside in case anyone else has a question."

The priest lingered for a moment. He was about to turn around and head back up the stairs when Sean had a thought that was needling his mind.

"I'm sorry, Father. Could I ask you one more question?"

"Certainly."

Tommy and the others didn't know where he was going with this.

"When we were inside, you said that these statues replaced the ones created by Paolo di Mariano."

"That is correct," the priest said with a nod. "You really do have a good memory, don't you?"

"Don't get me started," Tommy said.

"Anyway," Sean went on, ignoring his friend's jab, "I'm wondering, did they replace both statues?"

"Yes," the priest answers. "Both of these are nineteenth-century reproductions that are similar to the previous ones. They are much larger than the older versions."

"So, what happened to the old statues?"

Totti cocked his head to the side. He had a beleaguered grin on his face. "You know, that's a good question. Once more, you have presented me with a question no one has ever asked me before."

"So you don't know?" Tommy asked.

"Actually, as it would happen, I do. The originals were removed from Saint Peter's Square and placed in the Vatican Library."

"Oh," Sean said in a disappointed tone.

"If that is all, I'll leave you to your tour. Don't worry about the guard inside. I'll tell him to let you four back in with your tickets."

"Thank you," Sean said.

The other three threw in their thanks and watched as the old man slowly ascended the steps.

"Well, that was a huge waste of time," Tommy said when the priest was out of earshot. "The altar is a solid piece of stone, and there's nothing about this statue that suggests where the sword might be."

"It's not even the right apostle," Adriana added.

"I don't understand," June said. "Were you thinking this sculpture might contain the sword? I thought it was in the altar or maybe underneath it."

"Underneath the altar is the catacombs," Tommy said. "We could get down there, but it might take days or weeks to get into one of those groups. They only allow a limited number of people each day since space is at a premium down there. And even if we could get down there, I'm not so sure we'd find anything."

"He's right," Adriana said. "They've done many excavations under the basilica through the years. If the sword was there, they probably would have found it."

June processed what they were saying. "So that's why you wanted to take a closer look at this statue," she said.

Tommy nodded. "I figured it was a shot in the dark, but a shot nonetheless. It's a statue of an apostle holding a long sword. It looks out on Saint Peter's Square where the obelisk is. I hoped there might be a connection."

Sean stared up at the massive figure. "I don't think you were that far off, Schultzie."

Tommy turned and followed Sean's gaze. "What do you mean?"

"Well, for starters, that sword looks eerily similar to renderings I've seen of Excalibur."

"There are millions of those kinds of renderings," Tommy said. "Some look the same. Others look different."

"Yes, but this isn't the kind of weapon that was used by the Romans at the time of Peter or Paul."

"The priest said the sculpture was done in the nineteenth century," June argued. "It's probably in the style of weapons made during that era."

Sean shook his head. “Nope. Swords made during that time were thinner, lighter. Sabers, rapiers, and swords like that were in fashion. Of course, they were weapons from a dying age since firearms were making bladed weapons obsolete.”

“You’re right,” Tommy said. “But that still looks more like a medieval sword rather than one from ancient Rome or before. Remember, we’re looking for a sword that was made before the time of Christ.”

The discussion dropped off for a minute as each person considered every point.

“Excalibur wasn’t only a sword of mystical power,” Adriana said. “It was an innovation, something that no one else had at the time. A sword such as this, in an era with much smaller weapons, would have been seen as something fit only for a king. It would have been an intimidating sight to behold, a king riding toward an army with a blade longer than anything they’d ever seen before.”

Her point lingered for a moment before Tommy commented. “So you’re saying that Excalibur was just as much a means of psychological warfare as it was an actual weapon?”

“Precisely.”

“Not that it matters,” June said. “We don’t have any more leads. It’s a shame we can’t get in to the Vatican Library to have a look at the original sculpture. I guess we’ll never know if it held the sword.”

Tommy wasn’t about to let go of all hope yet. His parents’ lives depended on him finding Excalibur.

He'd wrestled his emotions for the last few days after learning they were still alive. All the pain, the lonely holidays as a young man, the memories he never got to experience with them gone, all kept trying to pry their way back into his mind. He pushed them away again as he spoke.

"The priest said that the original sculptures were taken into the Vatican Library. We can't gain access to the archives. Very few people are allowed down there. The library, however, is open to those who can get permission."

Sean frowned. "Yeah, except we don't have permission. And I'm sure that to get that kind of clearance we would have to submit an application, go through some sort of vetting process, and then finally be issued a permit, all of which could take months. We don't have that kind of time." He looked around the square. His last comment reminded him of the two potential threats lurking around the corners or hiding in the shadows.

"No," Tommy shook his head. "I mean, yes, you are correct. There is a process in place for all that. However, I'm wondering if we didn't just meet someone who could expedite the process for us?"

The other three followed Tommy's gaze up the stairs where the priest had stopped to speak to two children who were there with their parents. He was smiling pleasantly, as he had been through the entire duration of the conversation with the four Americans.

"Totti?" June asked. "You think he could help us get in there?"

"It's worth a shot," Sean said. "Never hurts to ask."

"Yeah," Tommy said. "Let's just hope he gives us the answer we want."

They hurried back up the steps and waited until the priest was finished speaking with the other visitors. He didn't notice them immediately and started to head back into the building when Tommy's voice halted him.

"Father Totti!" Tommy shouted a little louder than intended. "Father Totti, wait!"

The priest turned around. His seemingly permanent smile twisted slightly to a look of curiosity.

"Yes?"

"I'm so sorry, sir," Tommy said, panting for breath after the short run up the stairs. "I have a very strange, and pretty unorthodox, request."

"Oh?" Totti said. "What is it?"

"We were wondering if you could arrange access to the Vatican Library for us."

He might as well have asked the priest if he was wearing boxers or briefs. The surprised look on the older man's face told the Americans exactly how much they were asking.

"I'm sorry," Totti said. "There is a system in place for that sort of thing. You'll need to get your credentials checked. Then they will examine why you want access. They'll also want to check references and your records concerning your level of expertise in regards to history and that sort of thing."

Tommy and Sean turned their heads toward each other and then back to the priest. “Would a reference from the president of the United States help?”

Chapter 30
Vatican City

Totti led the group through a long, wide corridor with a high arched ceiling. The surface overhead was painted with magnificently bright colors that featured the Papal seal in several locations, as well as murals from biblical stories and symbols none of the visitors recognized.

They turned from the first hallway into another that opened up into the library. More elaborately painted arched ceilings soared overhead as the group walked down the aisle between shelves packed with thousands of books. To the right, empty tables were lined along the wall underneath high windows. The bright early afternoon sun poured light into the library, making the need for artificial light nearly unnecessary.

"You have very influential friends," the priest said as he turned into a corridor on the left. "Were I a more curious person, I'd be inclined to ask how it is you have a direct line to the president of the United States."

"Let's just say we've done him a few favors in the past," Sean said.

Totti wasn't sure what that meant, and from the looks of it he didn't care to know.

Sean's line to the president wasn't exactly direct, as the priest insinuated. The connection to Emily was, which is who Sean called to get to the president. Fortunately, the commander in chief wasn't in a meeting. He was actually playing golf when Sean called.

The two joked about the president's handicap and chatted about playing a round together at some point. When the pleasantries were over, Sean asked President Dawkins for the favor.

While John Dawkins wasn't Catholic, that didn't mean he was completely powerless when it came to persuading the Vatican. He and the pope had been on good terms during the extent of his presidency.

As soon as the phone conversation was over, an email was sent from the desk of the president asking that his friends be allowed access to the library. The message also included a few additional items such as Tommy's expertise, experience, and some of the successful campaigns he'd engineered. The president was only aware of a few projects the IAA had carried out, but the ones he'd had his secretary list were pretty high-profile ones.

The men in charge of giving access to the library were impressed, to say the least.

Totti was given the responsibility of showing them around and making sure they left at the end of the day. Tommy and Sean assured the priest that they would only need a few minutes.

They made their way into another open room where there were fewer books and more pieces of art.

Exquisite paintings lined the walls. While art wasn't specifically Tommy and Sean's area of expertise, they knew Adriana would appreciate it.

She stared in wide-eyed awe as they strolled by the masterpieces, each one more impressive than the last.

Ancient vases from all over the world stood in the center of the room, protected by velvet ropes and glass.

"This area is more like a museum," Totti said before the visitors could ask. "We have artwork from some of the greatest masters of all time stored in these rooms."

"It's impressive," June said. "I never knew a place like this existed."

Adriana did, but she said nothing. Her background in hunting down lost or stolen art from World War II had led her to a crazy theory that suggested some of the art had been salvaged by the pope and brought here to the Vatican.

She'd run out of leads that could connect the location to any of the art, and so she dropped the idea. Having seen some of the pieces in the Vatican's possession firsthand, she wasn't so sure it was a crazy notion after all.

Adriana's idea didn't suggest that the pope or anyone else at the Vatican had stolen the priceless pieces of art. She simply thought they'd been taken there for safekeeping, possibly stored in the archives or a secret chamber somewhere underground.

While her focus was primarily on paintings, one particular treasure had always tugged at her curiosity. The Amber Room. It was such a huge work of art that hiding it would take incredible resources and ingenuity.

The Vatican had both. Her theory was that agents of the Vatican saved the amber panels and brought them here to keep them safe from a world full of greed. She'd run out of proof, though, and dropped the idea.

Walking through the maze of sculptures and paintings made her wonder if she'd given up the pursuit a little too soon.

"Over here is where you'll find the original sculpture," Totti said. His voice echoed off the walls and hard floor.

He turned at the end of the hall and pointed down a short corridor with a dead end. "In there, you'll find an alcove that displays the sculpture of Paul. Feel free to take your time. I'll be back to get you before we close for the day, unless of course you leave before then."

"Thank you so much, sir," Sean said. "Really, I am very sorry if we've been an inconvenience."

"Not at all," Totti smiled. "I'm happy to help anyone who is interested in learning more about our history. If you have any questions, I'll be in the main section of the library."

"Thank you," Tommy said.

They waited until the priest disappeared back into the art room. Once he was gone, they moved forward with a quiet apprehension that was half nerves, half reverence.

"Do you have any idea how valuable all this is?" Tommy asked in a whisper.

"A lot," Sean said.

"That doesn't even come close to what it's all worth. Some of those pieces we just passed are each worth millions. I bet there are some thieves who'd kill to get into this place."

As they drew closer to the alcove where Totti said the sculpture rested, they slowed their pace until the front of the statue came into view.

Just as Totti suggested, the sculpture looked almost exactly like the one in Saint Peter's Square. While the one on display to the public was bigger in every way, this one was no tiny piece.

Saint Paul towered over the room, looking out at several other vases and works of art scattered through the area, protected by glass cases.

They stopped in front of the huge sculpture and stared up for nearly a minute before anyone said anything.

"So what are we looking for?" Sean asked.

Tommy held up the key he'd put back in his pocket earlier. "Look for a keyhole."

Similar images to the ones on the outside statue adorned the sides of the base. The same papal emblem that seemed to be everywhere was on the front and sides.

"A keyhole?" June asked.

"I don't know why," Tommy said. "Just call it a gut feeling. But I think this key I found in that guy's pocket has some connection to the location of the sword."

He stood close to the statue and leaned in as far as he could without touching it. A velvet rope blocked visitors from entering the alcove, but that didn't keep Tommy from sticking his head over it.

The four scanned every inch of the sculpted stone for several minutes without any luck. They switched places and went over every curve and crevice in detail. Still nothing.

Sean twisted his head around and looked back into the main display area. Cameras pointed down from the corners in the room. Their angles suggested the lenses focused more on the things protected in glass cases. That made sense considering there was almost no way a potential thief could steal the massive sculpture in the alcove.

He returned his attention to the cavity and examined the archway. It had no sensors or security system that he could see. If the big statue was sitting on a pressure pad of some kind, that wouldn't affect him going in and having a look at the back. At least Sean hoped it wouldn't.

"Hey, guys," he said. "Do me a favor. The three of you stand side by side right here with your legs close together."

Tommy looked at him like he was crazy. "What?"

"Just do it," Sean said. "You stand next to the corner of this archway here. June, you stand next to him, then Adriana. I'm going to make it look like I'm taking picture with my phone."

"Okay…" June said.

Adriana caught on to his scheme. "Ah. You want us to block the cameras' view so you can sneak in there and get a closer look."

Then the other two realized his plan.

"You sure they don't have some other kind of security measures here for that?" Tommy asked, his voice full of doubt.

"Not that I can tell. Of course, there might be some kind of new thing in here I've never heard of before. I'm a little rusty since I haven't been in the spy game for a while."

"Rusty?" Tommy gasped. "That's not what I want to hear when you're about to trespass in the Vatican Library."

"Relax, Schultzie. It'll be fine. If I set off an alarm, we'll just tell our friend Father Totti that I fell over the rope by accident."

"Oh, so now we're lying to a priest?"

"Would you prefer it if I actually fell over the rope?"

"A little."

June glanced at Adriana. "Seriously, are they always like this?"

Adriana nodded. "You get used to it after a while."

Tommy and the two women pressed together. June picked up his arm and put it around her waist to further the impression that they were getting a picture taken.

No one bothered to question whether that was allowed or not, though all four had the impression it wasn't.

Having his arm around her waist sent chills up the back of Tommy's neck, but he didn't let on. Instead, he stayed focused on his friend who cautiously slid under the velvet rope.

Everyone held their breath until Sean was safely on the other side. When no alarms sounded, they all exhaled and watched as Sean slipped around the left side of the statue base and shimmied his way between it and the wall.

The space was narrow, pretty much ruling Tommy out of the task. And Sean wasn't about to ask one of the women to do it. If they got arrested, he would take full responsibility and tell the authorities his friends had nothing to do with it.

He moved sideways to the back of the wall and then shuffled behind the sculpture, disappearing from view.

"See anything back there?" Tommy hissed.

"Not yet. I just got here. Gimme a second."

Footsteps echoed through the museum. Everyone froze, too afraid to turn around and look.

"Sean," Adriana whispered. "Stay back there. Someone's coming."

He didn't respond.

The other three did their best to look casual, as if they were just normal tourists admiring an impressive work of art.

A priest suddenly appeared in the doorway. He wore a black suit with the white collar as is common for many men of the cloth. This priest was much younger than Father Totti, with thick black hair atop a tanned youthful face. The pleasant smile was there, though. And he nodded politely at the three visitors as he passed by and hung a right down the next aisle. He turned at the next corner and disappeared. A minute later, the sound of his shiny black shoes clicking on the marble floor faded.

"Hurry up back there," Tommy said. "That was a close one."

"No need to hurry," Sean said. "I found it."

"You what?"

"I found the keyhole."

Sean reappeared around the corner of the statue base and shuffled back toward the front. When he was close enough, he reached out his hand with the palm up.

"Quick, give me the key."

Tommy felt through his pockets and found the little skeleton key. He gripped it tight as he carefully stretched his hand out and pressed it into Sean's palm.

"Don't drop it," Tommy said.

"Thanks, Captain Obvious."

Sean shimmied his feet toward the rear of the alcove and worked his way back around the corner.

Tommy started to hunch over, but June tapped him on the shoulder. "Don't look like you're trying to keep a lookout," she said.

That's exactly what he was trying to do. If the previous priest or another priest/librarian came through and found them still standing at the statue, they might think something suspicious was going on.

"Look casual," June said in response to Tommy's questioning expression.

He tried to loosen up his posture, shoved his hands in his pockets, and even started to lean on the wall.

"Don't overdo it," she said.

"I don't understand what I'm doing wrong here," he said.

"Just try to look natural."

He adjusted his stance again. As he was about to ask if it was better, they heard something click behind the sculpture. The sound of stone grinding on stone came next, followed by a quiet metal clink.

Tommy fought the urge to ask what Sean had found and continued trying not to look like a thief.

A minute later, Sean reappeared from behind the statue and shuffled quickly back to the front of the alcove. The other three got back in their positions to hide Sean from camera view, not that they were sure it would matter now.

If they were in sight and someone was watching the monitor on the other end of the camera, they'd have noticed Sean's disappearance and then awkward reappearance a few minutes later.

"What is it?" Tommy said through a ridiculous toothy grin.

"I'll show you when we get out of here."

Tommy couldn't contain his excitement, or his heightened curiosity. "Did you look at it? What did you do with it?"

Sean didn't answer immediately. He was more concerned with getting out of there.

"In my pants," he said as he walked swiftly back toward the next exhibition room.

The other three had to walk fast to keep up.

"Wait. I'm sorry. It sounded like you said it was in your pants."

"That *is* what he said," June said.

Adriana rolled her eyes and snorted a short laugh.

Tommy was incensed. "You put a potentially priceless historical item—that we need, by the way—down your pants?"

"Don't worry. I already looked at what's on it," Sean said.

They reached the next archway and passed through it.

Sean slowed his pace, nearly causing the others to bump into him. He held out a hand to halt their movement.

"What?" Tommy asked.

Sean put an index finger to his lips, signaling his friend to be quiet.

"I heard something," he whispered.

He tiptoed the final few yards to the end of the corridor until he reached the main hall of the library. Voices carried through the gigantic chamber and almost seemed amplified by the acoustics of the room. *That's a silly mistake to make in a library*, he thought. *You'd think they'd want to make it quieter*.

Sean leaned around a pillar and looked back toward the library's entrance. He pulled back immediately.

The others saw the look of concern on his face.

"What is it?" Adriana mouthed.

Sean drew in a short breath and sighed. "The Brotherhood."

Somehow they'd tracked the Americans to the Vatican. Baldwin was talking to Father Totti, who'd pointed in Sean's direction. He'd not been seen, not yet anyway, but now the exit was blocked.

They were going to have to find another way out.

Chapter 31
Vatican City

Sean hurried back to the other end of the hall adjacent to the main library. When he and the others made it to the next intersection, instead of turning right and returning to the statue, they made a left. Sean's logic was that the entrance was that way.

They saw a door at the other end, but it didn't look like one that led outside or back into the main section of the Vatican.

Tommy knew better than to ask where they were going. If his friend had a plan, it was best to simply trust it.

When they neared the door, a sign to the right of it showed a drawing of a set of stairs.

Sean turned the latch as quietly as he could and pushed the door open. "Quick," he said. "Up the stairs."

"Up?" June asked.

"Yes. Up."

"But shouldn't we—"

"He's got a plan," Tommy said, ushering her into the stairwell. After she and Adriana were through the doorway, he looked at Sean. "You *do* have a plan, right?"

"It's fluid," Sean said. "Come on."

Tommy eased the door shut and followed the other three as they flew up the flight of stairs, taking them two at a time. Sean stopped at the next level and carefully opened the door. He peeked out through the opening. The floor was vacant save for the high shelves stacked with thousands of books. Study tables were spaced between the shelves for anyone needing a quiet place to do research.

"Okay, now what?" Tommy asked.

"Follow me," Sean said in a barely audible tone. "And stay low." He pointed to a short wall to the right that acted as a protective railing.

Sean took off, keeping his knees bent to stay crouched as he moved across the floor. When he was around the first row of shelves, he turned left into the aisle. Once he was clear from a downstairs view, he stood up straight and waited for the others.

They copied his movement and joined him at the other end of the row. When they'd caught up, he waved his hand for them to follow again.

Sean moved fast, careful to make sure his shoes didn't make much noise on the floor. He even kept his legs apart to silence the swooshing of his pants. The entire time, he kept his eyes locked on the far end of the back row, anticipating that Baldwin or one of his men would suddenly appear, effectively hemming them in.

No one appeared, though, and when Sean reached the other end, he allowed himself to feel a moment of relief. Another door was just around the corner, opposite the one they'd come through a moment before.

He waited for the others, and when they'd caught up he motioned for them to stay low again. His eyes shot up to the ceiling and found a camera observing the room. If they hadn't been spotted before, they certainly were as they crossed the second floor. The only thing that gave Sean any sort of comfort was that he and the others had permission to be here. If Baldwin hadn't warned Totti of why the Americans were there, they might still have a chance to get out.

Sean crouched down again and made his way to the door on the left. As he turned the latch, he could almost sense the alarms about to start blaring. *No going back now*. He pulled down on the handle and eased the door open. Nothing happened except for a burst of new air coming through the crack.

He pushed it open all the way and stepped through, holding it on the other side until his friends were all clear. Just as cautiously as he'd opened it, Sean closed the door with no sound, not even a click.

They were standing in another exhibit room. This one featured various artifacts from ancient Egypt, including spears, shields, and even a chariot.

"Now what?" Tommy asked in a whisper. "Shouldn't we be going out the exit?"

Sean shook his head. "No. Baldwin will have men out there. We have to go out another way."

"What other way?"

"This connects to the papal apartments in the palace. We're going out that way."

"What?" Tommy hissed. "We can't go through the pope's house. Are you insane?"

"Probably."

"What?!"

"I'm kidding, buddy. Remember. I studied psychology. I'd know if I was crazy. Come on. We have to keep moving."

Sean didn't wait for a retort. He started toward a set of double doors on the far side of the room.

"No. Sean, wait." Tommy said in a vain effort to stop his friend.

Adriana nudged him. "The papal apartments have tours, too, Tommy. Pretty sure we're not going to try to break into the pope's private quarters."

"Oh," Tommy said. "Right. Okay."

"Well, not yet anyway. But who knows, right?"

She shot him a wink and then hurried after Sean.

Tommy was left bewildered for a moment and then at June's urging hurried after them.

At the set of doors, Sean hesitated for a second before he tested the latch. Luckily it gave way.

"You're sure the public part of the palace is through these doors?" Tommy whispered.

Sean looked at his friend like his head was on fire. "No. But we could always go back the way we came, you know, where we know Baldwin and his men are waiting for us."

Tommy sighed. “Point taken.”

Sean pulled the handle down and pushed the door open. A new burst of cool air rushed in through the opening along with a new scent that smelled like a mixture of lavender and jasmine.

On the other side was a hallway, much smaller than the ones in the library but still larger than an average home. Sean could see paintings lining the far wall from one end to the other, each one featuring a likeness of a pope from the past. The corridor was well lit by sconces every ten feet or so and a collection of chandeliers that hung intermittently from the ceiling. Off to the right, Sean noticed a group of people walking the other direction.

“Quick,” he said to the others. “There’s a tour group to the right. Let’s join them.”

No one argued.

Sean held the door while the other three rushed out and into the adjacent hall. When they were through, he gave one last look into the library before joining his friends.

They walked at a brisk pace down the corridor, barely catching up to the tour group before they passed through into another section of the palace. Sean eased his way into the mass of people who were listening eagerly to what the tour guide was saying. He found himself standing next to a large woman with short blonde hair and huge earrings dangling from her lobes. The others mixed in with the group, too, doing their best to look like they’d been there the whole time.

The tour continued through one more section of the papal apartments before making its way down a set of opulent marble stairs to the exit. The rest of the journey only took five to ten minutes, but to the four companions, it felt like an hour.

They knew that any second the Brotherhood—or worse, the Swiss Guard—could descend on them like a pack of angry wolves.

The ambush never came.

Back in the fresh air of Saint Peter's Square, Sean kept moving, hurrying down the stairs and into the plaza. His friends stayed close behind, none willing to linger longer than necessary. Every second they spent on Vatican property was a second they could be arrested.

"Need to get back to the car," Sean said as they jogged around a mob of schoolchildren waiting for their teacher to finish giving them instructions.

The group reached the relative safety of the colonnade and ducked in behind one of the columns on the first row. Sean peeked around the big pillar and stared back at the entrance to the basilica. There was no sign of trouble, at least not that he could tell. He was savvy enough to know that sometimes those signs weren't always obvious.

Every bit of paranoia his subconscious could muster rushed to his mind.

He had to push it away and focus on getting everyone out without getting caught.

"Keep going," Sean said. "I don't see anyone coming after us, but once we're off of Vatican property we should be okay."

"From the Vatican's security, sure, but what about the Brotherhood?" Tommy asked.

"No sign of them. We'll deal with that when the time comes."

"What about the North Koreans?" Adriana asked. "You know they could be skulking around here somewhere."

"Yeah, I know. Which is all the more reason for us to stay on the move. Tommy, take the lead, and head back to the car. I'll watch our backs."

Tommy nodded. "You still have the thing you found back there?"

"Yeah." Sean pulled the rolled-up vellum out of his belt and showed it to the others.

"Um, please tell me you're wearing underwear today?"

"That's private, and I'll thank you for staying out of my personal affairs."

"Seriously, man. You're—"

"Yes, Tommy. I am. Boxers, if you really want the details. Now if you don't mind, I'd like to get out of here so we don't run into any more problems."

"That sounds like a good idea," a voice said from behind one of the columns.

The Americans spun around and saw the North Korean leader standing in the shadows with a pistol pointed at them. None of the four were armed, having left their weapons in the trunk of the car before heading to Saint Peter's Square. They knew there was no point in taking guns since there was no way to get them into the basilica. Security was tight.

They checked for guns, knives, bombs, pretty much everything before letting tourists inside.

Now that fact played to the advantage of the North Koreans.

June spun around to see if there was anyone behind her. Shaved Head appeared like a ghost from behind one of the columns in the second row. Buzz-Cut stepped into view to her right. They all had weapons leveled and ready to fire.

The companions huddled together like frightened prey surrounded by a pride of lions.

"I don't suppose you have any ideas on how to get out of this one?" Tommy said in a hushed tone.

"Sorry, buddy," Sean replied. "I'm fresh out at the moment. We really need to work on getting some gadgets for situations like this."

"Silence," Han-Jae ordered. "You have caused enough trouble for me. Now you are going to do things my way. Give me what you found inside the basilica."

"What are you talking about?" Sean asked. "We didn't find anything in the basilica."

"Liar!" Han-Jae said, full of indignation. "We know you went in there looking for something. You wouldn't have left without finding it."

"Well, you're wrong," Tommy said. "There was nothing in the basilica we found to be of any help. We thought the sword was there, but it wasn't."

"Do you think I believe you, American dog?"

"Dog? Well, thank you. Dogs are very loyal and extremely intelligent animals. Unless you were trying to be offensive. In which case, I might recommend you use something like a cat."

"Cat?" Sean said, pretending to be offended. "I love cats. Cats have it figured out, man. They just sit around all day waiting for people to love and feed them."

"Shut up!" Han-Jae said, boiling over. "Where is the sword?" The gun shook in his hand as he nearly shouted.

Sean and Tommy glanced at each other and then shrugged.

"Seriously, does it look like we have the sword? I mean, it would be difficult to hide something like that in our pants."

Sean's answer didn't impress the North Korean leader.

Han-Jae forced himself to calm down. "Yes, pants. I overheard you saying you had something in your pants."

Sean raised a wary eyebrow. "Tommy, did he just say he wants to see what's in my pants?" He turned to Han-Jae. "Sorry, man. I'm spoken for."

Han-Jae ignored the comment. "Give me whatever it was you were hiding, or I will kill you all right here."

"I don't think so," Sean said. "Too many witnesses, even with those suppressors on your guns. It will be way too loud. So unless you've got some other plan for killing us, it ain't gonna happen here."

"You know, Sean, you're right. I'm not going to kill you here. We're going to take you somewhere else, to a place we have someone I think both you and your friend would like to see. Perhaps if we tortured them a bit, you might change your tune."

Tommy's and Sean's hearts dropped into their stomachs.

"If you do anything to Joe and Helen," Sean said, clenching his jaw.

"Joe and Helen?" Han-Jae laughed. "No. We don't have anyone by those names."

The feeling worsened in Tommy's gut. His face drained of all color, and he turned a ghastly pale.

"That's right, Tommy. We have your parents, here, in Rome. If you want to see them alive, your friend will give me what he found in the basilica. Or you can do this the hard way, and I can let you watch as the man I have guarding them cuts off their fingers and toes, eventually working his way up to their eyes, ears, nose, tongue...he can make dying a very long and painful process."

Tommy raged inside, but what could he do? They were surrounded.

Sean knew he was out of options. If he didn't cooperate, bad things were going to happen to people he cared about. And now the leader of the North Koreans was playing the ace up his sleeve.

"Okay," Sean said, putting up one hand. He held out the rolled piece of vellum with the other. "Take it easy. Here's the scroll. Just don't hurt anyone."

Han-Jae flashed a devilish, toothy grin. "I thought you might come around." He motioned with a flick of his head for Shaved Head to grab the scroll.

The henchman did so with caution, as if he was taking a piece of meat from the mouth of a crocodile. As soon as he snatched it from Sean's grip, he stepped back, wary that the American might try something.

Han-Jae reached out his hand and waited until his assistant had placed it in his palm.

"What does it say?" he asked.

"We don't know," Tommy said. "We haven't had a chance to look at it yet. We were trying to get out as fast as we could."

"Ah. Very well. We'll all know soon enough, won't we?"

Han-Jae carelessly shoved the scroll into a jacket pocket and waved his weapon at the four companions. "Now get moving. It's time for a little family reunion."

Chapter 32
Rome

The drive to the outskirts of Rome took more than a half hour. Traffic seemed ever-present in the ancient city, and the laws of the road were more like guidelines.

Mopeds and motorcycles zipped in and out of lanes, weaving between slower vehicles in a dangerous dance of speed and guts.

The four captives had been thrown into the back of a conversion van—probably a rental. Guns were kept trained on them at all times in case they considered jumping out the back door. That idea wouldn't have been prudent considering a violent death by car tire probably awaited anyone foolhardy enough to try it. So everyone sat as still as possible, contemplating how they were going to get away.

The van pulled off the main road and into an industrial area much like the one the companions had seen in Cologne, although the buildings were sparse, unlike in the German town.

Sean craned his neck to see out the windshield. A tanned brick building covered in ivy was just ahead. It was surrounded by a chain-link fence with a warped gate bent just enough for the van to get through. A tall smokestack stood off to the side of what appeared to be the main building.

"At least they didn't cover our heads," Tommy said. He'd been silent during the entire drive out of the city.

"That's a bad thing, buddy," Sean said. "When they don't care if you see where they're taking you, it means you're not getting out alive."

June's eyes welled, and she wiped her nose.

"Oh, it's okay," Tommy said. "He didn't mean it." He turned to Sean with an angry look on his face. "Did you?"

"No," Sean said in an unconvincing tone. "I was just joking around. It's going to be fine. We'll be okay."

Tommy put his arm around June to console her.

Sean and Adriana exchanged glances. Neither of them actually thought they were going to die, but they didn't know how they were going to get out, either.

The van bumped along the gravel road, jostling the occupants sitting on the floor in the back. The driver slowed when he neared the gate and carefully navigated the vehicle around the damaged blockade. He drove around the brick building to the side where a metal door hung open. A rusty padlock hung from a latch near the doorknob.

When the driver brought the van to a stop, Han-Jae turned around and faced the passengers with a menacing gaze.

"We're here."

The back door flung open, and the Americans were herded out, through the door of the foundry, and into a huge space where old machinery sat silent, rusting for the better part of some decades. The ceiling was at least fifty feet high at its zenith. In some spots, the roof had rotted away or collapsed, letting in sunlight that shone down as bright spots on the concrete floor.

Sean took inventory of the area. "Reminds me of that factory in—"

"Quiet," Shaved Head ordered, jamming the muzzle of his gun into Sean's back. "Keep moving."

Sean didn't think pressing the man's patience was a good idea, so he hushed for the moment.

They were ushered through the cavernous factory space and down an old set of stairs into the smelting areas below. An old light hanging in the stairwell allowed them to see where they were going, albeit barely. Tommy nearly slipped on one of the steps but caught his balance on the railing. He was lucky they hadn't bound their wrists, otherwise he would have tumbled painfully down the steps to the bottom.

Once they were in the basement, the group turned left into a four-hundred-square-foot room with a few naked lights burning in the ceiling. The power would have been off for years, which meant the North Koreans had circumvented the problem, possibly with a generator somewhere.

They found a man standing in the middle of the room, holding a gun aimed at two other figures sitting on the floor with their backs pressed against the wall.

Han-Jae walked over to the man and said something to him in their native tongue. Sean and the other prisoners didn't understand what he said, but by the man's body language and his sudden disappearance up the stairs it was a good assumption that the guy was being sent up to guard the entrance.

Buzz-Cut shoved Tommy in the back, and he stumbled toward the couple in the shadows against the wall.

"Time for you three to get reacquainted," Han-Jae said.

He pushed Sean in the back and then corralled June and Adriana into the corner near the others.

Tommy stopped a few feet short of the older couple. The woman had gray hair that fell down past her shoulders. In spite of her age, she had a natural beauty that would have been the envy of any woman. Her eyes were kind but tired.

The man had a head of gray hair as well, and a worn, wrinkled face. He still had a strong jaw and a rugged handsomeness like a lumberjack. The gray beard on his face helped complete that imagery.

Their clothes were worn down and old, probably given to them by the general years ago.

They both looked up as Tommy stood over them.

Up until that point, he still hadn't really believed his parents were alive. It was impossible. For so long he'd accepted the fact that they were gone, taken tragically before their time.

Now there was no denying it as he stared into the faces he'd not seen for nearly two decades.

Tears streaked down his face as he lost control of his emotions and collapsed in front of them.

"I...I don't believe it."

They both reached out and enveloped him in their arms.

"Son," Tommy's father said. "I thought we'd never see you again."

His mother was crying too hard to say anything.

Sean watched, fighting back tears of his own. He'd grown up with the Schultzes. When they died, or supposedly died, it was like he'd lost his second parents. Seeing them again brought back so many memories, and so many regrets.

"I...I don't understand," Tommy said. "I thought you were dead."

His mother shook her head while she sobbed. "No, Son. We...we had to stay alive...if for no other reason than to see you again."

June cried openly at the scene. Even Adriana—normally as hard as a diamond—wept at the sight of the reunion.

"You see?" Han-Jae said. "I kept my end of the bargain. Your parents are alive. Now tell me what this means."

He pulled out the paper and held it up to the light, unrolling it to see what was written on the ancient animal skin. His eyes narrowed as he stared at the vellum. Then his head cocked to the side, and he started laughing.

Sean turned around and faced the three gunmen. "What's so funny?" he asked, wiping the tears from his face.

"You know, I thought we might need your help interpreting whatever was on this thing." He held up the scroll. "Turns out, we don't need any of you. This scroll tells us the exact location of the sword."

Tommy let go of his parents and stood up. He spun around and stared hard at Han-Jae. “So let us go. You have what you want. The sword is yours. We can’t stop you.”

“Yes…well…I can’t risk having you interfere with our mission anymore. So unfortunately, you all have to die now.”

“No. What if you get there and you don’t know where to look. Or what if there’s something you need translated and you can’t figure it out. We could still be of use to you.”

Sean didn’t care for his friend’s begging, although he understood it. He was in no hurry to die either. Sean, however, had one more card to play.

He eased his hands behind his back and waited.

Han-Jae seemed to consider Tommy’s offer, if that’s what it was.

“You know,” he said after a moment’s thought, “I think you might be right. We could end up needing someone with your expertise in case we have any trouble figuring out how to get to the sword.”

Tommy nodded, seeing a sliver of hope in the man’s eyes.

That hope was squelched almost immediately.

“Then again, men like you probably take advantage of situations like that. An old proverb says it’s better to kill the few rats now than deal with an infestation later.” He motioned to Sean, June, and Adriana. “You three, get over there by the wall with the others.”

Sean knew what was about to happen. It was an execution. He’d witnessed a few just like this one before, haunting images that he'd tried to wash away with years of good deeds. He'd been unable to stop them from happening. But in this case, he wasn't entirely helpless.

June moved closer to Tommy, who wrapped his arms around her.

"Mom, Dad, this is June. I never thought I'd actually be introducing a girl to you."

Adriana shuffled near Sean and waited for him to make his move. If there was a move to be made.

"Please," Han-Jae said, "don't draw this out longer than necessary. If you just do what we say, we'll make sure you all die quickly. We'd prefer it that way. Fewer bullets, less screaming and moaning. Just a few shots to the chest and head, and it's all over. You won't feel a thing. Well, you won't feel it for long. Unless, of course, you want to."

"Tell me something," Sean said as he stepped between Adriana and the gunmen. "What are you going to do when you find that sword and there's nothing special to it?"

"What?"

"What if it's just a blade, an ancient weapon with no magical properties? What if what you've been searching for turns out to be nothing? What then? Your little revolution goes away. Your general goes away. And you return home to a pathetic country and an even more pathetic leader."

Sean could tell his words were getting to the man. Han-Jae's eyes blazed with fury, and he had to force himself to remain calm.

"You doubt the power of the sword?" he asked. "I don't think so. You wouldn't come all this way just to find something unimportant."

"Oh, I didn't say it was unimportant. I just said it might not have any sort of weird powers."

"Then you are a fool, Wyatt. You and your friends. And you are unfit to wield such a weapon. Not that it matters. Soon we will possess Excalibur, and the armies of the world will bow to us." He lifted his weapon, aiming it at Sean's chest. "Unfortunately, you won't be around to see it all burn. If you have any last—"

The lights overhead exploded and plunged the room into darkness before Han-Jae could finish his monologue. One of the other weapons fired, sending a bullet ricocheting off the hard walls, the sparks provided the only light until it stopped.

Sean charged forward toward the spot where Han-Jae had been standing. After three steps and grabbing nothing but air, he knew the man had moved.

Sean swept his leg around. Still nothing.

"Sean?"

"Yeah, over here. Everybody okay?"

One after the other, everyone else in the room chimed in that they were unhurt.

They were surrounded by a pitch-black, cave-like darkness. Sean put both hands out in front of him and felt his way over to the wall.

"I think our captors took off," he said.

"What?"

"He's right," Adriana chimed in as she also felt her way around. "They ran off."

"What caused the lights to blow out?" June asked.

The sound of shuffling feet echoed down through the stairwell and into the darkened basement. It was soon followed by lights dancing around on the walls on the stairs.

"Someone's coming," Sean said. The residual light coming from above gave him a minimal field of vision, enough to let him see his way over to the corner just behind the doorframe. If whoever was coming through that door had ill intentions, Sean was going to get the drop on them.

He waited with his back pressed against the wall. His breathing slowed, instincts from years of experience calming his nerves as he focused on the ambush. The sounds of multiple footsteps told him that there was more than one person coming. Was it the police? He doubted it. It was either the North Koreans or the Brotherhood. Either way, Sean wanted to get an advantage.

Always let the first guy go through, he thought, recalling training scenarios and real-life experience. By letting one enemy come through the door first, it prevented him from being attacked from behind. That tactic also placed him behind the first person, giving options to either take them out from behind or clear the door with any other enemies coming through.

The flashlights grew brighter and more intense. Sean kept his fingers loose as he continued drawing in slow, even breaths. He watched the bright circles shaking along the bottom wall of the stairwell.

One of the lights turned and pointed into the room. Sean's muscles tensed. The first person stepped through. He waited for a moment until the second appeared in the doorway.

Sean sidestepped silently behind the person and wrapped his arm around their neck, ready to snap it if necessary.

"No, wait!" the man shouted. The voice was oddly familiar.

Sean let go and spun the man around. The first person turned and looked back, aiming a pistol at both of them.

"Mac?" Sean said, confused.

The man lowered his weapon. "Sean. Thank goodness it's you. I thought you were one of the North Koreans about to snap my neck."

"You were half right."

Helen flashed her light around the room and found Tommy and June huddled next to his parents by the back wall. Adriana was close to the door, ready to help Sean with defense.

"How did you know where to find us?" Tommy asked as he stood up.

Helen smirked. "Let's just say we had a little help."

More footsteps thundered down the steps accompanied by several beams of light. Baldwin and his men stepped into the room, shining their lights everywhere.

Tommy took a step back, getting between June, his parents, and the Brotherhood.

"What are they doing here?" he asked.

"Who do you think helped us find you?" Mac said.

Baldwin slowed to a stop just inches from Sean's face. "You broke our bargain, Sean. You were supposed to drop this mission and go home."

Sean rolled his shoulders. "We had to get his parents back. Getting the sword was the best way."

"Except you don't have the sword."

One of Baldwin's men came from a side door on the opposite end of the room. "They're gone, sir. No trace of them."

"They couldn't have just vanished," Baldwin said. "Sweep the area. They have to be here."

"I know where they went," Sean said. "But you're not going to find them here."

Baldwin's eyebrows knit together. "What are you saying?"

"They have the scroll we took from the Vatican. We had no choice."

"Scroll?" Baldwin said, clearly unaware of the clue.

"Yeah," Tommy said. "They took it from us before we could take a look at it and see where to go next."

Baldwin let the information sink in. "If they get to the sword, all will be lost."

Sean raised a mischievous eyebrow. "Well, what my friend said wasn't entirely true."

Every eye in the room locked on Sean for what he had to say.

“I went ahead and took a peek at it while we were in the Vatican Library.”

“You what?” Tommy said.

His parents and June stood up, moving closer to the group to hear better.

“Yeah, so while I was behind the sculpture, I went ahead and took a glance at the scroll. I know what was on it.”

“And?” Adriana asked.

“There was a circle. It had some unique markings on it. I think it might represent the Round Table of King Arthur.”

Tommy and the others waited for more.

“That’s kind of vague. Was there anything else?” he asked. “I mean, that’s great to maybe have a connection to the Knights of the Round Table, but that doesn’t exactly tell us where to look.”

“No,” Sean said. “It doesn’t. But it also had something else.”

Everyone in the room leaned in closer.

“Just below the circle was written Deuteronomy 34:1.”

No one was able to connect the dots, not even the men from the Brotherhood.

Sean was surprised that no one else knew the verse. “Seriously, none of you know what that verse says?”

Adriana shrugged. “Doesn’t ring a bell.”

Sean sighed. “It’s the chapter that talks about the death of Moses and where he was buried. It’s the place where Joshua’s story as Israel’s leader begins. And it’s the place where the sword is hidden.”

The answer hit Tommy suddenly. "Oh my goodness," he gasped. "It's on Mount Nebo."

"Exactly. And if we want to beat the North Koreans there, we need to hurry."

"Hold on," Baldwin said, stepping between the two. "Your journey ends here. We cannot let you go any farther."

"Look, B," Sean said. "Mind if I call you B?" Baldwin frowned, caught off guard. Before he could contest Sean's pet name for him, the American continued. "We've come a long way to get to this point. Especially Tommy's parents. We've earned the right to see this through, whether you want us to or not."

"And besides," Tommy said, "if it weren't for us, you wouldn't know where to go next."

"If it weren't for you, we wouldn't be in this predicament. The North Koreans wouldn't have a map that leads them straight to the sword."

"Fair point," Sean said. "However, I'm noticing you're light a few guys. That means you're going to need all the help you can get."

"We are highly skilled in the arts of combat, so forgive me for saying that you will only get in the way."

"I beg to differ, pal. You know what it is? I think you're scared."

"Scared?"

"Yeah. I think you're afraid that we may get to the place where the sacred sword is hidden and find nothing. Then all these years of...whatever it is you all do would have been for naught. And that just eats you up inside. What would you do next if you didn't have the sword to protect?"

It was unclear whether or not Sean hit a nerve with his comment, but Baldwin grew oddly silent.

"Look," Tommy said. "We all want the same thing: The sword needs to be kept safe and out of the hands of bad guys. We're not looking for it so we can sell it or do something else with it, although it would be an important historical piece for pretty much any museum in the world. We seriously just want to preserve something that is clearly a priceless relic from ancient times."

Baldwin took several deep breaths in through his nose as he considered the offer. "You're suggesting we work together, that we all go to Jordan together to stop the North Koreans from getting the sword?"

"Yes," Sean and Tommy said simultaneously.

"And if we find it, what will you do with it?"

Sean glanced at his friend, who answered. "We will do with it whatever you say." Tommy looked over his shoulder at his parents. "If you want to hide it, fine. If you want us to take it to a lab to be researched, we'll do that. At this point, I think we just want to know if it's real or not. Honest. And if us helping you can keep it out of the hands of evil men, that's what we want to do."

Baldwin contemplated Tommy's remarks for a moment. He glanced over at the guy with the bandage on his head. The man nodded.

"Very well," Baldwin said. "What exactly do you have in mind?"

Tommy looked at Sean for the answer.

“No plan yet. First things first. We need to get to Jordan.”

Chapter 33
Mount Nebo, Jordan

The small convoy of SUVs rolled down the desert road at the base of Mount Nebo. Sean stared out the window at the passing countryside of rocky hills smattered with a few short trees here and there.

Getting Baldwin to agree to work with them had been easy enough once Sean revealed the sword's location—which was a fairly large assumption. The *Bible* verse certainly suggested that there was *something* to find at the top of Mount Nebo. Whether or not it was the actual sword remained to be seen.

Helen and Mac had to return to France to continue overseeing the operations there, though they'd wanted to come along. With everyone else already going to Jordan, it would have just been too many people, which the McElroys understood.

One thing was fairly certain. The North Koreans would likely be there, which would mean trouble.

Luckily, Sean and the others had them greatly outnumbered. The trick would be making sure no one got hurt.

There was a possibility, however small, that the North Koreans didn't understand the meaning of the *Bible* verse on the scroll. Sean doubted it. They'd been smart enough to get this far, even if they had been leaning on Tommy's parents.

Sean looked back in the rearview mirror at the SUV directly behind them. Tommy, his parents, and June got their own vehicle when arriving in Jordan.

Sean thought it better that they ride together to give them a chance to catch up.

What a heavy thing to think about. Sean couldn't imagine how Tommy was feeling. The emotions going through his mind must have been like a tornado, an earthquake, and a hurricane all rolled into one. Spending the better part of twenty years thinking his parents were dead only to find out they were still alive would have shaken anyone.

It certainly had roiled Sean's emotions.

"What are you thinking about?" Adriana asked from the passenger seat. She'd been watching him for the last half hour.

"Oh, me? Nothing. Just...thinking."

She intensified her gaze at him, which told him she knew he was lying.

Sean sighed. "That obvious, huh?"

"Yep."

"It's just...I hope Tommy's okay. That's a lot to take in, you know? Meeting his parents again for the first time since we were kids. I just hope he's okay."

"I thought that's what was on your mind." She turned her head and looked out at the passing desert hills as the caravan of SUVs turned onto the narrow road leading up the mountain. "Tommy will be fine, Sean. It will take some adjustment, probably for a long while, but this is a chance for him to reconnect and make up for lost time."

"Yeah," Sean said with a nod. "Although I have to admit, I wish they would have stayed in a hotel or something. I don't like the idea of bringing them to a gunfight. The North Koreans are still out there somewhere. Odds are, we're going to bump into them again. I'd hate to get his parents back just to have something bad happen to them again."

"They're grown adults. They chose to come along. Honestly, there's nothing you could have said or done to keep me away. If I'd done all the years of research and searching they've done on the sword project, you'd have to chain me down to a bulldozer to keep me from seeing it through to the end."

She made a good point. Tommy's parents had spent the better part of two decades trying to figure out the location of the sword, all the while throwing the North Koreans off the trail but giving them just enough to keep believing in the story. They deserved to see it, if there was anything *to* see.

Sean steered the SUV around the curves of the winding road as the convoy left the desert plains behind and ascended the mountain. At the top, he slowed down and found a place to park near an outcropping of trees. They'd decided on that spot before heading to Jordan based on aerial photos from the internet. The parking spot under the trees was far enough away from the church and other buildings atop the mountain, but close enough that they could walk to everything. At the same time, it gave them a chance to approach from a safe distance that allowed an open view of the area.

The other three vehicles pulled up next to Sean's. After everyone got out, they huddled near one of the larger trees and took a quick look around.

On the other end of the plateau, a line of cars was parked on both sides of the driveway leading up to a cluster of buildings. People meandered around the area, some laughing, some taking pictures, and others just taking in the incredible views from atop the thirty-four-hundred-foot mountain.

"Shame we can't enjoy this beautiful panorama," Tommy's father said as he gazed out toward the valley below and the plains beyond. "It's pretty amazing."

"We are standing on the same ground where Moses looked out over the promised land," his mother added. "I would have never imagined that this was where they would have brought the sword."

"They?" Tommy asked.

"The first of their order," his mother said, pointing at Baldwin. "They were the ones who brought it here to keep safe."

"At some point, I'm going to ask how you guys managed to find him and his Brotherhood pals. For now, we need to get moving."

"Two of my men will go up the left side over there," Baldwin said. "The others will go around to the right. They'll go wide to make sure they don't get ambushed from behind. It will take them longer, but it's the safest way to proceed."

"And we go down the middle?" Sean asked.

"Yes. Of course, if they are waiting for us, that will make us easy targets if my men are delayed in flanking their positions. It could be dangerous." He made no effort to hide the fact that he was speaking to the women and the older couple.

"We'll be fine," Adriana said.

"Nothing's going to stop us from seeing this through," Tommy's father said. "Like we mentioned before, we've come too far to quit now."

"Very well," Baldwin said. He motioned to two of his men, who immediately took off beyond the trees and started looping around to the left through a field of tall golden weeds. The other two went the other way, taking a similar tack around the road and another stand of trees. The field on the right was narrower, which meant they couldn't go as far wide as the other two men. The good news was that also meant it was less likely an ambush was coming from there. The steep slopes would have made it difficult for anyone to hide safely without tumbling toward sharper cliffs just beyond.

"Shall we?" Baldwin asked, sticking his hand out toward the drive.

"You gonna give us some weapons?" Sean asked.

Baldwin balked at the question. "Weapons? Do you think I have extra guns I carry around everywhere? And why would I trust them to you if I did?"

"Because I think you do have extra guns. And because you know what we can do. You arm us, you're helping your own cause. You don't, well then, the odds just got a lot more even."

"Fine," Baldwin said after a brief moment of thought.

He flipped open the trunk, revealing a slew of handguns, submachine guns, shotguns, knives, and even a tomahawk.

Sean recognized the latter. “Is that a tomahawk from RMJ Tactical?”

Baldwin looked surprised. “Yes. Why?”

Sean pointed at Adriana with his thumb. “I gave her one of those. Useful little item.” He turned his attention to one of six Glock 17s lying in a case. “Looks like you were planning on arming us after all.”

“Well,” Baldwin said with a shrug, “like you said, you might as well make yourselves useful. No sense in just being targets.” He flashed the first smile Sean had ever seen out of him.

The six Americans each took a weapon, though June and Tommy’s parents were a tad apprehensive about it.

“I don’t use guns often,” June said.

“That’s okay,” Tommy said. “Hopefully we don’t have to. The way you use your feet and hands, though, if I was one of the North Koreans I’d be way more worried about that.”

The comment brought a crease to her lips.

Baldwin closed the trunk and started off down the driveway. He tucked his weapon into an inner jacket pocket but kept his hand on it just in case. The Jordanians wouldn’t approve of foreigners walking around with guns exposed, much less on a holy site where tourists and pilgrims came to visit and pray.

Everyone tucked away their weapons as they moved down the road. The hot sun beat down on the group from high in a cloudless sky, and Tommy wiped his forehead numerous times to try to wick the sweat off.

As they reached the first few cars, everyone's eyes immediately began searching the cars for signs of the North Koreans. Passing each one, they realized that all the vehicles were empty.

"Doesn't look like they're hiding in any of these cars," Sean said in a quiet tone. "You think they went in one of those buildings?"

"It's possible."

"We should split up," Adriana said. "We can cover more ground that way."

"Yes, but then we lose the advantage of numbers."

"That advantage won't matter anyway with us out here in the open. At least if we divide up, we can work through the area faster. If we don't find anything or any of the bad guys, let's meet back here."

Baldwin thought about the proposal and then agreed. "Fine, but if you get in trouble, we might not be able to save you."

"Thanks for the warning," Sean said. "We'll take that building over there." He pointed at a structure with a sandstone base and matching stucco walls. It featured a cross made from wires or some kind of sticks on top of the roof. "You and Headwrap go around the outside and check out the area below. Looks like there's something down there like a lookout that people are visiting."

A Muslim man in white robes walked next to a woman in flowing black robes. They appeared to be coming from the old church.

Baldwin acknowledged the orders with a reluctant nod and then took off with his partner in tow.

During their research of Nebo on the plane, Sean and the others found it interesting that the mountaintop was considered a holy place by both Jews and Muslims alike. Both religions believed Moses to be an important spiritual figure. Indeed, many of the tourists and pilgrims visiting the site were dressed in traditional garb from Judaism and Islam.

"Let's go," Sean said.

He led the way onto the crushed-rock pathway that led to the entrance of the building. A sign made of stone was propped up next to the old church. It claimed the property as belonging to the Franciscan Order, written in both English and Arabic. It also read, *Memorial of Moses*.

What caught everyone's attention was the symbol at the top of the sign.

"That's the circle I saw on the scroll from the Vatican," Sean whispered. "It looked exactly like that."

Tommy gazed at the object. He recognized the emblem, though he didn't want to jinx the mission. "That definitely looks like the Round Table," he said.

His father and mother stepped nearer to the sign to get a better look.

His father ran his finger along the smooth stone, outlining the black circle with his fingernail. "That looks an awful lot like a Templar cross."

"Yeah," Tommy said. "I was thinking the same thing."

“You don’t think Baldwin and the Brotherhood are…” Sean asked.

“The Brotherhood of the Sword is an ancient order,” Tommy’s mother said. “They’ve been around for thousands of years, and they predated the Templars. One possibility we considered was that they might have founded the Knights Templar. There wasn’t much evidence to that theory, though, and trying to prove that point seemed a bit unnecessary at the time. Still, it is intriguing.”

Sean’s eyes scanned the area, making sure they weren’t being watched. “We should probably get inside and see what’s there.”

He held the door until everyone was in, gave one last look around, and then followed them into the building.

Seeing artifacts hadn’t been part of the plan when they’d left to come to Jordan, but the inside of the ancient church was too breathtaking to ignore.

Big stone blocks were exposed along the base of the walls, telling the age of the original structure. One of the signs inside the cool foyer said that this place was called the Basilica of Moses.

Intricate mosaics covered the floor from front to back. They featured stories from Greek antiquity, pictures of animals from long ago, as well as people and even activities that would have been part of daily life when the church was originally built. The vibrant colors were remarkably preserved through time, almost as if the tiles had been laid in recent years.

The building's interior smelled of rock and dust, a common characteristic of old stone structures. In spite of the church being built in the desert, the stone walls kept it remarkably cool, almost like an air conditioner was running full time.

The six visitors moved cautiously through the first chamber, walking by mosaic images of birds, oxen, people, plants, fruits, and pottery. One of the mosaics bore words written in Greek.

Adriana read them in English for everyone. "Offering of Caesarion, at the time of Alexios and Theophilos priests." She stared at the tiles for a moment. "Incredible this church has remained in such good condition. It's so old."

"Climate can do wonders for that sort of thing," Tommy's dad said.

At the end of the room, a stone baptismal font made from slightly more orange rock stood close to the far wall. Two circles were cut into the front with more Greek inscribed within them. A cross was cut into the stone between the circles.

The group turned into one of the adjacent rooms where more mosaics decorated the floors and parts of the walls.

They made their way through the rest of the building but didn't see any sign of the North Koreans or anything that looked like a clue as to the whereabouts of the sword. After spending another five minutes investigating the church, Sean suggested they go back outside and see if Baldwin and his men had found anything. He led the way to the entrance and stepped outside into the warm, dry air.

Once outside, everyone's senses heightened at the renewed feeling of being exposed.

"Let's keep moving," Sean said.

Tommy nodded as he and the others followed Sean around the edge of the building, down a crushed-gravel path that wound around the church to a slightly lower observation area. A large sculpture of a cross stood over the landing. It was designed to be an artistic replica of the cross used by Moses when Israel became afflicted with an overwhelming number of venomous snakes. A symbolic serpent wrapped around the huge bronze sculpture.

Sean stopped suddenly and put his hand up behind his back, signaling the others to halt as well.

"Quick, into the woods," he ordered, motioning to a thick stand of trees that ran from the base of the church down to the edge of the lookout point.

No one questioned him. They all climbed over the short rock wall and took cover behind the biggest tree trunks they could find.

Only when everyone was out of sight did Tommy dare ask Sean what was going on.

"What is it?" he asked.

Sean peeked around his tree, holding the weapon Baldwin gave him in front of his nose. "They're here."

"The Koreans?"

Sean nodded. "Yeah. And they have hostages."

Chapter 34
Mount Nebo

"Hostages?" Tommy hissed.

"Yeah. One of Baldwin's men, and another man and woman. All being held at gunpoint. Their leader has a gun aimed at Baldwin, probably twenty feet away from him. Looks like a stalemate."

"It sounds like a massacre waiting to happen."

Adriana was listening closely. "What do we do? Go around and hit them from behind?"

Sean shook his head. "No good. They're positioned in such a way that they'd see any movement. Unless Baldwin ran his mouth, the North Koreans don't know we're here yet."

"Unless they saw us," June said.

"Right, but we'll just have to work with the assumption they didn't."

"You know what happens when you assume, right?" she said.

Sean grinned. He liked her. A little snarky with just the right amount of sweetness. "Yeah. In this case, we don't have much choice."

"So, what?" Tommy asked.

"Looks like they are saying something to Baldwin. Too far away to hear. If we wait too long, though, people might get hurt."

"Maybe we could use a diversion," Adriana suggested.

That idea had crossed Sean's mind, but a sudden noise or movement might startle one of the villains and cause them to fire a weapon by accident.

“Too risky,” he said. Sean didn’t want to wait it out. As time passed, bad things could happen. One important lesson he’d learned long ago that had repeated itself over and over again was that a window nearly always opened if one was patient enough. “We have to wait for an opportunity.”

“Opportunity?” Tommy asked.

Sean shot him a look that reminded his friend of all the times he’d been right in the past.

“Okay, so we wait. For what?”

“A tactical advantage.”

Sean poked his head around the tree and continued watching the standoff at the overlook. He could see the fear in the man’s and woman’s eyes. They were innocently visiting a holy site, minding their own business. They had no idea when they woke up that morning that they’d be held at gunpoint, jammed squarely in the middle of a battle they had nothing to do with.

Baldwin was holding his gun by his hip, a signal that the North Koreans had gotten the drop on him. There was a reluctance about his posture and facial expression. Sean didn’t need to hear what was being said to understand exactly what was going on.

Han-Jae wanted Baldwin to put down his weapon. That was the first step. What the Korean leader would do next was up in the air.

Sean didn’t have to wait long to find out.

Baldwin slowly raised his left hand to surrender and bent his knees to lower the gun to the ground. He dropped the weapon on the rocks and stood up straight. The Korean leader shook his head and motioned with his weapon, saying something else.

Baldwin kicked his gun over to Han-Jae, who picked it up and tossed it over the wall and down the cliff. Then Baldwin gradually got down on his knees with his hands over his head. His other men dropped their weapons and did the same, kicking them over to Han-Jae before joining Baldwin on his knees.

When Han-Jae had thrown all the guns over the cliff, he issued an order to the man holding Baldwin's guy hostage. Shaved Head had been pressing the muzzle of his gun against the hostage's head. He shoved him forward toward the others who were already kneeling. A second later, he joined them and faced their captors.

The window was opening, and Sean knew it. One problem had just solved itself. Leading an assault on a group holding multiple people hostage was problematic. Sean trusted his aim. He knew he could take out one of the North Koreans without harming the hostages, but three could be tricky. He would have had to rely on two others in his group to execute the shot. Adriana would be his next choice. After that, maybe Tommy—who was slightly less accurate than Sean would like.

Now there were only two hostages: the man and the woman. If he could get one of those gunmen to release....

Just as he had the thought, Buzz-Cut released the woman, and the other gunman released her husband. She ran to him and hugged him, but the gunman forced them to get down on the ground like the others.

Sean had hoped for one hostage to be released. Now he had two. That took away the danger of accidentally hitting one, even though they were still pointing their guns at the couple and the men of the Brotherhood.

"We're going to have to make our move soon," Tommy said, watching things play out from his cover. "Looks like this is about to turn into an execution."

Sean nodded. "Yeah." He looked at his friend and Adriana. "You two come with me." Then he addressed the other three. "You stay here and cover the path back up to the church. If they try to run, take them out."

Tommy's parents exchanged an uncertain glance. They weren't used to being in such a position.

"Is this the kind of thing you do on a regular basis?" his mother asked.

Tommy rolled his shoulders and put on his best innocent-looking face. "I try not to."

Sean pushed ahead, careful not to step on any twigs or dead branches. Tommy and Adriana followed close behind, keeping to the shadows to stay out of sight.

The men holding the hostages dipped in and out of view between the trees. Han-Jae was yelling something at Baldwin. He'd moved over to within a few feet of the blond man, pointing his pistol straight at Baldwin's forehead. He was yelling something, of which Sean was finally able to hear bits and pieces.

As he and his friends drew closer, the full conversation finally came into range. Sean found a cluster of large trees and motioned for Adriana and Tommy to take up positions. They were only fifteen feet from the observation point and another fifteen to the North Korean leader.

Sean pointed at Tommy and then at Shaved Head. Then he gave the same silent instructions to Adriana for Buzz-Cut. The two pressed against their trees and lined up their sights with the targets.

Sean aimed at Han-Jae. He'd take out the leader first, which would cause the others to look their way. Then he could take out the other guy while Tommy and Adriana cut down their men.

"This is your last chance," Han-Jae said. "Tell me where the sword is, or we will kill all of you where you kneel." There was no denying the sincerity of the menacing look on Han-Jae's face.

Baldwin breathed calmly, apparently ready to die for his cause.

Han-Jae raised his weapon high and smacked it across the blond's face, knocking Baldwin over on his side.

He grabbed the fresh cut on his cheek and struggled to get up. "If you kill us, you'll never find the sword. We are your only chance."

Sean knew Baldwin was bluffing. Deep down, he had to admire the guy's moxie.

Han-Jae stepped back and motioned to the couple kneeling close by.

“Oh no,” Sean hissed. “They’re going to use that couple to get Baldwin to talk.”

“But he doesn’t know anything,” Tommy whispered.

“Yeah. That means we have to go now. You ready to fire?”

Adriana stayed silent but nodded.

“One second,” Tommy said, adjusting his feet to a more stable stance.

His right foot slipped and he grabbed the tree to keep his balance. Doing so caused his left hand to grab a small branch that snapped easily under his weight.

The North Koreans heard the sudden sound, and all turned their attention to the woods.

“Aw, man,” Tommy said.

In an instant, the tranquil silence of the trees turned into chaos. The gunmen unleashed a barrage of rounds at the trespassers, turning branches, leaves, and sections of tree trunks into shredded splinters.

Sean, Tommy, and Adriana kept their backs against the trunks while bullets zipped by them, smashing into the ground and other trees just beyond.

Tommy’s parents and June were out of view, so for the moment Sean knew they were safe. That could change in a moment.

The gunfire came to a sudden stop, but Sean didn’t dare sneak a look. He knew the gunmen were waiting to see if anyone appeared.

Baldwin used the moment of uncertainty to his advantage. “Are you afraid of squirrels now?” His cheek oozed crimson, but there was a bit of sarcasm to his voice.

Sean waited for another moment. He didn’t see it happen, but he heard it. One of the North Koreans was loading a full magazine and dropped the empty one on the ground by accident. It was easy to recognize the sound and told Sean all he needed to know. They were out of ammo and reloading. It was the window he’d been waiting for.

He spun around the tree and raised his weapon, lining up the sights as fast as he could with the Korean leader. In his hurry, his foot stepped on a twig. The snapping sound alerted the gunmen to more danger. Sean fired three quick shots, but Han-Jae—alert to the trouble—dove for cover between the bronze sculpture and the wall near the cliff.

The man behind him wasn’t so lucky. His reaction was slow, and the rounds meant for Han-Jae caught him in the chest and abdomen. He stumbled backward a few steps and then dropped to his knees before toppling over.

Adriana and Tommy jumped into the fray, spinning from behind their trees and taking aim at the two targets they’d lined up a moment ago. The men had already moved, though, and were running up the hill toward the church.

“You gonna take them out?” Sean asked as he fired another shot to keep Han-Jae in his spot.

“On it,” Adriana said. She turned and charged through the trees toward the path.

“I’m coming,” Tommy said, lumbering after her.

Adriana squeezed off a shot. The round splashed into the gravel near one of the fleeing men’s feet.

Sean stalked toward the edge of the woods, ducking in and out of view as Han-Jae took aim and fired one, then two, then three shots. Sean returned fire, keeping a careful count of the rounds he had left in the magazine.

He stuck his weapon around another tree trunk and fired again, taking another step closer. The round pinged off the sculpture and ricocheted into the ether. Sean took a glance at Baldwin and his men who’d surrounded the young couple to keep them safe. Sean could tell the blond guy was looking for a way to help, but he was doing all he could for the moment.

Han-Jae peeked around the other side of the sculpture’s base and squeezed his trigger repeatedly. The muzzle popped loudly. Bullets ripped through the trees again. Two whizzed by Sean’s head. He waited until the volley was over and took aim once more.

Han-Jae wasn’t there. Sean’s forehead wrinkled with a frown. He twisted a little more and saw his target running away down a path to the left. Sean’s finger twitched, squeezing the trigger again and again. Some rounds sailed over the wall, a few smashed into it, but when his weapon clicked, he’d missed with every one.

“Guess we do this the old-fashioned way,” he said and sprinted through the trees.

Back up the hill, Adriana ran after Shaved Head with Tommy lagging behind her.

Suddenly, the trees erupted in a blaze of gunfire. Buzz-Cut turned and saw the shooters too late, catching a round in the thigh. He fell to the ground, clutching his leg.

The shooters in the woods ceased fire as Tommy and Adriana approached.

“Take care of him,” Adriana said. “I’ve got the other guy.”

She ran by the wounded man and stayed after Shaved Head, who disappeared around the circular base of the church.

By the time Tommy arrived where Buzz-Cut had fallen, the man had dragged himself off the ground and started limping toward the parking area.

“Where do you think you’re going?” Tommy asked, grabbing the guy by the collar and spinning him around.

Buzz-Cut swung hard at Tommy’s face, but the American caught the fist, twisted the wrist, and jabbed the guy square in the mouth. His opponent staggered back a moment and then touched his lips with two fingers. He looked at the blood and then at Tommy. His eyes blazed with renewed fury as he charged, forcing himself to forget the pain coming from his leg.

Tommy suddenly felt like he’d jabbed a hornets’ nest with a stick. Buzz-Cut moved quickly, lashing out with hands that constantly stayed in motion. One punch caught Tommy in the jaw. He blocked the second, but the third struck his cheek. Then the opponent kicked with his good leg, landing the blow in Tommy's midsection.

The American dropped to his knees and gasped for air, the wind gone from his lungs.

Buzz-Cut moved rapidly. Stepping over to the edge of the pathway, he pried one of the softball-sized rocks that lined the walk. He stepped back over to Tommy, who was desperately trying to recover normal breathing.

Tommy looked up and saw the man hovering over him with the stone raised high over his shoulder. Tommy's arms flailed, but it was no use.

Buzz-Cut started to deliver the mortal blow at Tommy's head when another gunshot came from the woods.

The Korean's body shuddered for a second. The rock fell from his hand and hit the ground with a thud. A look of confused fear filled his face as he spun around to see who'd shot him in the back.

June stood at the edge of the forest, holding a Glock in her hand. A trickle of gray smoke drifted out of the barrel and disappeared into the desert sky.

Buzz-Cut's legs wobbled. Then he fell over onto his side, his eyes fixing on a distant point on the horizon.

Tommy's breath returned, and his lungs started rising and falling dramatically as he took big gulps of air. He looked up at June, who lowered the weapon. It dangled for a second in her hand before dropping to the ground. Her fingers trembled, and she put her hands to her lips.

Tommy struggled to his feet and rushed over to her, wrapping his arms around her in a tight hug.

"You saved my life," he said.

She was still trembling. "Is…is he dead?"

Tommy lifted his head and looked at the villain on the ground. "Yeah."

A tear formed in the corner of June's eye. She sniffled and wiped her nose. "I thought he was going to kill you."

Tommy stepped back and gripped both her shoulders. "There's a lot more to you than meets the eye, June Holiday."

She forced a laugh and then wrapped her arms around him again.

Meanwhile, Adriana sprinted through the parking lot after Shaved Head. He was fast, but Adriana was faster. She closed the gap in less than ten seconds and jumped the last few feet, throwing her arms at the guy's shoulders.

The weight of her body and its momentum hit him like a sack of rocks. She drove him into the ground face-first, grinding his right shoulder on the gravel. Adriana put so much effort into the tackle that she couldn't stay on top of the guy and rolled over him.

He pushed himself up from the ground and unleashed a furious attack. From the onset, Adriana knew the guy had been trained in various martial arts. His stance, the balance, the constant movement all belied mastery of hand-to-hand combat.

He slid both feet toward her and jabbed with the left. She swatted the punch downward only to find a follow-up from his right. One after the other, Adriana blocked and deflected every effort Shaved Head could throw. Her wrists ached from the blows, but she kept at it until she saw an opening. Her leg snapped out quickly, her foot striking him in the knee.

The blow did little to deter the attacker, but it bought her a split second of time to regroup. She retreated a step and invited the next round. Shaved Head pressed the assault, firing his own kick at Adriana's face then readying himself to pummel her face as he landed.

He couldn't have anticipated her next move. Adriana spun to the left and brought her arm around, clotheslining the guy in the neck. The power of the blow combined with his momentum flipped him onto his back with a heavy thud.

Adriana stomped her foot at his face, but he grabbed her by the ankle, twisted, and jerked. She twisted in midair, tumbling twice before crashing onto the gravel.

Shaved Head rolled to his feet. It was his turn to hit his opponent while she was on the ground. He swung his boot hard at her head. Adriana rolled out of the way, the tip of his foot missing her temple by inches. He repeated the kick with his other foot. Again, she rolled away. He tried a third time. Adriana didn't try to get away. She rolled toward the man, catching his foot before it could gain any force, then drove the base of her hand into his groin. Her fingers squeezed and twisted hard.

The man howled in agony. Adriana slid through his legs, keeping her grip tight. He doubled over, which played right into her plan. On her back, Adriana kicked her right heel up, plowing the bone into his nose.

His head snapped back, and his feet shuffled on the gravel as he tried to gain his balance while grabbing his face.

Adriana let go and stood up. She grabbed her opponent's shoulder and spun him around. He lowered his hands from the bloody nose in an attempt to ready himself for her attack, but it was too late.

Adriana drove a fist into his left cheek, then his right, then left again. His head rocked from one side to the other and back. Now he was fighting against gravity *and* the fierce Spaniard.

He drove a weak punch at her face, but she grabbed his wrist, yanked him forward, and drove her knee into his gut. He grunted and doubled over, stumbling to the ground face-first. Adriana jumped on his back and grabbed the back of his head. She lifted it and smashed it into the ground over and over again until she felt the resistance in his muscles go limp.

Adriana released the clump of hair, letting the man's bloody head drop to the ground.

She gasped for breath, only now realizing how much exertion the fight had taken. She wiped her nose with the back of her hand and stood up, rolling the guy over onto his back with the tip of her shoe.

His face looked like he'd just lost a prize fight against a cheese grinder. His chest rose and fell, signaling that he wasn't dead.

Adriana looked off toward the woods below the church and wondered what was going on with Sean.

Chapter 35
Mount Nebo

Sean weaved in and out of the trees, keeping an eye on Han-Jae as he ran down the path away from the sculpture. The North Korean looked back several times to see if he was being followed. Even though he didn't see anyone, he didn't dare slow his pace.

Sean made no effort to stay quiet as he ran through the woods. The path looped around to the other side of the little forest, to what he didn't know, but he knew he could cut off Han-Jae's escape this way.

The North Korean skidded to a stop at a huge circular stone propped up on its side between two large blocks on the ground. He took cover behind the far side and waited, panting for air.

He pressed the button on his gun and released the magazine, letting it fall to the ground. Then he reached to his belt to get a full one, taking another quick look back around the stone to make sure no one was coming.

The gravel crunched behind him without warning. Han-Jae spun around to see a fist coming at his face.

Sean's knuckles smashed into the man's forehead right between the eyes.

The gun dropped to the ground, and Han-Jae took a step back. He winced from the pain but was alert enough to catch Sean's next shot. He grabbed the American's fist, letting his fingers slide down to the base before squeezing hard, and twisting.

The sudden move bent Sean down and toward the enemy, who drove his knee into Sean's jaw. Han-Jae didn't let go, instead pulling the American down again and once more into his knee. After the second kick, Han-Jae drove his fist into Sean's cheek. He pummeled him repeatedly in the temple and side of the face.

Sean's vision blurred. He knew one or two more blows to the side of the head would end the fight and probably his life. Desperate, he reached out and grabbed the Korean's pants. With the last ounce of energy he had left, Sean tugged at the pants as hard as he could.

Han-Jae raised his fist again as the American pulled on his pants. His foot slipped on the gravel and he lost his balance, toppling over backward and hitting the top of his head against the stone. He fell to the ground and groaned, planting both hands on the gravel as he tried to get up.

Sean spit blood through his lips and crawled toward the edge of the wall overlooking the rolling desert plains and hills. He grabbed the wall's lip and pulled himself up. He blinked rapidly, bringing the scene below and the Dead Sea in the distance into focus.

His head throbbed, his lip stung, and both sides of his jaw ached.

Somehow he managed to stand up. The sound of gravel crunching underfoot alerted him to the approaching danger. He heard the pistol slide, chambering a new round. Han-Jae's shadow stretched out around Sean's feet. He saw the shadow of the man's arm stretch out, pointing the weapon at the back of Sean's head.

"Now you—"

Sean didn't let him finish the sentence. He ducked his head to the side, twisted his right arm back, and grabbed Han-Jae's wrist.

The weapon fired a bullet harmlessly into the air.

The Korean struggled to wrest his hand free of Sean's grip, but the American wouldn't let go.

Han-Jae drove his knee into Sean's chest, weakening his grip for a moment, but within a split second Sean regained his strength and pulled his opponent toward the wall.

Han-Jae punched with his left hand. Sean caught the fist with his palm just inches from his face. He torqued the enemy's hand into an awkward angle. Han-Jae screamed and released his grip on the pistol. The weapon clacked on the outer edge and then fell over the side, down the cliff.

Sean twisted Han-Jae's hand a little more and then drove his elbow into the arm. The bone snapped easily, bending the appendage at a gruesome angle and sending a fresh surge of pain through the North Korean's nerves.

Han-Jae yelled and smashed the bridge of his other hand across Sean's face, knocking him back to his knees.

Everything went blurry again in Sean's eyes. He braced himself with an elbow on the wall's surface and gasped for air. The world was spinning. He was barely able to process his opponent standing up and stepping away.

Han-Jae staggered a few feet toward the stone and then spun around, holding the broken arm with his good hand.

Sean struggled to his feet and faced the man, uncertain he could fight much longer.

"You interrupted me before," Han-Jae said. "I was saying it's time for you to die."

He took two steps and jumped. His right foot lined up squarely with Sean's chest. The move was so swift and sudden, Sean barely had a half second to react. He sidestepped and swung his right arm. Han-Jae flew by as Sean's elbow caught him in the back with just enough force to send him over the edge.

Sean turned around and saw his opponent's fingers clutching the outer lip of the wall in a desperate struggle of skin on stone.

Leaning over the edge, Sean saw the man balancing his weight on a narrow ledge. His toes looked to be slipping, and with only one good hand there was no way he could stay there for long.

Sean braced himself on the wall by planting both hands flat on the surface and looked down. His fear of heights mixed with the constant dizziness nearly caused him to vomit.

"It was you," Sean said. He tried hard to focus on his enemy's face. "It was you who killed that scientist in Cologne."

"So? I'd do it again. All for the glory of—"

Sean had heard enough. He made a fist with his left hand and hammered Han-Jae's fingers.

The North Korean shrieked and let go, simultaneously losing his balance and falling backward. His voice echoed up the slopes as he fell, the sound of his screams breaking off when he hit the bottom.

Sean pulled himself away from the ledge and put his back to the wall, sliding to the ground.

He panted for breath. So many parts of his body hurt.

"I'm getting too old for this," he muttered. He spat another clump of blood out onto the gravel and looked up at the stone.

Then it hit him what he was seeing. He started chuckling at first. Soon it broke into laugher until his chest started hurting.

Adriana came around the bend and saw him first. She was followed by the others who saw him sitting on the ground against the wall.

She rushed to his side and put her hand on his shoulder. "Are you okay?" she asked.

Sean looked up, still brimming with laughter. He nodded slowly. “I will be. Everything hurts right now, but I’ll be fine.”

Tommy and June joined them by the wall. Tommy stuck out a hand to help Sean onto his feet.

“You know what, thank you, but I think I’m just gonna sit here for a few days.”

Tommy’s parents stood by the giant stone, staring at it with wonder in their eyes. Baldwin and his men arrived, too. They also gazed in amazement at the big circular rock.

“Do you know what this is?” Baldwin asked.

“I’m fine. Thanks for asking.”

“What happened…you know, to the other guy?” Tommy interrupted.

“Oh, he needed some air,” Sean said and jerked his thumb back toward the cliff. “And to answer your question, Baldwin, that appears to be a rolling stone they used to seal up tombs back around the time of Christ.”

“It doesn’t *appear* to be one. That is exactly what it is.”

“So?” Tommy asked. “What’s the significance?”

Sean answered for Baldwin. “That, my friend, is what was drawn on the clue I took from the Vatican.”

“Wait,” June cut in. “Are you saying that the sword is…”

“Yeah.” Sean gave a nod. “I’m saying the sword is hidden right here, under this stone. The very stone some say covered the tomb of Jesus.”

"He's right, Son," Tommy's father said. "We always thought this might be the location, but we weren't sure."

"And getting information in North Korea was like trying to learn how to fly a plane in the Stone Age," his mother added.

June shook her head. "This is incredible."

Adriana put a hand against the stone. "So Arthur's Round Table...on the surface it was about equality and being of one voice, but in reality it was a representation of where he found Excalibur. The sword in the stone."

"Or under it, as it were," Sean said.

"And the lake," Tommy said. "One of the legends talks about a lady in the lake." He looked off into the distance. "You can see the Dead Sea from here. I wonder if that had anything to do with it."

"Probably."

"I just can't believe it. We found it. We found it!"

The moment of victorious jubilation was cut short as Baldwin stepped closer to Sean. He stood over the American as he spoke. "You have done well. You will always have friends in the Brotherhood for as long as you live. Should you ever need our assistance, you know where to find us."

Baldwin stuck out his hand. Sean hesitated for a second and then shook it as firmly as possible.

"Actually, we don't know where to find you."

Baldwin let go and straightened up. "I know," he said with a wink. He turned and motioned for his men to get moving.

"Did he just make a joke?" Sean asked Tommy.

"I think he did," Tommy said, amazed.

"What about the sword?" Adriana asked. "What do you want us to do with it?"

Baldwin stopped and looked back over his shoulder. "Do whatever you feel is right."

He and his men trudged back up the path and disappeared around the bend.

"So...what?" June said. "We get equipment up here to move this stone out of the way and then start digging? What's the normal process for something like this?"

Tommy looked at Sean, then Adriana, and then into the eyes of his parents. His mother and father stared at him with a warmth in their eyes.

"No," Tommy said finally. "We're going to leave it here."

"What?" June said. "I don't understand. We've been through so much. Your parents...they've waited their whole lives to see this."

"I know. I know. It's just that...this sword, if it's as powerful as we think it might be...it could be dangerous to take it out of its hiding place. In the wrong hands, it could cause a whole lot of trouble."

"But if we don't dig down there, we won't know if it's really there. Don't you want to know for sure?"

"I have a pretty good feeling it's there," Tommy said. "The only question is, can you keep it a secret?"

He wrapped his arms around her and pulled her close.

June had a pouty look on her face that cracked as Tommy moved nearer. He pressed his lips to hers and squeezed her tight.

"Oh, thank goodness," Sean said. He looked at Tommy's parents with a relieved expression on his face, like a two-ton yoke had been taken off his back. "You have no idea how bad he needed to find a girl."

They didn't get the joke.

"Hey," Tommy said, pulling away from June for a second. "We're right here."

June pressed her fingers to his face and twisted his head back around to face her again. "I think you boys have had enough fun together for one week."

"You're probably right."

Sean stared at the stone. He rested his arms on his knees, finally catching his breath. Adriana sat down next to him and followed his gaze.

"Amazing, isn't it?" she said. "This sacred place where Moses was shown the promised land is the same place where the sword he gave Joshua is hidden. That stone sits atop Excalibur."

"It sure is. A lot to take in when you think about it."

She tilted her head over and rested it on his shoulder. "How is it we keep finding ourselves in these kinds of situations? You know, shootouts and fighting for our lives?"

Sean sighed. "Because we're the best people for the job, I guess. Would anyone else have been able to take these guys down or figure out all the clues to get here?"

"Mmm. I don't know. But we'll have to slow down some day. Can't do this sort of thing forever."

He snorted. "You're right about that. I guess when the time is right we'll know."

Tommy and June joined his parents standing by the stone and gave them the biggest hug of his life. Sean wondered if he'd ever let go.

"Well, I'm glad it's over," Adriana said.

Sean kept his thoughts to himself.

Not quite.

Chapter 36
Pyongyang

General Min-Woo walked into his apartment and locked the door behind him. He wasn't afraid someone would try to break in. No one would be foolish enough to do that. He was one of the Chairman's most trusted advisers. If a criminal tried to enter his home, that person would be put through their own personal hell before dying.

Min-Woo stepped into the kitchen and switched on the lights. He pulled a bottle of water out of the refrigerator and poured half the contents down his throat.

It had been another long day of ridiculous meetings, war room briefings, and more meetings, followed by watching soldiers perform military marching drills for two hours.

Min-Woo made his way over to the living room and turned on the television. State-approved television was pretty awful, but it beat sitting around in silence. He eased into his big vinyl chair and put his head back, taking a moment to relax and forget about the stupidity of all the things he'd done over the course of the day.

Maybe after he rested for a few minutes he'd call one of the girls on his list. While Min-Woo hated much of the way the Chairman ran things, he had to admit that being one of Dear Leader's most trusted advisers did have its privileges.

After sitting in his favorite chair for ten minutes, Min-Woo realized he was still wearing his full uniform. He shook his head and got up, walked into the bedroom, and started taking off the medals from his jacket. He kicked off his shoes and was about to remove his pants in favor of some sweats when his phone started ringing in the living room.

It wasn't his burn phone, the one he used to keep in contact with Han-Jae. It was his day-to-day phone.

He hurried back into the other room and pressed the green button. "Hello?"

"I'm sorry to bother you, General. Something has come up."

Min-Woo didn't recognize the voice on the other end, but that wasn't anything out of the ordinary. He got calls from different people all the time. As soldiers were promoted up through the ranks, new ones came in under them to take their place.

"What is it?" Min-Woo asked.

"The Chairman requires your presence. Something has come up, and your expertise is needed."

The answer was cryptic, but again, nothing out of the ordinary. North Korea was a place full of paranoia. Citizens knew not to say anything stupid on the phones because the government was always listening. Every now and then, the secret police would go out and pick up random people just to reinforce fear in the minds of the people.

Fear led to respect. Respect led to following the rules.

Min-Woo also knew better than to ask if whatever the Chairman needed could wait. Dear Leader was soft. He couldn't make decisions on his own, like a kid in a candy store unable to choose which sweet to buy.

"Very well," Min-Woo said. "I'll put my shoes back on and head that way."

"Not the usual place, General. We're afraid there might be a security breach. The Chairman has requested to meet you at backup headquarters."

"Security breach? What kind of security breach? I wasn't aware of anything like that."

"I've been asked not to discuss the details on the phone, sir."

Min-Woo sighed. "Very well. I'll be there in fifteen minutes."

He ended the call and slid the phone into his pocket. As he put his clothes back on, he glanced over at the burner phone sitting on the glass table. He'd not heard from Han-Jae in days, which either meant his operative was still in pursuit of the sword, or something worse....

He pushed away the second thought. Han-Jae and his men were some of the best North Korea had to offer. They knew how to move in and out of the shadows, keep a low profile, and avoid security checkpoints in every country in the world.

Still, it was unlike Han-Jae not to check in.

Then Min-Woo remembered the last thing he'd told his asset. He'd told him not to call until he had the sword in his possession.

Easy enough explanation. Han-Jae was still looking.

Min-Woo left the apartment and walked down the stairs. The elevators would be shut down by now to save power, just one more irritation brought about by the current leadership.

At the bottom of the stairs, he made his way through the empty lobby and out the glass doors in front. A black sedan was sitting there with the engine on and the back door open. A soldier stood next to the door.

"General," he said with a quick salute. "The Chairman sent his car to pick you up."

Min-Woo was surprised by the act, but it wasn't the first time something like that happened. He got into the back seat without thanking the soldier, who closed the door and rushed around to the front.

In his years of serving the Chairman and his father, Min-Woo had only been to Headquarters 2 on three occasions. One was when they believed an assassin had infiltrated the country. It turned out to be nothing more than a hoax, probably instigated by the south.

The driver pulled the car out onto the empty city streets and did a U-turn, heading out of town toward the mountains.

Pyongyang was a ghost town. No lights burned in any of the apartments, though some citizens had circumvented the power rationing by lighting candles after dark. No one walked on the sidewalks or drove on the streets, partly because of strict curfews, partly because there was nothing to do anyway.

Ten minutes after leaving the city, Min-Woo noticed the secret road to Headquarters 2 pass by on the right.

"Excuse me," he said. "Where are you going? You just missed the road."

"Oh, I'm sorry, General. I got word that the Chairman has another location in mind. He's very concerned about this security breach."

There it was again. More worry about a security breach. Min-Woo had been in contact with his contemporaries all day. Whatever this breach was, it had the leader concerned enough that he wanted to meet in the middle of nowhere.

Another ten minutes passed before the driver made a left turn onto a worn-out gravel road. It was more dirt than gravel now, filled in by years of erosion.

The car bumped and jostled in the ruts and holes, causing Min-Woo to wonder if the vehicle could finish the journey.

"Maybe the Chairman should have sent a truck," he half joked.

The driver said nothing and maneuvered the vehicle around a left-hand curve, then a right. When he straightened out the wheel, he drove the car straight ahead into a grove of trees. The canopy blocked out the starry sky above, leaving nothing to look at but the skeletal trunks passing by on either side.

Finally, more cars appeared in a meadow directly ahead. Soldiers were standing around at attention.

In the middle of them was the Chairman in his usual suit.

When the car came to a stop, Min-Woo didn't wait for the driver to come around and get him. He opened the door and stepped out, anxious to find out what was going on to cause such a panic.

He walked toward the Chairman and stopped a few feet short to salute him.

"What's going on, sir? I heard there was some kind of security issue."

The Chairman stared at Min-Woo for a long moment and then put his arm around him. "Thank you for coming. I've heard some troubling news, and I wanted to have your opinion on it in person. I'm afraid over the phone wouldn't do."

"It's no problem, Chairman. What's going on?"

"We have a traitor in our midst. Someone is plotting against us." The Chairman kept his arm around the general, walking away from the cars toward the darkness of the forest. "I need your advice on what to do."

The general raised an eyebrow and looked at his leader. "This traitor, he's involved with the security breach?"

"Yes. And I need to know what you would do. I need your counsel. You have always been one of my most trusted advisers."

"Understood, sir. Get me the details on this traitor. Who is he? Where does he live?"

"What would you do to him if you found him?"

"What we do with any traitor, sir. Execute them like the dog they are."

The Chairman nodded. "That's what I thought you'd say."

His arm slid off of Min-Woo's shoulders. The general felt something press into his back. Before he could react, the gun fired.

Min-Woo felt the bullet pierce his skin and come out of his abdomen. It severed his spinal cord on the way in, and instantly he lost all feeling in his legs. With no control over his lower extremities, he dropped to the ground and clutched the wound in his gut with both hands.

"I received word," the Chairman said, "from an outside source. They told me that you assigned a team to find the sword called Excalibur and that your plan was to use it to overthrow me." His voice swelled with every word until he was yelling. "I trusted you! This is how you repay that trust and the generosity I've shown you!?"

"Please," Min-Woo said. He coughed several times before he could speak again. "Please, sir. You're mistaken."

"Mistaken? I'm mistaken? How then did I receive this picture of one of our operatives in captivity?" He held up an image of a man Min-Woo knew was a part of Han-Jae's team.

"Sir, please. You don't understand."

"Enough, Min-Woo. You betrayed me. And you have condemned yourself with your own words."

The Chairman raised the weapon and aimed it at Min-Woo's head.

"Sir, please. Don't do this. I was only working for the glory of our—"

The muzzle erupted, and Min-Woo fell instantly silent.

The Chairman stuffed the gun back in his jacket and motioned for two of his soldiers to dispose of the body.

He returned to one of the big cars sitting in the meadow and looked at the officer standing next to it.

“They didn’t say anything about the location of where the other operatives were, did they?” the Chairman asked.

The officer shook his head. “No, sir. They didn’t.”

“Just as well. They’re all traitors. Perhaps now we can put this foolishness about a mythical sword behind us.”

Chapter 37
Mount Nebo

Sean stood close to the camera crews shooting video and snapping hundreds of pictures.

The decision to leave Excalibur in its hiding place had, at first, seemed to be the right one, but after a day or two of reflection Tommy felt his parents at least deserved to see the relic they'd worked so hard to find.

They protested, of course, telling their son that it wasn't important. Part of him wondered if they feared the location on the mountain wasn't where the sword was hidden. There was an odd comfort in not knowing for certain.

After a discussion with Sean, Tommy knew what he had to do.

Getting the permits from the Jordanian government had taken time. Fortunately, the king of Jordan was swelling with pride at learning one of the most sought-after artifacts of all time was in his country.

Tommy promised that if they were to find the blade, it would be well cared for and presented to the government.

After weeks of working through red tape and months of carefully running the excavation, the crews finally found something: the corner of a stone box.

The workers toiled around the clock, in shifts to allow for rest. Tommy and his parents barely slept once the box had been found. They spent more time on site than anyone else.

Finally, the slender container was opened. Its lid was sealed with wax to prevent intrusion of air and water, a measure that managed to preserve the weapon in nearly perfect condition.

When Tommy's parents laid eyes on the blade, their faces reddened as they tried to force back the tears. Twenty long years they'd waited to see this, never knowing if they would or not.

Now, they stood by their son as he spoke to the crowd from behind a podium. He was saying something about the research involved. He thanked everyone involved with the project, including the Jordanian government.

Security surrounded the area around the overlook to make sure the king, who was determined to be at the event, was safe. Soon, Tommy would present him with the sword, which would then be taken to a museum.

Sean watched the whole thing with a smug grin and crossed arms.

He'd been gone for the last few months, working on a different project, but there was no way he was going to miss this.

Tommy's stage presence for public relations was top notch. While he came off as lacking confidence in many areas of his life, speaking to a crowd of people seemed to be natural for him. He spoke clearly and with a kind of confidence Sean rarely saw from his friend.

"I present to you...Excalibur," he said at the end of his speech.

Two assistants carried a long sword cradled in red cloth and encased in glass. They propped it on a table next to the podium as the crowd erupted in applause. The blade's metal glimmered in the bright sunlight as if on cue.

When the speech was over and the sword presented to the king of Jordan, the crowds dispersed, and soon the only people left were Sean, Tommy, his parents, and a shadowy figure lingering near the shade of the trees near the inner wall of the overlook.

Sean had noticed Baldwin earlier, but the man from the Brotherhood wasn't there to cause trouble. He'd been involved with the decision to dig up the sword and had agreed with it. Baldwin suggested that something as powerful as Excalibur shouldn't be left for someone else to find.

While his thoughts on the matter had surprised Sean, he agreed with the mysterious monk.

Tommy finished shaking hands and chatting with the dignitaries and media on hand, then made his way over to where Sean stood.

He stopped a few feet away from his friend, and they both looked over at Baldwin. The man gave them an approving nod and then made his way around the corner, disappearing behind the little forest.

"You really are good at those speeches," Sean said.

Tommy snickered. "I'm surprised you're not giving me a hard time about a slip of the tongue or something."

Sean grinned. “Me? Give you a hard time? That doesn’t sound right.”

Tommy faked a laugh.

“No, seriously. You were great. Being in front of a crowd is your bag. I mean it.”

Tommy blushed.

“Your parents must be on cloud nine right now.”

“Yeah,” Tommy said, looking over his shoulder at them. “They’re still recovering from the ordeal of being imprisoned for two decades. But they’re doing better than I would be if I’d been the one captured.”

“That generation is just tougher than ours, I suppose.”

“Indeed.”

Sean looked his friend up and down, then changed the subject. “Speaking of tough, have you lost weight? You look stronger. Slimmer.”

Tommy tilted his head forward to check himself out. “Yeah, well, I got tired of you giving me grief over being out of shape. Plus, falling over that fence didn’t help.”

“Hey, I hope I never hurt your feelings with any of that. You know I was kidding, right?”

Tommy nodded. “Yeah, but you weren’t wrong. Plus, I have other motivation to stay in shape, too.”

Sean’s lips creased into a smirk. “How *is* June?”

“She’s good. She couldn’t make it down for this whole shindig. Work calls, it seems. Oh, that reminds me: my parents are probably going to want to be involved with things at the agency once they get acclimated to things.”

“I think that’s a great idea.”

The two friends fell silent for a minute before Tommy spoke up again. “Where you headed next? Got any leads on your latest project?”

Sean rolled his shoulders. “I have a few. Going to head back to the States and visit New England. I’ll let you know what I find.”

“Tommy?” his mother said, interrupting the conversation. “Could you come over here for a picture?”

“Duty calls,” Tommy said. “I’ll catch you later.”

“Go do your thing. I’ll be in touch soon.”

Sean turned toward the pathway and started walking back up toward the parking lot.

“Sean?” Tommy said.

Sean stopped and spun around.

“Thanks for coming. Thanks for always being there for me.”

Sean gave a curt nod. “I always will be.”

GET FREE BOOKS

If you haven't joined the Ernest Dempsey VIP reader list, you should. You'll get two free, full-length novels, plus a couple of novellas just for signing up. On top of that, you get exclusive updates on new releases—and VIP pricing when the new books come out. It doesn't cost anything to be a member, so what are you waiting for?

Visit http://ernestdempsey.net to learn how to get your free digital books today.

AUTHOR NOTES

This story was an absolute blast to create. As with all of my Sean Wyatt tales, Excalibur Key takes us on a journey through history and mingles it with speculation, theories, and fiction.

Everything about the kings and great leaders from the sculpture of The Nine Heroes is true.

All of them were renowned for their abilities in battle and for their leadership. The sculpture can be found inside the town hall (rathaus) in Cologne (Koln).

The dig site and artifacts found in France came from my imagination, though the location of that region was historically Bouillon land as the story suggests. The nearby monastery was also a figment of my mind's creation, but there are ruins of other real monasteries in that area.

The diamond that Sean recovered in Venice is very real and is still missing to this day. Some historians believe it was sold to the highest bidder on the black market, but its whereabouts are left to speculation.

Glastonbury Abbey is one of the most fascinating historical locations in all of Europe. Once a proud bastion of religion in that area, it has deteriorated through the centuries since Henry VIII shut down all the monasteries.

The sign on the lawn suggesting the location of Arthur's burial site is very real, though no one knows for sure if that truly is where the legendary king and his queen are interred.

St. Peter's Square really is shaped like a giant keyhole. It requires viewing from above, but a quick search on the internet can provide plenty of images to that effect.

The two statues near the steps of the Vatican are also real. It is a fact that they replaced the older ones, which were taken to the Vatican Library.

The location of the sculpture in the library was purely fiction, but is certainly plausible.

The ancient obelisks in Rome are all real and, as described in the story, feature unique pieces that sit atop them.

Mount Nebo is a very real place, as is the church from the story. There are many well-preserved mosaics from ancient times still visible to visitors.

The giant rolling stone and serpent sculpture are also real, and it is speculated that the stone really is the one that covered the grave of Jesus.

The burial place of Moses is a fascinating issue and could be a quest all its own. No one is sure where he was buried. Based on Deuteronomy in the Bible, it gives a location, but then suggests his body was later moved. Then the transfiguration of Jesus on the Mount of Olives suggests Moses was resurrected by God.

We will never know for sure in this life, I suppose, but it's fun to consider.

Of course, Excalibur being buried beneath the giant rolling stone is pure fiction on my part. Or is it...?

OTHER BOOKS BY ERNEST DEMPSEY

- *The Secret of the Stones*
- *The Cleric's Vault*
- *The Last Chamber*
- *The Grecian Manifesto*
- *The Norse Directive*
- *Game of Shadows*
- *The Jerusalem Creed*
- *The Samurai Cipher*
- *The Cairo Vendetta*
- *The Uluru Code*
- *War of Thieves* Box Set *(An Adriana Villa Adventure)*

DEDICATION

To my 1st-3rd grade teacher, Mrs. Hurt. Thank you for teaching me how to read and write. And thanks for your patience.

ACKNOWLEDGEMENTS

None of my stories would be possible without the great input I get from incredible readers all over the globe. My advance reader group is such an incredibly unselfish and supportive team. I couldn't do any of this without them.

My editors, Anne Storer and Jason Whited, must also be thanked for their amazing work and guidance in crafting these stories. They make everything so much better for the reader.

Last but not least, I need to give a big thank you to Elena at L1 Graphics for the incredible cover art she always delivers, along with beautiful social media artwork.

Photograph of Excalibur by Eduardo Otubo.

COPYRIGHT

The Excalibur Key is a work of fiction. All names, characters, events, and places are products of the author's imagination or are used fictitiously. Any resemblance to actual events, locales, or persons, living or dead, is entirely coincidental.

Ernestdempsey.net

Published in the United States of America by Enclave Publishing.

Printed in Great Britain
by Amazon

40939046R00225